PINK
ORCHIDS
AND CHEESEHEADS

other
CONFESSIONS
OF
April
Grace

In Front of God and Everybody

Cliques, Hicks, and Ugly Sticks

Chocolate-Covered Baloney

PINK ORCHIDS
AND CHEESEHEADS

further
CONFESSIONS
OF *April Grace*

KD MCCRITE

LEE PRESS

AN IMPRINT OF
OGHMA CREATIVE MEDIA

Lee Press
Oghma Creative Media
Fayetteville, Arkansas

www.oghmacreative.com

The characters and events in this book are fictitious. Any similarity to real persons, living or dead, is entirely coincidental and not intended by the author.

ISBN: 978-1-63373-071-7

Interior Design by Casey W. Cowan
Editing by Jessica Nelson & Gil Miller

Author's Note

The series, "Confessions of April Grace" and "Further Confessions of April Grace" are set in the 1980s. Readers frequently ask why I chose this era for these books. I have a few reasons.

Several small farms were still in production and had not yet sold out to large corporations or real estate developers. Today, in the Ozarks where the April Grace stories take place, only a handful of dairy farms remain.

In the 1980s, no one had smart phones. The internet was so new it was almost unheard of. Most of the technology we take for granted today did not exist back then. As I explained in an earlier book, I wanted to write stories where characters must use their brains solve their problems rather than turn to some website or device. I wanted to write person-centered stories, where families and friends interact and rely on one another, face-to-face, not screen-to-screen.

I hope the continuing tales of April Grace, the Reillys, Ian and Isabel, and the rest of the cast entertain and educate in the "most funnest" ways possible. With these books, grown-ups can revisit days gone by, and children can experience what life was like back in the "good ol' days."

I love to hear from my readers, so please feel free to interact with me on Facebook, at https://www.facebook.com/K.D.McCrite.

Dedicated to my daughters, Holly and Joy,
who grew up in the 1980s, just as April Grace did.
Thank you, girls, for providing me with much happiness...
and plenty of material to write about!
Mama loves you.

One

President of the Drama Queen Society of the Known Universe and Beyond

Late May, 1987

I tell you what. You plan and plan and plan, and you look forward to the last day of sixth grade until you feel like your brain cells are gonna explode and trickle out of your earholes, and then when the day finally arrives, and you step off the school bus, the Very Last Thing you want to hear is a bunch of hollering and squalling coming from your very own house.

Isabel St. James's pickup was parked in our driveway, so right off I knew that racket came from her. You see, ol' Isabel shrieks like she's about to be skinned alive if she breaks a nail or sees a gray hair.

Daisy, our big white Great Pyrenees dog who is so old she can probably remember dinosaurs, lumbered down the driveway to meet us. Good ol' Daisy wagged her fluffy tail and ignored all the noise, or at least she appeared unconcerned by it. Most any other dog would have done one of two things. Number one, it would've chased Isabel down the road to her house, or number two, it would've run away from home its own self. I reckon by this time Daisy has learned what a drama queen Isabel can be.

Myra Sue Reilly, my older sister, got off the bus right behind me. She is fifteen years old and will be a sophomore when school starts again, so you might think she has a little sense. She does not. Everyone, including her, thinks she's gorgeous. Let me be honest. She did not look in the least bit gorgeous hoarding five hundred tons of torn papers and dirty gym clothes like it was treasure. She looked like a hobo who refused to throw away a scrap of trash. All that mess probably stunk to high heaven, but at least I was upwind of her.

She stared toward the house for a few seconds, then dropped all those papers and books and sneakers and trash in the driveway like she'd lost all the muscles in her arms.

"Something is wrong with Isabel!" she screamed and tore off up the driveway to the house.

Eyeballing that pile of junk, I very nearly walked off and left it there. But Daddy had gone to the sale barn that day, and he'd be coming back pretty soon, pulling the stock trailer. If the pickup and trailer ran over Myra Sue's collection, it would get covered with dirt and crud and probably cow-doody. Not that I cared about my sister's rotten old homework papers getting squished and stinky, but I am trying to be nicer to her.

You see, she ran off earlier in the year and scared the puddin' out of all of us so bad that I promised myself I'd be kinder and become a Better Person. At least I'd try.

Carrying everything would have been easier if Myra Sue had used a backpack like a normal person, but she said using a backpack was dorky. Even a big black garbage bag would have been smarter than hauling all that mess in her arms. But no one ever said Myra Sue was smart.

With my arms wrapped around my sister's loot, I trudged up the driveway to the house like a bent-over old woman, the straps of my backpack biting into my shoulders.

Just between you and me and the rest of the world, I had purely despised sixth grade from the very first minute of the very first day until the last bell rang on that Friday afternoon. I was so happy I had the whole entire summer ahead of me that the sound of Isabel's screeching voice failed to darken my mood. When I opened the door and walked in, I would've sung "The Hallelujah Chorus" if I'd known all the words.

Mama must have been baking that day because good smells filled the house, and whatever it was, I wanted some of it. I hauled my burden into our yellow and white kitchen where the good smells originated and all the noise was taking place.

Mama and Isabel were at the breakfast table, two glasses of iced tea in front of them. Myra Sue stood near Isabel, all big-eyed and tearful. She twisted her fingers together so hard it hurt me to watch.

Mama and Myra Sue stared at Isabel, whose top half lay stretched across the table with her head between her arms. Her short dark hair stuck up all over like a porcupine who'd been wallowing in pine needles.

She moaned.

She sobbed.

She wailed.

Myra Sue's mouth worked like she was fixin' to holler and blubber a duet right along with her idol. And I still did not know what had brought on this drama festival.

Mama patted Isabel's arm and said, "There, there" about 396 times. Poor Mama. Every time Isabel has any crisis—and by crisis, I mean anything from a run in her pantyhose to seeing a snake in the yard—she comes running and screaming to Mama. Isabel and her husband, Ian, have lived on Rough Creek Road for nearly a year now, so by this time, Mama understands Isabel tends to go off the deep end this way. She's come to expect it.

"What's going on?" I asked.

"Can't you see Isabel is upset?" Myra snarled at me.

I'd have to be blindfolded in a cave with the lights out not to see that.

"But why?" I asked.

Mama ran her gaze over the huge clutch of clutter in my arms. She frowned. Even when she frowns, Mama is pretty. She has shoulder length, dark red hair that curls soft and shiny and makes her eyes look like sparkly emeralds. Her skin is fair and sprinkled with freckles. People say I look a lot like her, but I don't know… I don't see it.

"Goodness, April, what is that you're holding?"

"It's Myra's." I shifted from one foot to the other, trying to keep from falling sideways from all that weight I carried.

"Why do you have it?" Mama asked.

"Because I'm trying to be nice to her."

I could practically hear my sister roll her eyes. I refused to look at Myra Sue, because if I saw her roll her eyes at my good intentions, I'd've wanted to clobber her instead of help her, and that's no way to start a summer break.

"Myra Sue," Mama said, "don't make your sister carry your things. Take your stuff and do something with it. Do not cram it under your bed or into your closet. Go through all that, throw away the trash, and put the rest away. Neatly."

Myra huffed so loud I figured one of her lungs exploded.

"But Mama! What about Isabel?" She grabbed her blond curls with both hands. For a second, I thought she was gonna tug on it like a tantrum-throwing three-year-old.

Isabel was still sprawled across the table. Hearing her name, she wailed like a police siren.

Now, to tell you the honest truth, while I know that woman is the President of the Drama Queen Society of the Known Universe and Beyond, I was still curious as all get out about what had got to her this time. But all her noise was giving me a headache that started in my ears and settled in the middle of my cranium.

"I'll take care if this for Myra," I said, as generous as a day in May. "I don't mind."

But as I turned to leave Mama stopped me.

"April, your sister will do just as I told her. Hand over that..." she waved her hands toward my load, "... whatever it is. You carry your own things to your own room."

She watched this transference of plunder, and let me tell you, Myra Sue put on a face and attitude that said she was the world's biggest martyr.

"When you're finished upstairs," Mama said as we left the room, "come back for a snack. I made cookies for tonight's cookout, but you may have a couple with a glass of milk."

You might be interested to know that we Reillys celebrate the end of the school year with a cookout. It's a tradition of which I wholeheartedly approve. If Isabel St. James had somehow mangled it, I would have been purely put out.

Myra stopped at the top of the stairs. Tears swam in her eyes and her face was flushed bright pink.

"What do you think is wrong with Isabel?" she whisper-screamed. "I hope she isn't dying."

Oh brother.

"She is not dying, Myra Sue. Maybe she gained a couple of pounds, or maybe her lipstick company quit making her favorite shade. Maybe Ian went with Daddy to the sale barn to buy more goats. You know how much Isabel hates goats."

Myra pulled a dreadful face to prove what she thought of my theory, or goats, or both. For someone who has lived on a farm and been around animals her whole entire life, my sister likes neither animals nor country living.

Call me crazy, but I don't understand that. I couldn't wait to go on long walks with Daisy, or Grandma, and explore the woods and fields. I wanted to wade in the creek and try to catch crawdads. This summer, I wanted take my sleeping bag outside and lie in the dark all by myself, so I could listen to the frogs hollering and crickets chirping and the wind blowing the trees and grass. I wanted to try to count the stars. And I wanted to breathe in all the sweet country smells.

When Myra Sue goes outside at night by herself—which isn't very often—she lugs around a huge flashlight, a can of bug spray, and a baseball bat. And let me tell you something—she's not planning on playing nighttime baseball.

Also, she is afraid of butterflies. What does that tell you?

Once I got through putting my things away—and you should know I keep my room clean and neat, unlike Myra whose bedroom can look like the Zachary County landfill if Mama doesn't remind her to tidy it up every single day—I grabbed a book off my shelf and went back downstairs for a cookie. There is nothing tastier than a chocolate chip cookie warm from the oven. Plus, I wanted to get the scoop on what had Isabel so beside herself.

She was sitting upright when I walked into the kitchen, her long bony fingers wrapped around her iced tea glass. Dark tracks of mascara trailed down her pale cheeks, and her eyes were red-rimmed and puffy. Her long pointy nose looked like a pink bone with dribbles. I handed her a fresh paper napkin from the holder in the middle of the table.

She wiped her nose and said in a shuddering voice, "And n-n-now, I don't know wh-wh-what I'm going to d-d-dooooo!"

Instead of the whiny-baby wailing she had been doing earlier, Isabel now cried like her heart was broken. Her face got whiter and whiter

Mama leaned forward and her gaze never left Isabel's face.

"April Grace, honey," she said, leaping up, "get me two cool, damp cloths. Quickly."

I grabbed a couple of clean dishtowels from the drawer, wetted them at the kitchen sink and handed them to her. She placed one on the back of Isabel's skinny neck, and the other she used to dab at the woman's face.

"I am so very, very sorry this happened to you, Isabel," she said. She brushed back Isabel's hair with her fingers.

Out of the clear blue, it occurred to me that Something Dreadful had happened to good ol' Ian, Isabel's long-suffering husband. The mere thought made me feel so sick and weak I sat down hard in the nearest chair.

"What's wrong?" I asked in that whispery kind of voice you're supposed to use at funerals and weddings.

I imagined several different situations. Number one, because Rough Creek Road is a bumpy, narrow dirt road, maybe he'd been a car accident. Isabel nearly killed herself in a wreck on it last year. Number two, maybe he'd keeled over with a heart attack because Isabel had finally driven him over the edge. Number three, he'd run away from home because Isabel had finally driven him over the edge.

None of these scenarios were above the realm of reason.

Myra Sue came galumphing into the kitchen, wide-eyed and breathless. She flung out her arms and practically sailed toward Isabel.

"Don't faint, Isabel-dearest! Shall I get the smelling salts?"

"What smelling salts?" I asked, but she ignored me. I bet she thought smelling salts was Morton's salt with Avon Timeless perfume poured on it.

I heard a truck coming up the driveway with the stock trailer rattling along behind it. It was noisy, but I loved to hear it because it meant my daddy was home. I jumped up and looked out the door of the service porch. He waved as he drove by on his way down the slope to the barn. Ian St. James sat in the passenger seat and he looked perfectly fine. I took a deep breath of thankfulness.

I went outside and trotted toward the barn. The stock trailer was empty, which meant Daddy had sold the calves he'd taken to the sale. I hated when it was time to sell the calves, but we're a farm family and that's part of how Daddy makes money. That, and selling our milk to a certain big company, which you probably see their bottles and cartons on the shelves in your supermarket. Just think. When you pour milk on your cereal in the morning, you might be getting some of the milk produced right here on the Reilly farm in Arkansas.

Daddy and Ian were talking earnestly about something and hadn't even gotten out of the truck yet when I walked up and tapped on the passenger door. Ian turned and saw me.

"Hey there, Miss April," he said with a grin. "What're you up to today?"

"Not much. Are you OK, Ian? You aren't sick or anything, are you? You aren't going to leave Isabel, are you?"

He raised both eyebrows like he thought was I speaking in Japanese or Latin. He looked at Daddy.

"Did you hear that?" He turned back to me. "Of course not, April Grace. What makes you ask such things?"

He and Daddy got out of the pickup.

"It's Isabel." I pointed to the house. "Ian, she's upset for real, not for drama."

He lost his smile and you could see the worry leap all over his face. Without another word, he hightailed it to the house. Daddy and I followed right on his heels.

Ian squatted down next to Isabel and said, "Lambkins! What's wrong, sweets?"

She raised her teary, mascara-smeared, blubbery-nose-stuff streaked face to him.

"Oh, darling!" she wailed. "It's the worst of all things. It's the end. The absolute end!"

Two

Lessons ol' Isabel Needs to Learn So She Don't Have to Keep Taking the Class

"Oh, Isabel-dearest!" Myra Sue yelped, then burst into a crying jag like you wouldn't believe. She squalled so loud, she woke up Eli, my baby brother.

"Myra Sue, hush that noise," Mama said as she went to get the baby.

Daddy laid one strong hand on Ian's shoulder. "What's wrong, Isabel?"

We all stared at that woman, waiting for her to compose herself enough to explain. Daddy turned to my sister.

"Myra Sue?"

"I don't know," she whimpered. "Oh, poor Isabellll."

Mama returned with Eli in her arms. He was rubbing his eyes and he was very cranky. I can't say I blamed him a bit, getting yanked out of sleep by all this mess.

"Lily," Daddy said to Mama, "do you know what has Isabel so worked up?"

"It must be something horrendous," I blurted, "because she looks worse than she usually does."

As soon as the words were out, I wished someone had sewn my lips together at birth. You see, there are times when I just say things I don't even know I'm going to say. It's like my mouth has a mind of its own.

Boy howdy. You should've seen the look Mama gave me. And daddy frowned. He almost never frowns. I gulped, and clamped my lips together, then held them that way with my teeth. It might have hurt less if I'd used safety pins.

Isabel sat straight up in her chair, pointed her sharp chin, shmooshed her lips together in that way she has, and blinked about 452 times. She cleared her throat and sniffled. Hard.

"My dear friends," she began in a voice that was way stronger than you'd expect from a skinny woman like her. "Today, before the last class of the day, Mrs. Farber called me into her office."

Let me pause in the telling of this tale to remind you that just the name of the Cedar Ridge Junior High principal brings a cold chill to my heart. The square-built, flat-footed, frowny-faced Mrs. Patsy Farber is scarier than a roomful of spiders and snakes.

Isabel sniffled again.

"She told me that the school board… that the school board… sch-sch-school board…" She paused and sniffed again. This time she sniffed so hard I thought she might swallow her sinuses and tongue and half her cranium. "The school board decided… d-decided…" She stopped and blinked.

"Isabel!" Myra Sue grabbed up one of that woman's scrawny hands and held it to her chest like she thought it was her favorite teddy bear.

Isabel gave her a trembling smile then looked around at the rest of us with red-rimmed, tear-filled eyes.

"They decided not to renew my c-contract. I won't be t-t-teaching next year, a-a-after aaaaaaall!" Her voice went up and up in pitch until I thought my ears might bleed. "I am ut-ut-utterly undone!"

"Oh, my sweetness, my lamb," Ian said, gathering Isabel to him with her hand still trapped in Myra Sue's clutches. The three of them looked like some kind of weird modeling clay sculpture where arms and legs and heads are all molded together.

"You mean you won't be teaching theater or dance next year?" Myra Sue hollered right next to Isabel's ear.

"Nooooooo!" the woman howled.

"Ohhhhh!" Myra Sue howled right back.

Good grief, you should have heard that sob-fest. And poor baby Eli, who is often so smiling and happy, looked at those two howling females and set up to bawling his own self.

Mama cast a stricken look to Daddy, "I need to feed this child and change his diaper."

"Go ahead, honey," he said. "I'll take care of this situation."

She gave him a grateful smile, and scurried out of the kitchen with the baby.

"Myra," Daddy said, "let go of Isabel. Right now."

Ol' Myra Sue looked at Daddy as if she'd never heard of letting go of someone before she finally extracted herself from her idol.

"Now please put out a plate of cookies," he told her. "And April, freshen up everyone's tea, please."

While my sister slogged around, fumbling with cookies and plates like she had no idea how that worked, I gave Daddy and Ian each some sweet tea then filled up the glasses for Mama and Isabel. I poured milk for myself and Myra, but she curled her nose up when I set it on the table for her. She can be an ungrateful brat sometimes.

I helped myself to a cookie and sat down, but Myra stood behind Isabel like she was her guardian angel or something.

"Now," Daddy said, turning to Isabel, "why don't we start at the beginning. Isabel, you said the school board decided not to renew your contract?"

Ian continued to hunker there next to Isabel's chair. Other than accepting the tea from me, I don't believe he'd taken his gaze off her face. She twitched, and began to clench and unclench her fists like she was gonna claw something.

"Stay calm, sweetums," he said in a soft voice. He stroked her hand.

I'd be embarrassed to the roots my toenails if anyone ever called me some of the pet names those two St. Jameses use for each other. Of course, their pet names are better than what they spew at each other when they are fighting mad. Listening to them fight is enough to dry up your gizzard.

"Don't tell me what to do. I am trying!" Isabel snapped, pushing at him and glaring until her eyeballs nearly turned inside out.

See what I mean? Isabel has come a long way in the last year, but she's still got a long way to go, believe you me.

"It's very hard to stay calm when I'm without a job I have loved and slaved over," she said. "A job that brought culture to these backwoods."

I bit my two lips together so hard I nearly hollered in pain. Isabel is always complaining about life in the Ozarks. She completely ignores the beauty of the hills, trees, rivers, and creeks. Instead, she whines for traffic and smog and noise and lots of people. If she'd just hush her bellyaching for a while and look around, she'd see that she's in a pretty nice place.

Her "bringing culture" job was to teach performing arts for the Cedar Ridge School System. She taught dance and dance history at the junior high and theater history and dramatic arts at the high school. I don't know about those theater classes, but one thing for sure her dance classes were pure-dee torture for us students. Not only did we have enough homework to choke an army of horses, she made us dance until we had blisters on our feet.

She scared the kids and annoyed the teachers, so I wasn't surprised in the least the school board refused to have her return.

Still, if you had half a heart, you couldn't help but feel sorry for ol' Isabel. She's the kind of person that needs to have purpose to her days. And let me tell you, if she doesn't have a purpose, she can be the biggest drip in the whole entire world, I kid you not.

I laid my hand on her shoulder and could feel those bones poking my palm. Isabel believes being skinny is one of the Ten Commandments.

"I'm sorry you lost your job," I said.

"Thank you, dear," she sighed, sniffled, and patted my hand. "I don't know what to do."

"We'll figure out something," Ian said.

"Of course we will," Daddy said.

"Yeah," I put in.

"Yes, Isabel," Myra Sue said, "the world is your oyster."

Oh brother. My sister probably thinks oysters grow on trees in Alaska.

"I gave those students the benefit of my vast experience. I nurtured them as I would my own children. I suffered and sacrificed myself. To be betrayed this way is my darkest hour."

Well, that was just too much. Isabel was not a saint, no matter what she said. If she couldn't see the truth for herself, someone needed to point it out to her. I figured I could do that as well as anyone else.

"Isabel," I said in my serious, grown-up tone, "stop and think about it, please. From the very first day of the spring semester—your first day as our teacher—you were hard as nails. You yelled and fussed and bossed us kids around like we had no brains. You called us hillbillies. You made nasty remarks about parents and houses, and how we talk. You tried to be a boss, not a teacher. I'm fairly sure that is why the school board fired you."

"April Grace Reilly!" Myra Sue huffed out my name like a fire-breathing dragon.

Everyone else stared at me, and Daddy's frown looked like a thunder-cloud on the Day of Doom. He pointed that frown at me and boy, oh, boy I knew I'd had it.

"April," he said in that quiet way that will curl your toenails. He started to say more, but Ian cut him off.

"No, Mike. She has a point." He turned to Isabel. "Darling, if you will recall, you came home from work and daily ranted about school. Making ugly, personal remarks has always stirred up trouble for you."

As he spoke, she drew her lips in tighter and tighter, until it seemed she had no lips at all, just a thin line between her nose and chin. With every word he spoke she jerked as if someone poked her rump with a sharp stick.

"This is none of your business, Ian St. James, and I will thank you kindly to stay out of it!"

He got to his feet and walked away a few feet with his back to us all. The part of his neck you could see between his sandy blond hair and his collar turned really, really red.

Isabel glowered at his back, and I thought for sure she was gonna clobber him good with the iced tea pitcher, or maybe her fist. After a minute, though, she sighed deeply and slouched in her chair as if the weight of the world rested on her narrow shoulders.

"The thing is," she said in a quieter voice, "I see how things are, and how they should be. I try to help others improve themselves by pointing out their flaws and explain how they can fix them." She sighed again. "I'm beginning to realize people around here do not want me to help them change."

No one said anything, and even though I knew I was already in trouble, I figured I couldn't get in any worse trouble if I spoke up.

"Well, golly, Isabel, think about it. Maybe it isn't everyone else who needs to change. Maybe it's you."

Good gravy, you could've heard a pin drop. But I said it and I wasn't taking it back because she needed to hear it, even if I got grounded for the next three-quarters of a century. Ian turned around and faced us. He even gave me a quick nod and wink.

"You've done pretty well since you've moved here, all things considered." I hoped my saying so smoothed any feathers I may have ruffled. "Everyone knows it's been hard for you to leave the city and move to the, um, backwoods."

"That's right," Daddy said. "Your change has been so slow, you don't even recognize it."

"Obviously it isn't enough. No one here cuts me any slack." Her voice rang with despair. "They don't make even the least effort to do what I tell them."

Well, there you go. What we told her just didn't sink in.

Ol' Isabel and I have had this discussion on more than one occasion. It was plain as day that she'll be at least a hundred years old before she learns this lesson.

Mama came into the room with my freshly-diapered, well-fed baby brother.

"Just keep your heart open, Isabel," Mama said, "and do your very best to find the good in everyone."

"You do that better than anyone I know, Lily dear," Isabel said, as gracious as you could hope for. "I endeavor to follow your example." They exchanged warm smiles, then Isabel added, "Give me my sweet little man, please. I want to kiss those darling cheeks."

Her face lit up as she held out her arms for Eli. He wriggled and grinned as Mama handed him over. He loved Isabel. Well, actually it seemed Eli loved everyone. I reckon he got that from our mama.

Three

My Grandma,
She Gets Around

"Where's Grandma?" I asked while Mama and I were skinning boiled potatoes for potato salad. "And why are you and me doing all the work?"

"Grandma went to Blue Reed with Ernie today. Or was it Reverend Jordan? It was an unexpected trip, and she was in and out so fast this morning, I'm not sure who she went with."

For those of you who don't know, my grandma, Myra Grace Reilly, has three—count 'em, three—boyfriends. Ernie Beason, who owns Ernie's Grocerteria. Rob Estes, who owns the pharmacy. And Reverend Trask Jordan, who is the Methodist minister.

Grandma. She gets around.

"You know Isabel is in the front room, taking care of Eli. Myra Sue is helping."

I rolled my eyes and started to make a snotty remark, like "Myra Sue is helping to make sure you 'n me do all the work because sometimes she is lazier than two toads in the sun."

But I kept my big mouth shut.

By the time Mama and I got all the food prepared and the picnic table set up outside, Daddy and Mr. Brett, the hired man, had finished the evening chores and Ian had charcoal briquettes smoking in our big ol' black Weber grill.

I hoped Grandma would make it to the cookout, because in my whole entire life, she had never missed an end of school celebration.

By six o'clock, all of us were outside—Eli in his playpen surrounded by colorful toys, Myra and Isabel putting out the white Chinette plates, Mama making sure all the condiments and side dishes on the table were covered to keep off the flies. Daddy, Ian, and Mr. Brett had gone to their separate homes and showered off the chores from themselves and put on clean clothes so no one would bring the odor of cow or goat poop to the table.

Let me tell you, farm animals are not the cleanest folks to work with. They will do their business anywhere, at any time, for any reason, and if it gets on you, too bad. *They do not care.*

The three men stood around that smoking Weber grill as if it held the secrets of life, death, and the hereafter. I guess maybe it did, to them, if the secrets were kept inside steaks, hamburgers, and hot dogs.

I kept watching for Grandma to show up, and she didn't. This was so worrisome, that I like to have paced a hole in the ground.

"I'm gonna go see if Grandma came home and we just never noticed," I said at one point, and started to strike out across the hayfield. Mama called me back.

"She'll be here when she gets here, April. Stop fretting."

And then she spoiled the calming effect of her words by looking across at Daddy. The worried expression on her face was as obvious as Daisy lingering hopefully near the grill.

"I'll go call," Daddy said.

I trailed right behind him, and no one stopped me. Before we got inside the house, though, a brand new green car pulled into the driveway and sat there a bit. Grandma and Ernie were inside it. Thank goodness Ernie was behind the wheel, because Grandma is a driver who doesn't know her driving scares the entire population of Zachary County.

Daddy stopped walking, planted his hands on his hips and grinned.

"I knew Ernie was getting himself a new car but didn't know when, or what kind. A Chevy Caprice. That's nice."

I took about three running leaps toward the car before Daddy called me back.

"But, Daddy," I said, "I want to find out why Grandma —"

"They don't need you hovering, honey. Come back here."

Boy, oh boy. Sometimes what people do not understand gives me a giant pain in the patoot.

I didn't care two owl hoots about that ol' new car. My focus was on my very own grandmother who was just sitting there like she was stuck to the car seat. I paced and fidgeted, hoping and praying Grandma hadn't got sick or something while they went to Blue Reed.

"Come on, punkin." Daddy put his arm around my shoulder and led me to the others.

I went with him, but I kept looking over my shoulder until I saw Grandma get out of the car. She stood slightly bent from the waist, her right hand on the door, talking to Ernie. Then she straightened and closed the door. She waved as he backed out and drove away.

"Now may I go to my grandmother?" I asked.

And in case you're wondering, yes, I was peevish, but good grief, wouldn't you be peevish if people kept you away from your grandmother when you were concerned about her?

"Go ahead," Daddy said.

I shot off across the yard to her. From a distance, she *looked* the same as ever, with her short sandy blond hair—she dyes it 'cause it's gray for real—in its usual neat style. She wore maroon slacks and a white blouse with black loafers, so nothing real odd about that. But there was something peculiar....

"Hey, Grandma!" I hollered. "I thought you'd forgot."

"Forgot what? The cookout? Not in a million years."

I hugged her as if I hadn't seen her since before she was born, then grabbed her hand and walked with her towards everyone else. Up close this way, I could see her makeup was strange and streaked, and beneath it her face seemed pasty, like raw bread dough. The worst thing, though, was that look in her eyes, like she was lost. That look scared me.

"Are you okay?" I asked. "Did you get sick?"

"Mercy, child, what wild hair is ticklin' you into thinking such a thing? I'm fine."

"Well, you've been gone so long, we thought maybe something had happened, like an accident or something." I paused a couple of seconds then added, "You look sick. Are you sick? Did you have a car wreck?"

"Forevermore, child!" she said, like I was being foolish instead of concerned. "I went with Ernie to help him pick out his new car." As soon as we got within earshot of the others, Grandma called, "Lily, who has been filling this girl's head with flapdoodle?"

Mama sent us both a startled look. "What flapdoodle?"

"Accidents and illness."

"Because you were so late!" I insisted. "And you have *never* missed our end-of-school cookout. That is *not* flapdoodle. It is the Very Opposite of flapdoodle."

"We were a little concerned that you were gone so long," Mama said, "but certainly no one mentioned a word about illness and accidents. You know April's runaway imagination."

"Ah. I see."

Both of them looked at me like I was a bug in a jar. Well, let me tell you something. I might have a big imagination, but I see things that go on right in front of everyone's very noses that they never seem to notice. If that's what you call a runaway imagination, then, well, I guess that's what I have. And they ought to be glad for it, as it has proven true in many cases.

I was plumb put out and went to sit next to Daisy who had plopped herself not that far from the grill to watch the proceedings with her tongue hanging out of the side of her mouth.

"Honest to goodness, Daise," I said to her, "you'd think these people would finally realize I'm not a dumb little kid."

She twitched her eyebrows, looked up at me, then put her head in my lap and sighed. The two of us sat there and watched everyone else. I knew something was going on with Grandma and I was going to figure it out.

Here's what was obvious to me. Number one—that strange look in Grandma's eyes, as if she was somewhere else in her mind. Number two—she looked pale and nervous. Number three—she wasn't paying the least bit of attention to anything anyone said, and they had to repeat themselves. Now, that was so obvious it was like a slap in the face with cold cooked spinach. But did anyone other than me notice?

Nope.

I might have been peeved and put out, but that detail was powerless to change my appetite for a big ol' heaping spoonful of Mama's famous potato salad and a generous helping of baked beans on my plate. I practically drooled as I piled my smoky, barbecued burger a mile high with sliced tomatoes, onions, and lettuce and drenched in spicy mustard and ketchup. I added some potato chips on top then smashed the bun down on the whole thing so it would fit in my mouth. That first bite made a mess all over my chin and plate and some got on my shirt, but did I care? Nope.

"Mercy, April Grace," Mama said, handing me about 510 napkins. "Wipe your face, and cut that hamburger in half before you take another bite."

"If you were to go to the Taj Mahal and eat like that," Myra Sue said, all snooty, "they would probably carry you outside and set you on the sidewalk."

"They don't serve hamburgers at the Taj Mahal," I told her.

I didn't know if they did or not, but considering it was one of the Seven Wonders of the World, it seemed unlikely. Besides, I figured Myra Sue didn't have a clue that the Taj Mahal was a mausoleum, not a fancy restaurant in New York City.

"Too bad Ernie couldn't stay for supper," Daddy said as he helped himself to the potato salad.

"Why didn't he stay?" Ian asked. His burger was piled nearly as high as mine. Isabel was eating her half a hamburger wrapped up in a lettuce leaf. At least she'd stopped blubbering like a baby.

Grandma refused to look at anyone as she waved one hand like she was shooing flies from the table. I think she was trying to shoo away questions.

"I didn't invite him."

Now, we Reillys are known for our hospitality, so ever' last one of us at that table stopped chewing to stare at her.

"Why not?" I asked because everyone else just sat there with their teeth in their mouth.

"Because. Pass the salt, please."

"Because is not an answer," I said.

How many times had I been told this? It seemed completely appropriate for the moment, but if you'd seen the frowns I got from my parents, you'd have thought I'd just busted out with some bad words. It would be the Worst Thing Ever, if I got sent from the table without finding out why my grandmother acted like she harbored the secret of making chocolate out of dirt. I clamped my lips together.

Isabel passed the salt, holding it prissily between her thumb and forefinger, with all her other fingers splayed as if touching the shaker might cause her to turn into a pillar of salt like Lot's wife.

"Grace, darling," she said, "you look wan. Are you feeling all right?"

At last! Someone else finally noticed something was off. As an added bonus, Isabel focused on someone other than herself for a time.

Grandma took the salt shaker and set it down without even using it. Then she picked up the ketchup and squirted it right on top of her potato salad. Everyone noticed that.

"Mom!" Daddy said.

His sharp tone startled Grandma so bad, she dropped the ketchup bottle right smack in the middle of her plate.

"Ew!" Myra Sue screeched. What a sissy.

Mama handed Grandma a bunch of napkins and wiped off the bottle while Grandma cleaned her hands.

"Where's your mind today?" Ian asked with a knowing smile.

"I think her thoughts just drove off in that shiny new Caprice," Daddy said.

The food was getting cold on our plates but no one cared 'cause we were all staring at Grandma and waiting for some kind of an explanation.

She stood up as if she was going to either make an announcement or walk off, then her face turned chalk-white and her knees folded.

"Grandma!" I screamed, reaching for her. On the other side, Mama grabbed her arm. Between the two of us, we kept her from toppling right to the ground.

Daddy jumped up and brought her a fresh glass of water from the pitcher on the table. He checked her pulse and peered into her eyes. If there had been any smelling salts in our house, right then would have been the time to use it.

"What's wrong? Are you all right?" everyone seemed to be yelling all at once.

"I told you, I told you, I told you!" I hollered at that bunch of people. "I told you something wasn't right."

Isabel ran into the house and came out again twenty seconds later with a wet cloth. Just as Mama had sponged her neck and face earlier, she now did it for Grandma, making the same kind of clucking, cooing sounds Mama had made over her.

"What's wrong, Grandma?" I shrieked above everyone's voices.

"Ernie..." she said, gasping his name.

I could feel my eyes getting bigger and bigger as I tried to figure out why she was calling for Ernie.

"What about him, Mama Grace?" my mama asked.

Was Grandma calling for him, or was she talking about him? My heart pounded so hard in my chest, I thought it might break a rib or two.

She squeezed her eyes shut really tight then opened them again, really wide as if trying to see the whole world all at once.

"Ernie," she squeaked. She gave a little cough. "Er...nie."

Her voice broke his name and she reached for the glass of water Daddy held out to her. She guzzled, holding up one hand as if telling us to leave her alone. When she drained the glass, she set it down with a sigh. Color began to return to her cheeks.

"Ernie Beason..."

We waited, staring at her, silently willing her to continue.

"Ernie Charles Beason... has... has..." She gulped air.

I felt like the entire top of my head was gonna blow off and couldn't stand it any longer.

"Is he going to die?" I shrieked the awful words.

Grandma stopped gulping and gasping long enough to give me a look that said I had done lost all my sense. Then she started waving one hand back and forth like she was leading the song service at church. From the googledy-eyed, terrified expression on her face, you would have thought Ernie had just robbed a bank and asked her to drive the getaway car. She took in another whopping gulp of air.

"He has asked me to marry him."

There was complete silence for a minute while this news oozed into our heads.

"Congratulations, Grace!" Ian said, breaking all that quiet.

Daddy grinned from ear to ear, and gave her a big ol' smooch right on her pale cheek. I wondered if he had given even *one moment's thought* about getting himself a new daddy after all these many years? Because that's what Ernie would be.

And he'd be my grandpa.

Don't get me wrong. I like Ernie Beason just fine… but good grief. Didn't we just go through this wedding thing last year? Yes, we did.

Mr. Brett said nothing. Myra Sue rolled her eyes like she thought the whole situation was boring.

Mama and Isabel chimed at the same time, "When?"

Grandma's eyes stayed wide open without a single, solitary blink, and she worked her mouth a few times like she was fixin' to spit watermelon seeds. I couldn't figure out why my very own family was so all-fired excited about her getting married when it was obvious the very idea scared her out of her wits.

The way Grandma had been dating first one fellow, then another, if you didn't know better you would have thought she'd been taking applications for husbands.

But I knew better. I knew she'd been burned by that no-account rotten scoundrel wormy old weasel, Jeffrey Rance, who had tried to trick her into marriage last year just so's he could steal every blessed thing she owned.

I figured she was still trigger-shy about getting married, and poor old Ernie just hadn't figured that out.

"It's OK, Grandma," I said and gave all those folks at that table a stern look. "We understand you don't want to marry him and nobody is gonna make you."

I'm here to tell you that they turned and gawked at me like I was the Creature of the Slimy Depths.

"What are all y'all staring at me for?" I hollered. "Am I the only one at this whole entire cookout who is the Voice of Reason?" I put my fists on hips and continued. "Need I remind y'all of *Jeffrey Rance?* Do you remember Grandma almost went off the deep end with him? We cannot let that happen again."

Boy, oh boy. From the way they frowned and glared, you woulda thought my words had been dipped in curdled milk and spewed on the food.

For about one minute this glaring business went on, as if they expected me to take back everything I said and run out right then to buy Grandma a wedding dress.

"Ernie Beason is nothing, *nothing,* like Jeffrey Rance." Grandma's tone was so uppity she sounded like a clone of Isabel St. James. "And you know that, April Grace."

"April, go to your room and dust it," Mama said. "Then organize your underwear and sock drawer, and when you've finished, you may come back."

"What about my hamburger?"

Mama didn't blink. "Better get going before it gets any colder."

I knew better than stomp off like Myra Sue would've done. That would have earned me the chore of toilet scrubbing, or maybe organizing Myra Sue's underwear.

What kind of way was this to celebrate the last day of school? Boy howdy was I perturbed.

Boy howdy, boy howdy, boy howdy.

Four

Let Your Fingers Do the Walkin' and Your Big Mouth Do the Talkin'

If you know me at all, you know my room was *not* dusty.

Well, not much. The heat and dryness of summer had not yet turned Rough Creek Road into dust that billowed in thick clouds to invade our house any time a car drove by. That would happen in a few weeks. I ran a cloth over everything anyway, because Mama had told me to. I fumed so much I almost don't remember dusting at all.

But when I organized my underwear and socks—which meant I put the socks where the undies were and the undies where the socks usually go because they were already folded and tidy, I had to wonder what kind of punishment this was.

Then, like sun coming up on a bright morning, it dawned on me that Mama sent me upstairs so I could cool off for a bit.

What I did was this—I came up with a Plan. I can't honestly say it was a good plan, but I'm telling you, I hated to see my grandmother looking the way she looked that day. I had to do *something*.

I looked out an upstairs window and saw everyone was still sitting at the picnic table, eating all that good food as if nothing had happened. I mean, they weren't even concerned that I'd been banished while mine grew cold.

"Boy howdy," I whispered to the whole lot of them.

At least they were outside, and no one would be in the house to stop me.

I slipped out of my room and down the stairs. In the hallway, I picked up the phone book from the telephone table and looked up Ernie Beason's number.

Without a moment's hesitation, I called him.

The phone rang three times, then a deep voice answered. I kinda jumped a little at that, 'cause I'd never heard him on the phone before. For a second, I thought I was talking to someone else.

"Is this Mr. Ernie?"

"Yes, it is."

"Hi. This is April Grace."

"Hello, April Grace. How are you?" He sounded more like himself then, and I relaxed.

"I am concerned about my grandma."

"Oh? What's the matter?" Now he sounded all anxious. "What's wrong with her?"

I took in a deep breath.

"Well, I just want to explain…" I kinda choked a little at this point.

"Explain what, hon?"

My thoughts felt like dried-up leaves inside my head and they rattled around in there with no purpose for a few seconds. I swallowed hard and wished I'd taken a minute to write out what I wanted to say.

"Well, the thing is… well… she likes you, and all… and all of us like you a lot…"

"That's good to hear," he said, chuckling. "I'm fond of all the Reillys."

I had a spell of coughing and hated the way my skin felt cold, stiff, and jumpy.

"You see… um…" I cleared my throat real hard.

"What is it you're trying to say, honey? Just say it."

Ernie's voice was as kind and gentle as Daddy's, and I felt worse and worse and worse about what I had to tell him. But Grandma's happiness and peace of mind comes first for me. So I just opened my mouth blurted it out.

"Grandma does not want to get married, ever again, never, for the rest of her life."

You shoulda heard the silence from his end of the line.

"What did you say?" he asked, after a time.

I figured he heard me, but maybe the words didn't sink in.

"Ever since that old goat, Jeffrey Rance, nearly married Grandma last year, she don't want to get married to anyone. She likes you. A lot. Like I said, we all like *you.* You sell good groceries in your store, especially on Tuesday when Grandma gets the senior citizen's discount."

I heard that mess of words gushing up like backed-up toilet water.

"Didn't you notice how peculiar she was today?" I continued to gush.

A few silent moments passed, then he said, "Well, now that you mention it, once I popped the question, she did seem…"

"Peculiar?"

"Yes. Yes, indeed." He said nothing for the length of probably five seconds. His next words were stiff, like they had frozen in his mouth.

"Your grandma asked you to call me with this message, did she?"

"Uh. Well, no. Not exactly. But the thing is… we were all talking…"

"You all were talking." He repeated, as flat as drawing a straight line.

"At supper."

"Did Grace tell everyone she did not want to get married, or did she say she did not want to marry *me?*"

"Um. Well… um…."

Good gravy Marie. Where were the explaining words when I needed them? I had done stepped in it this time but good, and I did not know how to clean up this mess.

"Never mind, April. Thanks for calling."

The line went dead silent, and I decided that's what I'd do too. I'd never utter another mumbling word for the rest of my life.

Five

Strange Diseases and Healing Manicures

I felt hot and smothered all over. In the bathroom, I splashed cold water on my face until I thought I'd drown.

"I oughta just get in the shower and scrub until I wash myself right down the drain," I growled at my reflection.

The back door opened, and Mama called out to me.

"April, honey, you've been cleaning your room long enough. Come on outside and have your supper."

Are you kiddin'? Not only would I never speak again, I'd never be able to eat again. Talking and eating. Two of my three favorite pastimes. The third one is reading. I'd never give that up, no matter what kind of rotten person I turn into.

I dried my face and hands, then got a piece of paper from one of my school notebooks and wrote, "I don't feel well. I am going to bed."

I hauled my sorry backside outdoors and handed Mama my note, then started to trudge back to the house.

"Hold it!" Mama said. "Come back here."

I gulped, turned around and went to stand in front of her.

"Hold your head up."

I lifted my head but did not look at her.

"This came on all of a sudden, didn't it?" She laid her palm against my forehead, then frowned. "Your face is cold." She grabbed my hands and felt them like she was trying to count my finger bones.

"April Grace, look at me."

I dragged my gaze upward, rubbing my throat and head, and making an awful face. She leaned forward and peered into my eyes. Even though I wanted to turn away, I couldn't.

"You're up to something. What is it?"

If I said anything about calling Ernie Beason, my goose would be cooked from now until six years from next Christmas. Every person at that picnic table was looking at me, and I felt like a dirty pig. I moaned a little in the back of my throat.

"I don't want to eat a cold hamburger," I croaked. And just in case she didn't buy my pitiful excuse, I shuddered and massaged my tummy.

Mama narrowed her eyes, then sat back in her chair.

"Okay. Go take a warm bath, put on clean pajamas and crawl into bed."

I couldn't believe my good luck. No third degree. I didn't have to hang around everyone, feeling like a guilty dog. It was more than I'd dared hope for. I'd grab a handful of cookies for supper, and my book, and I'd be set.

But Mama wasn't finished.

"If you're so ill, what with your head, throat, and stomach, you need to go right to sleep. So no supper, no TV, and no reading."

"Oh, but Mama —" I began in my regular voice, but caught myself and set up the awfullest coughing fit you could imagine.

"Scoot!" she said, way more cheerfully than she should when talking to a sick child. Even though I wasn't really sick.

A little voice way in the back of my head whispered that Mama probably knew I wasn't sick at all. It told me this was punishment for not telling the truth. It reminded me I was lucky that I didn't have to scrub the cellar floor.

I scooted before I could louse up anything else by blurting out this bit of information.

The next few days were as dismal as cold spinach on stale crackers.

Grandma had decided she needed some "alone time," and stayed at her house instead of coming to see us. And guess what? She didn't want *any* company, and she didn't want to go anywhere. She didn't go to church on Sunday. She didn't even go grocery shopping on Tuesday, which is something she *always* does.

To make the world even drearier, Isabel dragged her gloomy self over to our house Every Single Day and sat around sighing like a lonesome polecat. Every time she sighed and drooped, so did my silly sister. I decided if I ever fixated on a role model, it would be someone with some spunk and joy, not someone who wilted like a hot house flower every time things didn't go to suit her.

Watching those two sighing females was enough to make me grab a book, whistle for Daisy and go for a long walk in the woods.

I would have called my best friend, Melissa Kay Carlyle, but every year since she turned ten, she has gone to camp that lasts most of the summer. She attends because of an endowment that is given to kids from lower income families. According to the little booklet they send out to folks when trying to raise money, this camp is supposed to "teach our youth value of life, independence of spirit, and preparation of living."

Melissa told me that mostly they have classes pertaining to manners and social activities. Sports are volleyball and field hockey, and art is making plaster of Paris wall art. She said they have to go to bed at nine, and get up at six, and every day they have to police the entire place from dining hall to shower houses. She said she wishes she didn't have to go, but her mother insists on it. At least she likes the food.

That's not saying much. Let me tell you something. Melissa's mother is the most awfullest cook in the southern United States and maybe in the entire northern hemisphere. I'm sure if that camp served boiled cardboard boxes, they'd taste better than Mrs. Carlyle's coconut hamburger casserole.

At any rate, I wished she was home because I sure could use someone to talk to. About the only one around our house I felt comfortable confiding in right then was Daisy. I'm sure she understands most of what I'm saying because she looks right in my eyes while I tell her stuff. Unfortunately, she has never learned to talk.

Late on Wednesday morning after the cookout fiasco, I came home from a trek through the woods and down to a fresh water spring on the far side of our farm. It's shady and quiet there, but we'd had rain the day before so it was muddy too.

The minute I stepped into the house, Mama said, "Forevermore, April Grace, what did you do? Roll in dirt?"

"Get away from me!" Myra Sue yelped. She was sitting at the table while Isabel St James painted her fingernails.

She reared back as if she thought I was going to hug her.

"I'm clear on the other side of the room from you. Chill out."

"Hold still, Myra-darling," Isabel said. "If you jerk your hand like that, the polish will end up on your knuckles."

She applied pink polish as if brushing powder onto a butterfly's wing, all soft and gentle.

I stood there and watched her for a while. For the first time in all those days of complaints and sighs, Isabel was almost smiling. An idea stirred in my mind. Myra Sue looked up.

"What're you gawking at?" she said.

"I'm just watching," I said. "You do that really well, Isabel. It's cool how you can take such tiny little strokes."

"Thank you, darling. I find it utterly relaxing."

She admired Myra's hand in hers, tilted her head one way, then the other, as if trying to get the full effect of painted fingernails.

My sister narrowed her eyes like she suspected I was up to something, but I wasn't. Well, not in the way Myra Sue suspected. That good idea she had interrupted a minute ago returned and formed inside my brain. It seemed to me if Isabel found something she could do well, and relax while she was at it, maybe she would stop feeling wretched—that's her word, not mine—and be happier.

"April," Mama said. "Go outside and brush that dirt off before you get it all over the house."

Myra Sue gave me a smart-alecky smirk, but I'm trying to be a Better Person, so I ignored her.

I went outside again and stomped around, trying to get the mud, leaves, and sticks off my shoes and pants and bottom. I started to go back to the kitchen, but Mama had been watching me real close lately, almost like she suspected I was up to no good. I wanted to stay in her good graces as much as possible, so I hurried upstairs and took a shower, washed my hair, and put on clean jeans and T-shirt. If that didn't win me some bonus points, I don't know what would.

When I walked into the kitchen, I did a little twirl so everyone could see I was no longer Piggy Ann McDirt.

There are people in the world who believe that when you are one month past your twelfth birthday, you should stop going to the woods with your dog and digging around in the dirt and leaves, and some of those people were in our kitchen. But here's the thing. I betcha when I'm really old, like Mama and Daddy, I'll still go grubbing in the woods, looking for cool bugs and rocks and plants. After all, Grandma showed me how.

Myra Sue's manicure was done, but she still sat next to Isabel with her hands splayed out like duck feet. She blew on them with her cheeks puffed out like two balloons.

Isabel pushed around the bottles of polish and all the doodads she'd used on Myra's nails, but it was like her mind didn't know what her hands were doing. Bit by bit, her face settled into that droopy pity-party expression again.

Before she could get started on how miserable her life was, I plunked myself down in a chair on the other side of her and stuck out my hands.

"I think I need a manicure."

Well, you shoulda seen those three females gape at me like I'd just my shaved my head.

"Really?" Myra asked. She blinked at me like I was a complete stranger.

"Yep."

Isabel's face lit up.

"Well, of course, darling. Scoot closer and let me see those little hands."

She picked up my left hand and eyeballed it, then picked up my right one and examined it too. I sorta felt like she looked for cooties and was glad I had taken a shower.

"April dear," she said, frowning down at my hands, "what on earth do you do, dig for gold in the backyard? Your nails are simply dreadful."

I squinted a little and stared at my fingers. They looked just like always to me, a little raggedy around the edges, but completely clean and usable.

"At least I don't chew on 'em like some people." I gave ol' Myra a significant stare.

She got all huffy and said, "I haven't done that in a long time. Not since Isabel explained that nail-biting is unhydrogenetic and low-class."

"*Unhygienic,*" I corrected, then told Isabel, "Sometimes I dig in the dirt, if I'm trying to get a cool rock or some other interesting thing out of the ground. Mostly, though, I use 'em for scratching."

"Oh my!"

She sounded like she'd never heard of scratching.

Let me enlighten you, in case you didn't know, but if you live in the Ozark Mountains like we do, you will get—mosquito bites, tick bites, chigger bites, poison ivy, sweat bee stings, wasp stings, heat rash, and sunburn—unless you stay inside all the time, and who wants to do that? Every blessed one of these things will give you an itch like you can't believe.

"If God didn't want us to scratch, he wouldn't have given us fingernails," I declared.

"Oh, April Grace," Mama said, as if she despaired of me.

All I had done was state the truth as I saw it. If Grandma had been there, she would've agreed with me, but she was still holed up in her house like a hermit. I dearly hoped she'd come out someday soon. I missed her like crazy.

Thinking about Grandma made me remember that awful phone call. I pushed it as far back in my mind as I could, but I knew it would come squirming to the front, sooner or later.

"Let's pick out a color," I said, hunching over the bottles of polish Isabel had, and boy, oh boy, she had about a gazillion of them. "Myra, what color is yours?"

Myra Sue held out her hands, and the tips of her fingers looked like little pink shells. As far as fingernails go, I reckon they looked nice enough, but that color was like something you'd see in a baby nursery. I was no baby.

I spotted a pretty color and picked up a bottle. It was reddish-orange and made me think of a sunset. I read the name of the color out loud.

"Tahitian Love." I read out loud and handed it over. "This one, please, Isabel."

"Hold it." Mama intercepted the bottle and scooped up one that was Barbie-pink. Not my favorite color, *at all.*

"This." She handed it to Isabel. "Or the color you used on Myra. April, you are too young for Tahitian anything."

I wrinkled my nose. "That's a yucky color."

"I'm serious, ladies," she said. "You'll have a nice pink, or clear, April Grace. Or none at all."

"Very well, Lily."

Isabel tapped the top of the pearly pink she had put on Myra Sue and lifted one eyebrow in question. I nodded. Pearly pink was better than that horrible pink. It looked like stomach ache medicine. If I had to look at it on my fingernails, I'd want to hurl, for sure.

While Mama fixed lunch, Isabel manicured me. Boy howdy, you wouldn't think having your fingernails done would hurt, but you'd be wrong. It was torture. Ol' Isabel filed and chiseled and clipped and cut like crazy. I almost expected her to send Myra Sue out to the tool shed for the hacksaw and staple gun.

I wanted to scream and shudder when she used that little file she calls an emery board. The scritchiness of it set my teeth on edge and raised goosebumps all over my skin.

"You should let Isabel do something with your hair, sis," Myra said.

I hoped the expression I turned on her was properly horrific, because I dislike anyone touching my hair. It's nearly waist length and very heavy, so I usually wear it in a single braid down my back. That's how I like it, and that's how I want it to be.

I failed to anticipate Isabel's complete rapture at such a suggestion.

"I'd love to!" She clasped her hands and held them against her chest like you see in pictures of the saints. She practically glowed like a Christmas tree, and I haven't seen her look like that in a long, long time.

Honest to Pete, after watching her droop and hearing her sigh all week, I didn't have the heart to tell her no.

"You have to promise you won't cut it, or roll it, or backcomb it, or put a perm on it, or color it, or make me look like any of those big-haired girls on TV."

Isabel blinked about twenty times.

"Well, my dear, what's the purpose of 'doing something' to one's hair if one isn't going to make a change?"

"I don't know. I didn't ask for a change."

She shmooshed up her lips and stared hard at my hair.

"Turn." She made a little twirly gesture with her finger. "I can do a lovely French braid."

I was unsure what that meant, so I asked, "Are you gonna cut it?

"No."

"Curl it?"

"No, dear."

"Rat it up and pouf it like a soufflé?"

"Not at all."

"Get a clue, April Grace," Myra Sue put in. "A French braid is very pretty and Isabel will make it gorgeous."

"I think that would be lovely, honey," Mama said, stroking my head a couple of times. "Try it. You might like it."

Lest we forget, she was the woman who a short time earlier had wanted me to wear the world's ugliest nail polish. I wasn't sold on the idea of a French braid. It sounded more like a pastry than a hairdo to me.

"If you like it, April, I will teach you how to do it yourself," Isabel added. "Myra Sue can help you until you can do it well on your own."

Oh good grief.

Six

Personal Space Invaders

I have to admit, when the manicure was done, my fingernails looked nice. After lunch, Mama even said she'd do the dishes so the dish water wouldn't mess up them up. Boy oh boy, that's as good a reason as I can think of to get your nails whacked and polished.

Myra Sue and I went outside and held out our hands so the sunlight could make our fingertips shimmer.

"See the pearls?" she said.

"I do."

"Aren't you glad Isabel did your nails?"

"I guess so, but it hurt, all that filing and clipping and stuff."

She flipped one hand. "The price of beauty is pain."

Oh, give me a break.

She ran one hand along the braid, lifting the tail to examine it closely.

"This looks really nice, April Grace. I can do this for you every morning, if you want."

I hated to admit that I liked the way Isabel had styled my hair. It wasn't all poufy and big. But I still couldn't stand anyone to touch my hair and pulled away.

"We'll see," I said.

She got all prissy-faced. "Well, if you want to go through life looking like a mess, that's your business."

It's difficult to keep my mouth shut most of the time and in the best of circumstances, as you know. My sister often stirs up that urge so I can hardly contain it. I bit my tongue just to keep from saying anything that might start a fight. I am trying to be a Better Person.

"I'm going back inside to keep Isabel company," Myra Sue said. As if Isabel was alone and adrift on the Sea of Life.

She flounced off to the house.

I figured if I went back inside right then Isabel might get the bright idea to complete my new look by slathering makeup all over my face. When she did a makeover on Grandma last year, the result like to have scared me out of ten years' growth. While that makeover certainly gave her a different look, in no way did it improve her. She went from looking like my smart, plucky grandmother to looking like a flashy, fluffy old lady who was trying to appear way younger than she was. But not as much as Mimi, my other grandmother, who is scrawny and faded and wears miniskirts with her red cowboy boots. She is sickly and now lives in Arizona for her lungs.

I'm not sure exactly why, but after Grandma got her hair cut and Isabel did an intervention on her face, Something Peculiar triggered in her brain. She was still funny and sweet and loving, but she acted flirty with her men friends and younger than she is and dressed all fancy and showy.

She even went out on dates. And I'm not talking about the dried fruit in a Christmas fruitcake.

I looked across the hayfield to Grandma's little white house with the red roof. Her white Toyota was parked next to it, so I knew she was home. I had not seen hide nor hair of her for five and a half days. Never in my whole entire life has that much time passed without me seeing my grandma. She hadn't even called to say "Hi."

No one seemed concerned about it but me. They all said things like, "She wants some time to think." Or, "She needs her space right now." Or, "When Grandma wants to us to tell us what's going on, she'll let us know."

Daisy plodded up to me and nuzzled in close, as if she understood my worry.

I shot a look toward the house. Mama, Isabel, and Myra Sue were still inside and unlikely to come out any time soon. Daddy and Mr. Brett were in the far hayfield mowing and raking that field's first cut of the season, and Ian was doing his own farm work.

For another minute, I gazed at Grandma's house, hoping she was all right and wanting to be with her.

"This has gone on long enough," I said to Daisy

And without saying a blessed word to anyone about what I was gonna do, I struck out across the hayfield. Daisy followed me a little way, then lay down under one of the walnut trees in the side yard and watched me go. I reckon she was worn out from all the exploring we did in the woods earlier.

By late May the field grasses had grown high, ripe, and dense. Walking through it took longer than usual. I jumped and squealed when a blue racer flashed past like a streak. I am not a big chicken like my sister, but if I had my 'druthers, I'd ruther never encounter a snake.

It felt good to reach Grandma's yard. There is something about her small house with its dark red roof, matching shutters and neat little shady lawn. Three big hanging pots of red geranium hung from hooks on the porch ceiling, and two white rockers sat comfortably side by side with a small table between them. She had the windows raised and the inside door open, and the breeze blew her yellow dotted swiss curtains.

Walking across her porch to the front door felt like someone opened their arms to welcome me. I paused, wondering if I should knock or just go in. Usually, I hollered to announce my presence then walked in. But if Grandma was still isolating herself like Miss Havisham in *Great Expectations*, she might not appreciate me barging in. Of course, Miss Havisham was okay with having company.

I knocked.

I heard dishes clattering in the kitchen, like she was cleaning up after her lunch. I knocked again, louder. This time I called out.

"Grandma?"

"Woo?" Grandma almost always says "Woo?" when you call out to her. She came out of the kitchen, drying her hands on her apron. "Well, land sakes! April, why are you just standing there? Come in, sugar."

I yanked open that screen door, ran to her and gave her the biggest hug I could without squishing her guts completely out. Her bratty white cat Queenie yowled like a crazy thing and streaked out of the room like she thought five German Shepherd dogs were after her.

"Mercy, child," Grandma said, gasping for breath. "Is everything all right? Have you had your lunch?"

"Not yet. But I had to see you." I let go of her and stepped back. "Here it is, the first week of summer vacation, and I've only seen you for about five minutes. Have you completely hermitized yourself, or are you ever coming back?"

She gave me a surprised looked then laughed. "Come in the kitchen and let me see if I can find you something good to eat. Why haven't you had lunch?"

"Mama's fixin' it, but I wanted to come over here for a minute or two."

"I see."

As I trailed behind her to the kitchen, I couldn't help but notice she was wearing one of her old dresses, what she called a "house dress." Hanging loose, it was blue with little pink and white flowers, and buttoned down the front. Instead of her hair being styled and stiff, it was wound around about a thousand little green brush rollers. And you know what else? She wasn't wearing any makeup. That day, she looked more like herself than she had in a year.

I sat down at her little kitchen table, and she fixed me apple slices and peanut butter with a glass of milk.

"How come you need your space?" I asked when she put the plate down in front of me. "Haven't you had about had all the space you need?"

She frowned. "It's not physical space I need as it is *time*. Time to think some things through."

I took a deep, hard gulp of air. If I'd had a piece of apple in my mouth right then, I'd've choked.

"Think about Ernie, you mean?"

She nodded and poured herself a cup of coffee.

"Among other things," she said.

I preferred to talk about anything other than Ernie because I was afraid I'd just blurt out with that whole mess with the phone call.

"What other things?"

She sat down and sipped her coffee.

"So what have you been doing this week? I like your hair that way. Did your mama do that?"

"Isabel did it. And you did not answer my question."

She reached out and examined my braid like she'd never seen hair before. "Isabel is a woman of many talents."

Useless talents, in my opinion. What good is twirly-toe dancing, project-ing your voice on stage, and fiddling with hair and fingernails? Not much.

"Why, look at your fingernails, April Grace!" She grabbed up one hand and eyeballed that pearly pink polish. "I don't believe you've ever had fancy nails before. Isabel did them too, didn't she?"

I did not want to get caught up in a conversation about Isabel St. James.

"Yes'm. But what other things have you been thinking about?"

Grandma examined her own fingernails and murmured, "I should get her to give me a manicure before too long."

"*Grandma.*"

She looked up at me like she'd forgotten I was there.

"What. Other. Things?"

"What other things what?" she said as if she was completely mystified.

I blew out a loud breath. "All those things you've been thinking about? Why haven't you come over to our house? Aren't you lonesome over here, all by yourself?"

From across the room, Queenie stared at me with her greeny-gold eyes and hissed as if she informing me that she was all the company Grandma ever needed. If Queenie was all the company anyone ever needed, I'd say the world was in sorry shape.

"Oh, dat puddy tat," Grandma said, smiling. She got up and took a carton of cream from the refrigerator. "Her wants her treat, don't her?"

It was all I could do not to clamp my hands over my ears and go "na-na-na-na-na-na" to shut out that awful babytalk. Why does Grandma do that? It sets my teeth on edge.

She put a saucer of cream down in front of Queenie, then stood there with her hands folded against her chest, smiling as though she thought the mean, cranky cat was a sweet little a newborn baby.

"Grandma!"

She jumped and gave me a startled look like she'd forgotten about me again.

"Oh, April," she said. "Do you want some more milk? Or another cookie?"

Number one, my milk glass was still full. Number two, she hadn't given me a cookie, so why did she offer me another one? Number three, was she losing her mind? Good grief.

She poured herself another cup of coffee, then sat down and stared at the first cup, which was still on the table and still three-fourths full. A frown pulled her eyebrows together as she stared at that cup.

"Well, forevermore...." She looked confused.

"Grandma, are you all right?"

"I'm fine. But, I guess I already poured my coffee." She laid a hand against her right cheek and shook her head. "Mercy on us."

She had such a look of confusion on her face, I wondered if I ought to go get Daddy or Mama. Had she been sick all that time and we just left her there, alone? I started getting mad at myself, because I should've known my very own grandmother who likes to be around people and laugh and talk would never want to be alone.

Of course my big mouth engaged before I put my brain in gear.

Seven

If My Mouth Was an Iceberg I Could Sink the Titanic

"Grandma, are you gonna die?"

She opened her eyes wide and ogled me like a gasping goldfish.

"What in the name of time are you talking about, April Grace Reilly?"

"Well, shucks alive, Grandma! You're acting weird. You look pale and messy, and your eyes are scary."

"What? Scary? Me?"

She jumped up and hurried into the living room with me following. At the small wall mirror next to the door, she leaned forward and peered into her own eyes. She pulled down the skin of her face until she looked like a cross between a dried apple and melted candle. It was frightful. Then she lifted her chin and examined at that business under it, wrinkles and sags and all. She grimaced at herself, turned her head this way and that, eyeballing her hair rollers. Her gray roots were about a half-inch long. She stepped back and looked down at her front, all the way from her bosoms to her feet.

"Good gracious," she muttered, then went to the recliner and flopped down on it. "Goodness gracious."

"Grandma? Are you okay?"

"It's beyond me how this came to be," she said to the air.

"Huh?"

"For years I was completely happy, living here in my little house with my family within yelling distance and Queenie in the house to keep me company." She was still talking to the air. "I had my garden and my quilting and sewing to keep me busy. I was happy."

I wasn't the air, but I had to ask. "You aren't happy now, are you, Grandma?"

Slow as a slow can be, she turned her eyes to me.

"I didn't realize I loved him as much as I do."

I blinked. Those were not the words I expected to hear. And I could tell that even though she was looking right at me, she didn't see me. Maybe she was gazing into memories of my granddad, who died a long time ago, way before I was born. Her lost expression filled me with something cold and dreadful. I read somewhere that when people are fixin' to die, sometimes they feel and see their dead loved ones.

I was so scared, I shivered like a wet dog.

"You mean Grandpa Voyne?" I asked, real quiet and calm.

She turned her head and looked out the window.

"He said it was time to choose. That's what he said. He says, 'Grace honey, it's time to decide.'"

I gulped. "Who? What?"

"He says, 'I've been a patient man. I've given you your freedom, and never said a word when it was eating me alive. But I can't stand it.' That's what he said. He says, 'I can't stand it no more. It's me or them, but it can't be all of us.'"

Her meaning started to fall into place, and I just let her talk, 'cause I figured she needed to say what was on her mind. She continued talking to the air.

"I said to him, I says, 'Why, whatever do you mean, Ernie?', and he says, 'I mean, I'm tired of it being you 'n me, and you 'n Rob, and you 'n that preacher Jordan.' He says, 'I was here first, Grace, and I love you like crazy. You know that. I'm tired of sharing you with 'em. So's if you want to be with them, then so be it. And if you want to be with me, that's fine. But it can't be all of us anymore.'"

And then she stopped talking and just sat there, staring out the window. Queenie strolled over to her and gave me a dirty look. She jumped up on Grandma's lap and shoved her face in Grandma's face. I bet you could hear that crazy feline purr clear up in Cedar Ridge. You might want to know that the only other person Queenie likes is Isabel St. James. So, believe me when I say that she is one crazy cat.

Grandma petted her head, but she never looked at her. She just kept staring outside like she thought the answer to the world's problems was in that big old oak tree in her yard.

I cleared my throat real soft and whispered, "Grandma? What did you tell Ernie?"

She kinda jumped a little, like I'd startled her again.

"I told him I'd think about it."

She did?

"You did?"

Uh oh.

"You mean you didn't tell him that marriage was Out of the Question? That ever since Jeffrey Rance had nearly dragged you into matrimony you'd never think of such a thing again?"

She turned to me. "Why, of course not. That would have been a silly answer."

Uh oh, uh oh, uh oh.

"So you told him you'd think about it for a long time?"

"For a few days, yes. I needed to cogitate and ponder, pray and meditate. I wanted to make sure I loved him enough to change my life for him. Making such a big decision needs serious rumination."

I swallowed hard.

"Marriage is more than having a good time, you know," she said.

Believe me when I tell you I had a bad feeling that was getting worse. Dread rose higher and higher until I thought I might actually choke on it. Hiding out in the little cave on the far side of the farm seemed like a good plan.

"But then last night," she said in a stronger voice, "after I said my prayers and before I went to bed, I was sitting here, watching the news on channel three, everything suddenly became clear and I knew the answer."

"You did?" My throat and mouth were drier than two pounds of cotton.

"Yes. As much as I like Rob Estes and Trask Jordan—they're both fine men, you know, April Grace, just excellent fellas—and as much I enjoy being squired around by each one, Ernie's the man for me."

I think I squeaked a little in my throat.

"And as soon as I realized that, I got right up and called him."

Boy howdy, it was like all the air and blood fell out of my body and went splat on the ground.

Eight

Quivering Liver
and
Slushy Brain Mush

I didn't want ask because I was afraid of the answer. But, I'm no coward, so I said, "Grandma, what did Ernie say when you told him?"

She stroked Queenie's fuzzy head with one hand and tapped on the arm of the chair with the other.

"He didn't let me get but a couple of words out then interrupted to say, 'You've obviously made your choice, so I'm not up to talking to you for a while.' And then he hung up. I tried to call again, but he didn't answer his phone. I'm thinking he may have misunderstood me when I told him I needed to think about his proposal." She heaved a great sigh. "I reckon I'd best clean up, change my clothes and go into town. I need to talk to him face to face."

It took me about 248 tries but I finally got the words out, "I'm sorry."

She smiled a sad little smile and held out one hand to me. I reached out and took it mine.

"Good gravy, April, your hands are colder'n ice." She tightened her grip and looked at me closely. "Are you sick, sugarplum?"

"No, ma'am." I paused. "Well, not sick in the way you mean."

"How's that?"

She still had hold of my hand, and boy, did I hate to say what I had to say and I didn't want to say it, but I knew it had to be said, sooner or later.

"I think I did something really rotten," I managed to strangle out of my voicebox.

A small frown crossed her face. "Oh? What did you do?"

I thought for sure I was gonna faint, or maybe throw up. I wished a hole would open up in the floor and I'd fall through, right smack to the middle of the earth.

"I, uh, I, um…"

Grandma hung on to my hand and stared into my eyes.

If I'd been Isabel St. James, I would have wailed, "My wretchedness knows no end!"

But I wasn't Isabel. I was April Grace Reilly, the mouth of the South who was, right then, at a loss for words.

"Just say it, child."

"Well, then… um…" I cleared my throat, and looked down at the floor. "Y'see, I was worried." I looked up to glance in her eyes right quick, then back down.

"About what?"

"Well, y'know. It was the end of school, and Isabel was upset about her job and all that mess…"

"Go on."

I resisted the urge to wring my hands.

"And you weren't there, and I was the only one worried because I knew you wouldn't miss the end-of-school-cookout unless something was wrong."

I gulped and choked for a minute.

She never moved except to say, "Go on."

"And you came home with Ernie in that new green car, and you didn't want him to have supper with us, and you looked just awful, all sick and pale, when you joined us, and, and…"

I breathed and breathed, and wanted to kick my own behind.

"April Grace, tell me what this is all about or I'm going to call your mother."

"Don't do that!" I hollered.

Grandma let go of my hand long enough to pluck Queenie off her lap and set her on the floor. Then she leaned forward and grabbed both of my wrists, pulling me closer. The look in her eye made my liver quiver and turned my brain to mush.

"What did you do?"

My mouth opened before my brain unfroze.

"I told him you didn't want to marry him," I blurted

Believe me when I say that time stood still. And so did my heart.

Grandma turned to granite, cold and hard. She did not move, not even so much as an eyelash.

"What did you just say?" she asked, finally, in a dreadful frozen voice that nearly ripped out my innards.

"I'm sorry. Sorry, sorry, sorry. Sorry as I can be. But you looked so upset. And you didn't want him at the party, and I remembered Mr. Rance, and… and… I'm soooooorry…."

I burst into a bawling fit that made Isabel's sob-fest the other day look and sound like a teddy bear picnic.

I want you to know that when Grandma finally let go of my wrists, I flopped to the floor and squalled until I felt like my guts had tangled and tied themselves together in a hard, painful knot. I lay on the floor, curled in on myself like an unborn baby.

Grandma sat in her chair with her hands folded in her lap. She watched me, but she said nothing and she made not one move to comfort me. I had stuck my nose where it did not belong and ruined Grandma's romance, and for the rest of her life, she'd be alone, growing older and older, while poor ol' Ernie would be all by himself in his house in town, heartbroken.

The more I thought about these circumstances, the more I sobbed and howled and blathered on about what a horrible, terrible, rotten person I was.

Grandma finally got out of her chair. I heard her voice but by that time, my ears and nose and throat were so full of snotty stuff I couldn't hear what she said. I didn't even have enough oomph to say "Huh?"

Lying the middle of the floor like a slug is not my style, as you know. But sometimes, you just can't help yourself. I stayed put, vaguely aware of Grandma moving around. I reckon she was straightening up the kitchen after our snack.

I wished she'd taken that broom of hers, that one with the hard, sharp straws, and swish me right out the front door. But then I wished she'd stop working, and gather me in her arms, and tell me she forgave me and everything was all right.

She didn't do either one.

Before long, I heard hurried steps on the front porch, and then the screen door opened.

"April Grace, what on earth…?"

Mama's voice washed over me like a warm soft wave. I opened one eye as she knelt beside me. Her face was full of worry.

"I'm s-s-sorry," I hiccupped. "I didn't r-r-realize…"

I sniffed hard and gagged. Grandma stood behind Mama and handed over a box of tissues.

"I'm the most awfullest granddaughter in the whole entire world!"

Mama wiped tissues over my face, drying it, then helped me to sit up. She put a fresh Kleenex in my hand and said, "Blow."

My eyeballs felt like they'd been removed, rolled in salt and pepper, then stuffed into sockets that were too small.

Mama and I sat there on the floor and she said, "Now, suppose you tell me what this is all about?"

Grandma stood behind her, arms folded. I'd never seen my grandma mad at me before and I'm here to tell you, it hurt me worse than anything I can think of. I turned my aching eyes to Mama who sat there looking sweet and concerned. Boy howdy, I hoped she didn't get that madder-than-a-wet-hen look on her face after she found out what a rotten person I'd been.

The whole mess came blubbering and spilling out. All of it, every disgusting little speck. When I finished, Mama's face remained soft and kind. She did not fold her arms and glare at me like Grandma did.

"Well, then," she said quietly.

"I'm sorry," I said. "And I told Grandma nine hundred and eight times I was sorry, and she just keeps looking at me like that." I pointed at her. "She might as well be a statue made out of ice and rock."

I sniffled.

"Don't be dramatic," Mama said. "And stop feeling sorry for yourself."

Oh, good gravy. For real? Dramatic? Me?

Me?!

Stop feeling sorry for myself? Was she kiddin'?

At that moment, I felt like the crust on the belly of the world's smallest worm. That was not feeling sorry for myself.

If Mama wanted to accuse someone of being over-the-top and full of self-pity, she should turn her eyes to Isabel St. James, who was probably over at our house that very moment conjuring up some kind of reason to feel wretched.

And then… and then my whole entire brain made a right-hand turn.

Do you reckon Isabel felt low-down and rotten on the day Mrs. Patsy Farber told her not to return to school? As if the world had reversed its spin and started going backwards because she'd said and done the wrong thing? Maybe she was so guilty and undone that the only way she could cope with how badly she felt was to indulge in a big, whiny-baby, wailing festival.

It soaked in, bit by bitter bit. Ol' Isabel and me. We're way more alike than either of us would care to admit. My own personal self, I saw no reason to announce it to the world, and I trust you can keep this just between us.

"What do you think should happen now?" Mama asked me.

I eyeballed Grandma, saw not the weensiest bit of softening in her, and realized it might take a while before she decided to forgive me, no matter how many times I apologized.

"I think I should talk to Ernie and explain that I stuck my nose in where it didn't belong and made a big fat mistake."

Mama nodded. "Anything else?"

I blinked. Right then, all I could think of was making everything right for Grandma, but it was like my brain stopped coming up with ideas.

"I'll do whatever you and Grandma want me to do."

Grandma got her phone off the little table where it usually sat and brought it to me, its long, black cord trailing behind like a tail.

"Call him. Tell him what you did. 555-9261."

"Yes'm." I hiccupped, and dialed with shaky fingers.

"Ernie's Groceteria," a chirpy voice said.

"May I s-speak to Er-Ernie, please?" I gulped back another hiccup and nearly choked.

"He's not here," she chirped back, cheerful as she would have said that Santa Claus just walked in the door.

I looked at Grandma. "He's not there."

"Where is he?"

I said to the woman, "Where is he?"

"He has taken the afternoon off."

I relayed this information to Grandma.

She gave me a steely look. "Where is he?"

"Ma'am," I said in the mouthpiece while eyeballing my glaring grandmother, "where is Ernie?"

"I can't tell you confidential information," she sniffed. Boy, she sure went from chirpy to snooty awful quick.

"It's a secret," I told Grandma.

She frowned so hard, she liked to have split her forehead. She yanked that receiver right out of my hands.

"This is Grace Reilly. Where is Ernie?" She listened and her face got pale, then snapped, "I see!"

She slammed the receiver down in the phone cradle so hard, the phone pinged. "Well, I'll swan."

I thought she'd looked mad a minute ago, but boy howdy, you shoulda seen her right then. I bet she could've bitten a fistful of nails in two.

"What's wrong, Mama Grace?"

She stood there staring at nothing for a bit, then she said, "That Ernie Beason has done gone out to lunch with that cake decorator at the Grocerteria bakery."

"Nancy Agnes Greenleaf?"

Grandma nodded, staring down at the phone in her hand like it was a rattlesnake.

"Oh, my," Mama said.

"But Nancy Agnes is about five hundred years younger than Ernie." I didn't need to point that out. Everyone knew the woman was young. And beautiful as a movie star. And as sweet and nice as the cakes she decorated.

Mama closed her eyes and let out a long, long breath.

"April Grace, go to the house and eat that meatloaf sandwich I fixed for your lunch. It's in the 'fridge. I'll be home directly." She spoke in that quiet, serious tone that Daddy uses when he gets good and ticked off. If I valued the rest of my summer vacation, I knew I better do what she said.

"Okay."

I slunk out the front door and back to the house like an egg-suckin' dog.

Nine

How Low Do You Have to Feel Before You Feel Higher Than a Worm Belly?

I was so all-fired depressed and aggravated that I went to Myra Sue's room. She was sitting in her bed, looking at a style magazine. She glanced up when I stepped through her door.

"You look awful," she said. "What's up?"

I wasn't about to tell that girl my troubles. Number one—She has no empathy for anyone but Isabel. Number two—She would have nothing to say that could help. Number three—My stupid blundering big mouth was none of her beeswax.

"Nothin'."

I looked around her room and shuddered. One thing I can't stand is a dirty, messy room and Myra Sue tidies it up only under duress— that is, when Mama threatens to ground her from the telephone. Ever since she hid secret letters in her mess under the bed, Mama refuses to let her get away with living in a complete pit. But she still never cleans it without being told.

I started picking up her dirty clothes and putting them in the hamper. She did not offer to help. Of course.

"You look awful," she said, watching me.

"I know. You told me that a minute ago."

"Are you sick?"

I stuffed a ton of trash in the waste can. "No."

"Hmm."

I shot her a sideways glance and straightened all the bottles scattered across her dresser top. Perfume and fingernail polish enough to fill a shelf in Blue Reed Five and Dime, where they display such stuff. Ol' Myra had her head cocked to one side, and if I didn't know any better, I'd figure she was thinking. But my sister is not the thinking kind.

"You want to take a walk?" I asked her. "Rough Creek is still running, and we could go wading. Or we can look for some sheep sorrel in the woods."

She curled her nose. Myra Sue Reilly does not like the tart taste of sorrel. Also, she is afraid of—snakes, bees, butterflies, frogs, ticks, chiggers, worms, ants, and moss. All these things are in the woods. Crawdaddies are in the creek before summer heat dries it up, and she's afraid of them too. I figured she'd say something snooty and hateful, but she just shook her head.

"No, thanks. And weren't you just in the woods earlier?"

"Yeah, but you can't get too much fresh air."

She rolled her eyes.

"Where's Isabel?" I asked.

"She went home when Mama went over to Grandma's. What's going on over there anyway? Mama left in an awful hurry."

"Nothing. Grandma just needed to talk to her, I guess. Where's Eli?"

"He's asleep. You think I'd be up here if he was awake?"

I plopped down on the edge of the bed and eyeballed my sister. Boy howdy, I needed to talk to someone about the trouble I'd caused and how bad I felt. But to tell you the honest truth, my mind didn't rest easy about spilling my guts to Myra Sue. We've been getting along a lot better lately, but she's still snooty and goofy. The last thing I needed was for someone to call me names and make me feel even worse.

"What are you doing in here?" She had slight edge to her voice.

I shrugged. "Just hangin' around."

I eyeballed that magazine on her lap. I guess reading something about Christie Brinkley is better than not reading at all. But not much.

"Well, go hang somewhere else. I'm busy."

That settled my quandary of baring my soul to her. I got up and slouched over to the door.

"See ya," I said.

I sat outside on the porch swing for a minute or two, then went to the backyard and climbed up my favorite box elder. The bark felt rough against my skin, even through my clothes, so I climbed down and walked to the hay barn.

Let me tell you city-slickers something. If you have never been in a hay barn, you do not know what smells good. Imagine what sunshine smells like—warm, sweet, and golden.

But even the crackling dry fragrance could not sooth my aching heart. Enough hay had fallen loose that I was able to gather some into a pile. I flopped down on it and cupped my chin in my hands.

If there is anything that makes you feel worse than hurting someone you love and maybe even ruining their lives, I'd like to know what it is so I can avoid doing it.

I shut my eyes. Behind closed lids I replayed the times with Grandma when we took nature walks, or baked cookies together, or looked at pictures in the family album. I remembered her face when she looked at photographs of my grandfather. She always looked soft and sad, but she always smiled, as if her thoughts of him were good ones. She always sighed every time she turned the pages.

"I'm so sorry," I breathed in a quiet prayer to God. "You know I did not mean to hurt my Grandma. Please forgive me and help me to make up for it. And if you can help Grandma understand, Sir, I surely would appreciate it." I paused just a few seconds, then added, "Thank you very much. Amen."

A sun-kissed breeze traveled in through the big barn door. It stirred up dust and bits of hay, but that soft wind felt comforting against my skin. I sat there in that quiet, peaceful place and waited for a change to come over me. I expected a big white light or something like you read about in the Bible. That did not happen.

But the longer I sat there, the more my insides untied themselves. I knew God forgave me for what I'd done because He loves us unconditionally. And isn't what love is all about? I knew Grandma would pardon me as well, in time, because even though she was ticked off as she could be, she loves me too.

My own personal self, I was unhappy with April Grace Reilly. It was going to take me a while even to like myself again, let alone forgive what I'd said and done. Maybe if I did my best to mend the rift between Ernie and Grandma, I'd stop feeling like such a worm belly.

I got to my feet, dusted the hay bits off the seat of my britches and walked out into the sunlight. Daisy lumbered up from where she'd been lying in the sun and came to meet me, wagging her tail and smiling her sweet doggie smile. I gave her a hug and she lapped my face with a lick. Boy oh boy, a dog hangs by you no matter what you've done, especially a good dog like ol' Daisy.

That night and the next day, the world drooped around me. In spite of my awfulness, it seemed nothing changed in our house. Daddy and Mama continued to be kind and to make goo-goo eyes at each other. Eli gurgled and cooed and smiled. Myra Sue was no better or worse than her usual self.

I was the only one who'd changed, and the rest of them left me alone. I figured Mama thought comforting me would just make me wallow and sob, kinda like it does Isabel, which is why Mama is kind to her when she's in a state but doesn't hover as much as she would if it was, say Temple Freebird who was having a spell. I was no Isabel and if Mama had babied me a little, I don't think I would have collapsed into a heap. But, I never got that chance anyway.

After washing the supper dishes with Myra Sue, I retreated to my bedroom and did my best to lose myself on an island with Robison Crusoe and Friday. I finished reading that book the next morning.

Grandma and Mama went shopping at J.C. Penney in Blue Reed right after lunch, leaving Myra Sue and me in charge of Eli. Even though they were only going to buy sheets, Myra pouted because she wanted to go shopping, and she was madder than a nest of wet hornets that sports were the only thing on TV on Saturday afternoons.

"Want me to get you a book from my room?" I asked, helpful as all get-out. Mainly because I did not want to listen to her bellyache about staying home when she could be looking at clothes and shoes and perfume and makeup at the mall in Blue Reed.

"No, I do not. If I want to be boring, though, I'll turn into you." Then she went off in a huff, flopped down on the sofa and stared at the blank television screen.

I bit my lips together so hard it hurt. Boy howdy, being a Better Person isn't easy when you have been called boring by someone who lives her life to watch as much TV as possible.

The mail carrier ran later that afternoon. Daisy and I ambled down to the mailbox to get whatever he'd delivered. We'd almost reached the end of the driveway where it joins Rough Creek Road when we heard the heart-stopping racket of gravel flying, metal crunching and someone screaming in pain and terror.

Beside me, Daisy stiffened, her muscles as hard as a rock, when I touched her. She looked to the right, the direction the noise had come. I squinted down the road and saw something red and a flash of chrome.

Without thinking, I tore off down Rough Creek Road like a house afire. Right smack in the middle of that old dirt road was a

red bicycle, its wheels still spinning and a dark-haired girl sprawled facedown alongside it. She lay still as a stone and just as silent.

Ten

Myra Sue Should Never Be a Paramedic

Daisy reached her and ran a gentle sniff across the girl's entire length.

I skidded to a stop, hollering, "Are you all right? Are you okay?"

The girl didn't make a sound. I squatted down beside her, and touched her shoulder.

"Hey! Are you okay?"

I knew from the first aid they taught us at school that when someone has been in an accident, you don't move them because you might cause worse injury. I softly poked her shoulder and patted her head.

"Are you all right?" I yelled, but she lay there, and I figured she was plumb dead.

Although our road is isolated and full of holes and ruts, and only a few folks live here, sometimes a driver will get a wild urge to speed along this old dirt lane like a crazy knothead. I needed to get help, but I couldn't just leave her out there in the middle of the road.

I screamed *"Help! Help!"* over and over so loud I nearly burst open my own head.

Then I stopped and listened. It was quiet as could be, no sound from our house, no car crunching gravel beneath its tires as it approached. I doubted Myra Sue heard me, and Daddy and Mr. Brett were on the far side of the farm, moving some heifers to another pasture. All the neighbors were too far away to hear me.

I wanted to bust out bawling, but right then was the wrong time and place for such carryings on.

Daisy stood next to the girl, her posture showing the world she was so alert that nothing would ever escape her notice. She might be old, but she's still savvy as all get out. And she's big enough that no one is going to miss seeing her standing in the middle of the road.

"Daisy, you stay right there and don't let anyone run over her. Bark like crazy if you hear a car coming." She looked straight into my eyes, and I knew she understood every blessed word I said.

I shot back to the house, screaming for help at the top of my lungs. Just as I reached the front porch steps, Myra Sue came flying out the door, her eyes wide and frightened.

"What's wrong, what's wrong?" she shrieked. "Has something happened to Isabel?"

"Call an ambulance! Tell them there's been an accident on the road. Hurry."

She jumped up and down, shaking her hands as if they were wet. "Is it Isabel? Is it Isabel? Is it Isabel? Is it —"

"No!" I screamed at her. "It's a stranger. Go call an ambulance right now."

She stared at me like she does when she's figuring things out.

"Run, Myra. Hurry. Call for an ambulance! *Hurry!*"

She turned and hightailed it back into the house. I yanked the old crocheted throw off the porch swing and rushed back to the injured girl.

Daisy had not moved, except to turn her head and keep watch up and down the road. She held her big fluffy tail high and unmoving as her gaze combed the entire area.

"Good dog," I said, panting like a dog my own self.

I hunkered down next to the girl and arranged the throw over her. It was yellow and white and as soft as a million washes could give it. Grandma had crocheted it way back when I was a little girl. There was a lot of good loving and gentle thoughts stitched into that afghan, so I made sure I tucked it snug.

She moaned, and I froze for a minute, watching her. She moaned again, louder. This time, she moved her legs and curled one hand.

"Take it easy," I said, as soothing as I could, even though I still trembled and screamed like a deranged banshee inside my skin.

"Ooh." She dug her fingers into the dirt. "Ohhhh."

"Lie still. Help is coming." I patted her shoulder and watched her fingers dig, relax, dig, relax.

Her next moan came out long and thin, like a high-pitched tone on a violin. She straightened her arms and tried to sit up, pushing her palms into the gravel.

"Don't!" I yelped. "You don't want to move a body that's been hurt in an accident."

It was like she did not hear me. She kept pushing her hands against the gravel and scrounging her legs into the dirt.

"Oh!" she said loudly as she sat up completely. That yellow and white afghan slid off.

The blood was running down her face so bad I was afraid she might bleed completely to death.

Behind me the sound of running footsteps.

"Here! Here!" I looked over my shoulder and saw my sister galumphing more awkwardly than she usually does. She had her arms full.

"I got stuff." She stopped next to us, huffing and puffing. "Gauze and alcohol and Band-Aids and Nyquil and wash cloths."

I ignored the presence of the Nyquil, but took a cloth and began to blot away the blood that poured from a cut on the girl's forehead.

"Ooo." That was Myra. She swayed and moaned and I was afraid she was gonna pass out.

Real quick I said, "Myra, give me that stuff, and run back for some water."

She nodded, let go of her burden so it fell willy-nilly next to me on the road, and off she went.

Let me tell you something. It took less time than you'd would have thought possible for blood to completely soak that cloth. I grabbed up another and pressed it against the girl's forehead where an egg-sized knot had swelled. Her nose was all skinned up, her lip split open and bleeding. Her eyes seemed unfocused and her head lolled backward. The next thing I knew, she fell over sideways.

Right then I heard a car coming toward us, fast. Daisy leaped over the girl's unconscious body and stood in the middle of the road, waving her tail like crazy and barking her head off. I stood up and waved my arms, screaming, "Stop, stop, *STOP!*"

It was Grandma's car and she slammed on the brakes so fast and so hard she and Mama nearly exited through the windshield. Both front doors flew open and they ran toward us. Myra Sue trotted up as far as the car, but stayed back, looking like she might barf.

Mama and Grandma dropped down on the road next to the girl. Mama grabbed the last clean wash cloth and pressed it against the wound.

"Myra," I hollered, "get lots more rags. Clean ones. Hurry."

Grandma tucked the afghan around her again. It was all splotched with blood.

"We better get her to the clinic, and right now," Grandma said.

"Don't move her!" I yelled. "Don't move an injured person."

Right then I heard the chugging engine of our tractor. It was Daddy and Mr. Brett coming back from the pasture to get the evening chores done. Daddy would be driving and Mr. Brett would be sitting on the fender of that green John Deere.

Faster than the roadrunner in a cartoon, I tore off up the road, across our yard, past the barn and met the men as the tractor pulled up the slope toward the barn.

"Daddy, Daddy, Daddy!" I screamed, jumped up and down like Myra had done earlier. "Come quick!" I figured he couldn't hear me over the noise of the engine, but I leaped around and pointed toward the road.

His expression changed from a tired grin to one of alarm. He turned off the tractor, jumped down from the seat before the sound of the motor died. He ran toward me.

"Quick! On the road. A hurt girl."

"Where?"

"On the right, past the mailbox. In the middle of the road."

Before I could blink twice, he and Mr. Brett had leaped into the pickup and flown down the driveway. The front door slammed, and Myra Sue staggered down the steps with an armful of rags and towels. I ran to her and took everything.

"You stay here with the baby," I said, "and I'll take these."

She nodded and dashed back into the house.

When I got to others, they were already laying the girl in the backseat of Grandma's Toyota. Daddy and Mr. Brett are part of the volunteer fire department, so they've had training and knew what they were doing. I quit worrying about moving that poor girl. Mama squished herself into the backseat and pressed clothes against the girl's head. She took all the rags and towels I had.

Daddy and Grandma got into the car—with Daddy in the driver's seat, thank goodness, because Grandma is the world's scariest driver, as you know.

"Brett, get the chores started, and call Ian to help if you need him," he said. "April Grace, you and Myra take care of the baby and fix supper. We'll be back as soon as we can."

He maneuvered the car around so they could drive back toward town. He gunned the engine and just like that, they shot down Rough Creek Road with dust billowing out behind the car. Mr. Brett and I just stood there a minute.

"Well sir," Mr. Brett said, taking in a deep breath when the dust settled. "Reckon we better get to our chores."

He picked up the bicycle, which looked brand new, except that red paint was all scratched up and the front fender was kinda bent.

"I'll come back and get rid of those bloody rags," he said.

He kicked them to the side of road and down into the ditch so they weren't visible, but there was nothing he could do about the blood on the ground. Looking at it made me shudder.

"Will they get her to the clinic in time?" I asked him. "Do you think she'll die on the way there?"

He shook his head and gave me a reassuring smile. "No. She's hurt, but not too badly. They'll fix her up just fine at the clinic."

Relief flooded through me so that I felt it from the top of my head to the tips of my toes.

"Good!"

"Who was that little girl, anyway?" he asked. "Somebody you go to school with?"

"I don't know," I said. "I'd never seen her before, and we know everyone who lives on this road."

"No one has moved in lately." Mr. Brett looked around the road as if he was looking for new houses he'd never seen before. He stroked his black beard for minute.

"It's a bit of a mystery," he said. I walked beside him as we went back to the house.

Boy howdy.

A mystery.

Eleven

Tracking
the
Tracks

Myra Sue was sitting cross-legged on a blanket on the floor of the front room, playing with Eli.

He looked up when I came in and grinned. He waved both arms up and down in the excited way babies do when they see someone they love. Two tiny teeth peeked out of his lower gums as he smiled, and two big dimples curved on both his fat little cheeks. The red hair he'd been born with had darkened and turned curly. He is the cutest little baby boy in the whole entire world, I kid you not.

I got down on the floor next to him and kissed his face and neck while he giggled and squealed. A long string of drool hung from his lower lip.

"Here," Myra Sue said as she pushed a cloth in my hand. "Wipe his chin. How can you stand to kiss his face when he has dribble on it?"

That girl is such a Miss Priss she makes my behind hurt sometimes.

"I don't mind." I wiped his chin, then I tipped him back and buried my face in his tummy and made funny noises. He laughed, grabbed a fistful of my hair and pulled. It hurt like everything, but that was okay.

"Myra," I said, as I carefully opened his little hand and freed myself, "have you ever seen that girl before?"

"The one who got hurt?"

Honest to Pete, who else did she think I was talking about?

"Yes. The one who got hurt."

"All I saw was blood."

She sat Eli upright on his bottom and played with his curls, fluffing and winding them around her fingers. She tipped her head to one side.

"Eli would make a pretty girl," she said.

Trust my silly sister to come up with that one.

"You heard anything at all about someone new moving to the road?"

She shook her head and glanced at the clock on the fireplace mantle. "It's nearly five o'clock. Think we should make supper now?"

"Since we don't know when they'll be home, maybe we should make something that can be warmed up."

"Or eaten cold."

"Like tuna sandwiches?"

She nodded.

"Or egg salad," I added.

"Or pancakes."

"Pancakes?" I curled my nose. "No one wants to eat a warmed up pancake." I got to my feet. "I'll fix some tuna salad."

It wouldn't be one of Mama's good suppers, but at least I wasn't going to run the risk of Myra concocting pancakes—she can't cook worth a hoot—and warming them up. Or eating them cold. I shuddered at the mere thought.

As soon as I finished the tuna, covered it and set it in the fridge, I told Myra, "I'm going to see if I can find out something about that girl."

She looked up from playing soft blocks with Eli and said, "Don't you think Mama and Daddy and Grandma will find out who she is?"

"More than likely. But what if she's an orphan who has been living by herself in some old shack, and no one ever saw her until now."

I paused to let that idea get past her big blond hair and sink into her brain, then said, "Or maybe she's taking a crosscountry bike ride and made a wrong turn at Albuquerque."

Myra tipped her head to one side and frowned.

I had pity on her and said, "Or maybe, just maybe, we have a new family in the neighborhood."

Her face cleared. "You are so not funny. I still think Mama and Daddy will find out who she is and let us know when they come home."

"You're right. But I'm itchin' to find out."

I left her with Eli and walked to the place in the road where the accident had happened. I stared at the blood that had soaked into the dirt. I saw where she had clawed at the earth while she laid there moaning. The whole thing was creepy, let me tell you. And sad. That poor girl was a stranger and whoever loved her, wherever they were, had no idea she was hurt.

At least the bloody rags were gone. Mr. Brett is a man of his word.

There were several loose rocks and a big spot where the hard packed dirt of the road had been scraped and overturned. I figured the mystery girl had driven her bike too fast over some loose rocks and lost control. That's easy to do on Rough Creek Road. If anyone ever asks you about bike riding on our road, you can tell them that April Grace Reilly, who has lived here forever, says it's not much fun. Mostly you get your intestines and your eyeballs shook loose.

I walked away a few steps, noticing the tracks of her bicycle tires in the dustier parts of the road. Walking along, head down, eyes focused, I followed those bike tracks. Sometimes they wobbled, sometimes they were straight. I spotted what I was sure were the imprints of Grandma's tires as she had driven over them on the way home, and where Daddy had driven over them going to the clinic. But as far as I know, no other car had come along since the accident to mar the bicycle's tracks. Night was still a few hours away, and I knew I'd get in trouble if I was out on this road after dark. I decided if those tracks took me as far as the highway, which was about two miles from our house, I'd come back home.

The creek for which the road is named runs along beside it for a while. If Rough Creek rises from the spring rains, it can wash out parts here and there. For all its hazards and obstacles, the road is beautiful as it winds around sharp curves, up and down hills, and along pastures where livestock graze. In some places, big trees grow on either side of the road and their branches meet over the top, making a leafy canopy prettier than any piece of lace you'd ever hope to see.

There were three neighboring families living between our farm and where Rough Creek Road meets Highway 542. At the first two driveways, by both mailboxes, the mail carrier's truck tires had left prints. The tracks of the bike were more to the center of the road and nowhere near those driveways. That told me the girl had not come from either house.

Late afternoon shadows stretched across the ground like they were crawling toward a hibernation hole. If I'd lifted my head, I'd be looking at the sun, eyeball to eyeball. As I walked along, my neck hurt from watching those thin tire prints, but I kept my focus on them.

And then they ended.

You see there is a dip where the creek crosses the road, and the rain we had a couple of weeks ago washed out the low spot, leaving nothing but a bunch of big ol' rocks. I reckon a grizzly bear couldn't have left a track in that spot.

I paused long enough to stretch the kinks out of my neck, then I picked my way across the washout, found tracks on the other side and continued on. The last stretch of road before you get to the highway is a steep hill. As I trekked up that hill, I spotted shoe prints next to the tire tracks, so I figured the girl had walked her bike down the incline. That had been a smart move. If she'd gone free-wheeling down that hill, she would have probably killed herself. Some roads are not made for bike rides.

The last house on Rough Creek Road before reaching the highway belonged to Chester and Theodosia Hopper. They are just about the oldest people on the face of the earth. Their house is a tiny little four room white cottage that sits on the side of a hill at the end of a long narrow driveway. They have a small pond behind it and a flock of white geese. Big old trees and bunches of flower beds surround that little house, and it's really pretty, like a picture.

Mrs. Hopper is a sweet old lady, but her mister can be crankier than all get out. Neither one of them hear very well. If you're ever outside their house, you'll probably think all that shouting and hollering is a big ol' fight, but it's just them two having a conversation.

That afternoon, Mrs. Hopper was standing next to her mailbox at the end of the driveway. The lowering sun made her white hair look pink. She was twisting the skirt of her overall apron between her hands, and gawking around like she'd lost something.

"Hi, Mrs. Hopper," I yelled.

She turned, squinted, then toddled out into the road and came towards me. The closer she got, the more I could see how pale and sick she looked. Mrs. Hopper might be older than the moon, but she has always looked healthy.

"Is that you, April Grace?"

"Yes, ma'am. Is something wrong? Is Mr. Hopper all right?"

"It's lacy," she said.

"Lacy?"

Mrs. Hopper wore plain cotton apron over her dress, and I had on jeans and a t-shirt. I glanced around, looking at fences and trees limbs. There was not a scrap of lace on anything, so her words completely confused me.

"Where? What do you mean?"

"She's gone." She twisted that apron so hard it looked like she'd break her fingers. "I think she ran away. Maybe someone took her."

I think Mrs. Hopper loved her geese as much as most people love their kids. She always kept a close eye on them.

Her tears dripped down her pale wrinkled cheeks. The sight like to have broken my heart.

I tried to comfort her. "If anyone tried to take her, she'd likely bite them a few times, wouldn't she? They'd let her go quick enough. Or maybe she flew over to one of our ponds to visit the ducks."

I want to tell you, the look she gave me said I must have been dropped on my head before, during, and after my birth.

"Honest, Mrs. Hopper, I don't think she'd just fly away. Do you? You take good such good care of your flock —"

"April Grace Reilly. I am talking about Lacey Paige Pickering, my little cousin. She's come to stay with us for a while, God love her. She went out riding her bike earlier this afternoon, and she hasn't come back yet."

She wrung her apron again and looked around at the gathering darkness.

"A red bike?" I asked, my heart leaping wildly.

Mrs. Hopper turned to me.

"Yes! Have you seen her?"

"Does she have long, dark brown hair?"

The old woman raised trembling hands to both cheeks, and her mouth worked like she wanted to speak and couldn't. She reached out one hand and grabbed my arm. Who woulda thought an old woman like her would have such strong fingers?

"Yes! Where is she, April Grace?"

Excitement shot through me so hard that I could barely stand still.

"Oh, my goodness! Oh, good gravy! Mrs. Hopper, she didn't run away. She had an accident on her bike a few yards from our driveway. Daddy and Mama and Grandma took her to the clinic in Cedar Ridge."

"An accident? Was she hurt? Is she all right?"

I chose my words carefully.

"She was able to sit up, so I don't think she broke any bones. She'd scraped her face on the dirt pretty good and it was bleeding. There's a bump on her forehead and I bet she's going to have some bruises. But she's at the clinic, and they'll fix her right up."

Mrs. Hopper looked so worried and scared, I left out how much blood there'd been, and that the girl had been knocked out. I said that last bit with a lot more confidence than I felt. And I'll tell you something else. I surely was glad Mrs. Hopper had not seen Lacey Paige Pickering's injuries or her lying there, unconscious, 'cause I think she might have toppled over, right there on the road.

"Oh. Thank the good Lord. But… why didn't one of y'uns come and get me?"

"We didn't know who she was, ma'am," I said before I thought.

"Didn't know who she was!? Why, didn't you ask her name?"

Uh oh.

The last thing in the world I wanted was to distress this old lady more than she was. I tried to figure out a way to tell her the condition we'd found Lacey in, but I was afraid I'd say the wrong thing.

I heard the crunch of tires on the road right then, and boy, howdy, was I glad to see Grandma's Toyota.

"There's Daddy 'n them."

The car stopped right next to us and the only two passengers were my daddy and mama.

Mama opened the passenger door right quick and jumped out.

"April Grace Reilly, what on earth are you doing out here when it's getting dark?" Without giving me a chance to say 'boo' or 'good evening' or anything, she turned to Mrs. Hopper and grabbed both her hands.

"We've been trying to call you, but can't get through."

"Chester done had the phone service cut off," she said. "He said we can't hear anyone, anyhow, so why should the phone company get rich off of us?"

Mrs. Hopper peered into the back windows.

"Where's Lacey? Is she all right?"

"She's just fine. Mike's mother is staying with her," Mama said. "They're keeping her at the clinic overnight, just for observation. Concussions are nothing to be taken lightly."

"Concussion? April said Lacey only had scrapes and bruises."

I squirmed a little because that's not quite how I put it, but Mama said, "April Grace didn't want to worry you until we knew more."

Daddy leaned over and spoke to Mrs. Hopper through the open passenger door.

"I need to get Lily home to the baby, but if you'd like, I'll be happy to come right back and drive you to the clinic to see Lacey."

"I want to go to her, poor child. She just got here last night… After everything that girl has been through in her young life, what a welcome into Arkansas this has been for her." She sniffled and wiped her eyes with the hem of her apron. "But you don't need to come back, Mike. I can drive Chester 'n me into town."

"Absolutely not," Daddy said in his firmest voice. "We forgot to get sugar and coffee while we were in town so I need to go back anyway. I'd be grateful for a little company."

Mrs. Hopper's wrinkles deepened as she smiled.

"Why, that's mighty fine, Mike. I'll go get washed up and be waiting right here."

"Get in the back, Mrs. Hopper. I'll drive you up to your house, then after I drop my girls off, I'll come back and pick you up there. Don't walk up here and wait for me. We don't want you or Chester taking a spill in the dark."

"You're a lucky woman, Lily, to have such a fine husband," Mrs. Hopper said as we climbed into the backseat.

"I know it." Mama gave her beautiful smile to Mrs. Hopper, then offered it to Daddy.

For a minute, I thought they were gonna smooch, but they didn't. It might be getting dark, but it was still light enough to see that nonsense.

And anyway, I agreed with Mrs. Hopper.

Twelve

Fixin'
What's
Broke

The next morning, I went into Cedar Ridge with Mama, Myra Sue, and Mrs. Hopper.

Jennifer and Jessica Cleland, Myra Sue's best friends, had invited her to spend the night. We dropped her off at the Cleland's big brick house in town, then drove to the Cedar Ridge Clinic. Kids aren't allowed where the patients are unless they're patients their own selves. I reckon the doctors and nurses think kids are germier and cootier than adults and shouldn't be able to spread their dirty germs to sick folks. To tell you the honest truth, that kinda annoys me because I have seen some scroungy-looking grown-ups.

But, anyway, that day I had a mission to accomplish, and I was glad for those restrictions.

As soon Mama and Mrs. Hopper went through the door leading back to where I couldn't go, I approached the woman at the front desk.

"May I help you?" She looked at me and spoke to me as if I were a real person instead of a pestering child, which is the way some people at some front desks do.

"If my mama and grandma come looking for me, would you please tell them I'll be right back?"

She raised one eyebrow.

"Who are your mother and grandmother?"

"Lily Reilly and Myra Grace Reilly. They are here for Lacey Pickering."

"Ah, yes. I know who they are." She gave me a sharp look. "And if they ask where you went…?"

"Just a walk." I could see by her expression she was fixin' to get all snoopy as to my intentions, so real quick I added, "This waiting room makes me feel weird and dizzy, like all the sick people are gonna hurl or something. I want to go outside before I barf my own self."

"Oh, goodness!"

And before she could say another word, I hightailed it out of there.

Ernie's Grocerteria was just a block from the clinic. I hurried through the store to the back and pushed through the big swinging double doors that lead into the stockroom. No one that works in that place said one word to me other than "Good mornin', honey!" as I passed them because they know who I am.

His office was upstairs, and I rushed up them two at a time. I looked through the glass panel in his office door and saw ol' Ernie behind the desk, squinting at a pile of papers on his desk. A small desk lamp spilled its light over all those pages. He signed the one on top, then put it in a basket full of other papers.

I knocked. He looked up and beckoned me inside. Ernie is a cozy-looking man, kinda round and stocky, with sorta messy gray-brown hair and a gray mustache. He wears glasses, but most of the time they're on top of his head unless he's looking at something real close. When I think of a grandpa person, someone like Ernie Beason is who I visualize.

As sweet and gentle as a newborn baby lamb, I went in.

"Well, Miss April Grace. What brings you here today?"

He sounded just like always but he didn't have his usual smile. In fact, he was watching me as if he expected me to tell him Grandma had run off to Mexico with the mailman, or something.

Standing as straight as I could, I locked my hands together behind my back and met his eyes. I cleared my throat.

"I'm as sorry as I can be for butting in where I didn't belong and for opening my big mouth and telling you the wrong thing when I called last week."

He got a startled look all over his face.

"Do what?" he sputtered.

"I thought Grandma didn't want to get married, because of all that mess with that old buzzard, Jeffrey Rance. I didn't know she needed some time to adjust her thinking. I didn't know she really *did* want to get married."

He kinda twitched, then moved his chair around so that he faced me. He leaned forward and eyeballed me without blinking even one time.

"Do what?"

I gripped my fingers together so tightly that it hurt, but I did my best to look serious and mature.

"You gotta understand..." I gulped and went on. "You see, I thought I was doing you both a favor, speaking for Grandma. I thought she'd told you marriage was Out of The Question, but you just hadn't understood."

I had to pause a second and take in some more air.

"But, well, the thing is, when I told her she got really upset. So then she tried to call you to clear it all up, but someone told her you went out to lunch with Nancy Agnes Greenleaf, and boy, oh, boy... Well, I think she's mad at you and me both. And Grandma has never been mad at me before."

My eyes stung, and I felt the tears just about brim over. I did not want to look like a baby in front of Ernie. I blinked real hard and sniffed even harder.

He sat back in his chair, his round eyes seeing right through me.

"But... I... we..." He reached for the phone.

"Grandma isn't home."

"No? Where is she?"

"At the clinic."

He jumped up so fast his elbow hit a stack of papers and they scattered all over his desk. He didn't even notice.

"She isn't sick!" I hollered, in case he was fixin' to get upset. "She stayed there last night with Lacey Paige Pickering."

"With who?"

I told him who Lacey was and all about the bicycle wreck and why Grandma stayed with her, and all that.

"Of course Grace would stay. She's that kind of lady," he murmured this almost to himself. Then he said, "That poor child. Is she okay?"

"Grandma called this morning and said she was ready to come home, so I guess she's all right. I came into town with Mama and Mrs. Hopper because I wanted to talk to you, face to face, so's you'd stop being angry at Grandma, and marry her, and not go out with Nancy Agnes Greenleaf. I mean, Nancy Agnes is a very nice lady and she's really, really beautiful, but, well, Grandma loves you."

The biggest smile you ever saw came over his face.

"She told you that?"

"Yep. Right out of her own mouth. But she's still mad at you, anyway."

His smile went away.

"Because of Nancy Agnes?"

I nodded.

He huffed and shook his head.

"Pilar Ruiz—she's the bakery manager—and I took Nancy Agnes out for her birthday. We went to Tico-Taco. Pilar's husband is the cook there. He made us a nice lunch. It wasn't a date or a romantic dinner or anything else. Your grandmother does not have one reason to be upset, or jealous." He gave me a tiny grin. "But it's sorta nice to know she cares that much."

"Then you better explain it all to her before she decides to go out with Rob Estes this weekend."

He frowned. "Yes, ma'am, I better talk to her."

"I better get back over to the clinic before Mama finds out I'm gone. I don't think I trust that gal at the front desk to be my alibi."

"They don't know you're here?"

"No, sir."

"And you said your grandma is still at the clinic?"

I nodded. He turned and clicked off the desk lamp.

"Let's go." He held open the door for me. "If we hurry, they might never know you left."

Good ol' Ernie.

Boy howdy, I didn't realize an old guy like him could move so fast. I trotted right along beside him. Ernie has never been much of a chatter-box, and he didn't say a word on the short walk down the street.

He opened the big glass door at the clinic and we went inside. There stood Grandma, Mrs. Hopper, Lacey, and Mama in a cluster near the front desk and didn't see us at first. Then Grandma spotted us and grabbed Mama's arm.

Mama turned. She frowned so hard at me, I don't think she even saw Ernie.

I think he hoped to save me a punishment, because he reached out with one arm, pulled me to him and gave me a big ol' hug.

"Thanks, April Grace," he said loud enough for those two women to hear. Then he smiled, gave me a wink, and let me go.

"Myra Grace Reilly," he said to Grandma, right there in front of everyone in that entire clinic waiting room—and there were a lot of waiting folks, believe you me, "you and me need to talk."

Mama's gaze shot back and forth between the two of them for a few seconds, then she looked at me. I couldn't help but grin at her, because I knew Ernie was gonna make everything right with Grandma again. Her face softened.

"If you women want to go now," he said to Mama, "I'll take Grace home later."

Grandma's mouth was wagging open and shut like a fish, but she'd not uttered a single solitary word yet. It seemed everyone in that clinic was watching us, grinning like a bunch of monkeys. Cedar Ridge is such a small place, that everyone knows everyone else. I betcha all the folks in town knew about Ernie and Grandma, and Grandma's other boyfriends, and that whole entire mess.

Mama herded "us women" into a little clump, out the front door, and into our Taurus.

"I'll swan to my time," Mrs. Hopper sighed once we were settled into the car. "What was all that about?"

"I'll explain on the way home," Mama told her. She turned to Lacey and me in the backseat. "April, this is Lacey Pickering." She looked at Lacey. "This is my daughter April Grace. She's the one who found you yesterday."

Lacey gave me a smile that seemed kind of shy.

"Hi," she said, in a soft voice.

"Hi. How are you feeling?"

That poor girl had a big old bandage on her forehead, and big purple bruise on her cheek. She skinned the tip of her nose, and split her lower lip open, so it was kinda puffy, but she had really pretty green eyes and long brown hair. Her right wrist was bandaged, and both knees were bruised and cut. Her skin had a nice tan, like she spent a lot of time outside.

"Did you break your arm?" I asked.

She held up her arm so that the white bandage seemed to glare in the sunlight.

"Just a sprain."

"Does it hurt?"

"A little. But not as much as my head, right here." She put the very tips of her fingers against that big ol' bandage and winced. "Five stitches."

"Oh!"

In the front seat, Mama was driving us out of town and telling Mrs. Hopper about Grandma and Ernie. Lacey leaned forward a little, as if she was interested, so I didn't say anything else for a while.

After a bit, she sat back and asked me, "Is Miss Grace your grandma?"

I nodded.

"She's cool. She stayed with me all night."

"She's the best grandma in the whole entire world."

Lacey smiled, then winced and put her hand to her lip.

"Oo," she said. "I have to be careful not to move my mouth too much."

"Me too! But my problem is, I say things when I shouldn't"

She tried to smile again. "What grade will you be in?" she asked.

"Seventh. How about you?"

"Eighth grade."

"Do you like school?" I asked her.

I had a feeling if she could wrinkle her nose, she would. "Not much. I don't like being inside all the time."

"Me, either! You'll have to come out in the woods with me while you're here. We have a creek and a fresh water spring, and a cave. Or maybe Grandma will take us on a nature walk."

"Sounds like fun." Her eyes sparkled. Boy, oh boy, it was going to be nice to have someone to spend time with. I hoped she'd be around for a while.

"How long are you staying with the Hoppers?"

It was like a cloud came over her face and the smile in her eyes faded. She looked out the window.

"I don't know. Maybe always."

More than anything right then I wanted to ask Lacey what she meant. But something about the way she sat, completely motionless and silent, persuaded me not to ask questions.

Thirteen

Thinking About
Life
and
Rotten
Scrambled Eggs

Grandma and Ernie came to the house right as we were finishing supper. They both practically glowed like two new flashlights.

Daddy invited them to sit and have some cake and coffee.

"Don't mind if I do," Ernie said. He held a chair out for Grandma, but she took a step back.

"I need to use the phone first," Grandma said.

Supper that night had been one of my favorites—chicken-fried steak with mashed potatoes and gravy. Mama had also made creamed corn and a spinach salad. I would have thirds, but I didn't want to spoil my appetite for cake.

One of the best things that happened that evening, no one punished or scolded or lectured me about my interventions on Grandma's behalf. At least they hadn't by the time we'd finished supper.

I could hear Grandma murmuring in the telephone but not what she said.

"Not a big piece for me, Lily," Ernie said as Mama began to cut a three-layered chocolate cake with icing so thick you could smother in it, if you wanted to. "Grace and I had a nice dinner at that new place on the square in Ava."

"You went to Ava?" Daddy said.

"It wasn't our destination, but it's where we ended up. We were just driving around, talking."

"It's such a pretty drive between Cedar Ridge and Ava," Mama said as she put a slice of cake in front of him. She poured him a cup of coffee, and I noticed the funny little smile on her face as she gave it to him.

Grandma came into the kitchen a minute later, and settled down in a chair next to Ernie. She eyeballed the slender slice of cake on his plate.

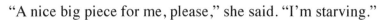

"A nice big piece for me, please," she said. "I'm starving."

"Wha...?" Ernie said with his fork halfway to his mouth.

"Don't look at me like that," she said to him. "I've not had the heart to eat for nearly a week, and I'm making up for it."

Everyone had a good laugh, and Mama put down a big slab of cake in front of Grandma.

"So I hear you have a new neighbor," Ernie said after he'd eaten a bite or two.

"For a while, anyway," Grandma said. "That poor, sweet little girl has surely had a long hard row to hoe before she got here."

"What d'you mean, Grandma?"

"Well, she didn't tell me a whole lot, but I –"

The front door opened and Ian St. James called out a greeting. A few seconds later, he and his missus joined us.

"Just in time for cake!" Daddy said.

Ian's eyes lit up, and Mama cut him a slab nearly as big as she'd given to Grandma. She offered Isabel a Yellow Delicious apple from the fruit bowl.

"No, thank you, Lily," she said. "We've had dinner. Ian, would you kindly bear in mind your waistline?" She turned to Grandma. "My word, Grace, you sounded strange when you called us just now. We got here as fast as we could. I didn't even have time to fix my hair."

I eyeballed that slicked-back style, which is how she always wears it and believe me when I say it does not flatter her one little bit.

"Looks the same to me," I said.

She blinked about ninety-five times. I was just stating truth. I didn't even insult her.

"Yoohoo! Reillys!" That was Temple Freebird's voice, coming from the front door.

"Come on in," Daddy called out.

Let me stop to tell you something right here and now. Anyone with a nose could smell the Freebirds before seeing them. In case you don't know it already, I'll tell you—those two gray-haired old hippies see no reason to bathe on a regular basis. And by regular, I mean at least a couple of times a month.

You should've seen Isabel's face when Temple and Forest joined us in the kitchen. She curled up her nose so hard she nearly turned her nostrils inside out.

While all the greeting of the visitors went on, Mama opened the kitchen window. Wide.

We have a big kitchen, but with so many people in there, it seemed really small. Like Isabel, the Freebirds think sugar is a plague. Maybe it is, but I like cake. And if staying away from it will make me look as stringy and scrawny as those three sugar-free people, I'd be sure to keep eating my sweets.

Of course, even as stringy and unpleasant-looking and foul-smelling as they were, I liked Forest and Temple. They were strange and interesting to talk to, and both had very kind hearts. Ol' Forest looked droopy and sad, but that's just because his face fell that way. And Temple's blue eyes sparkled a lot. Forest told me one time that Temple had been runner-up in a beauty contest when she was eighteen. Looking at her now, in a faded old prairie skirt, a stained tanktop, and a couple of teeth missing, I found it hard to believe. Sort of. But it didn't matter because Temple is beautiful inside. She has what I've heard Mama call "a pure heart." And if anyone should know what that is, it would be Mama.

"What a happy looking group!" Temple said, flinging her arms out as if she would gather us into a group hug. Boy howdy, I prayed hard that would not happen.

Isabel skittered to the far side of the room.

For a minute or two, everybody ate cake, or apples, or sipped their drinks, and chatted with one another. I shoveled cake into my pie hole. That creamy chocolate icing and the moist soft cake melted in my mouth and slipped down my throat without me even trying.

"Grace, darling," Isabel said, "I'm simply dying of curiosity. Why did you call us over here? What is it you wanted to tell us?"

She sipped her water with her pinkie extended. If Myra Sue had been with us, she'd have been doing the exact same thing.

"Yes, what is it?" Temple said. "You have my interest all a-twitter."

Everybody got quiet, and we all stared at Grandma. She gave Ernie goo-goo eyes, and he smiled at her like she was his favorite teddy bear. She turned to us and cleared her throat.

"We've set the date."

Boy howdy, for a few seconds it was so silent, you could practically hear everyone's hair grow.

"You have?" Mama said, smiling all over herself. "Oh, I'm so happy for you!"

"When's the big day?" Daddy said, grinning so big he nearly split his face.

"June 27," Grandma and Ernie said together.

"The last Saturday of the month," Grandma added.

"That's only a month away," Mama said, her voice kinda faint.

And then that whole entire kitchen turned into what Mrs. Patsy Farber, the principal of Cedar Ridge Junior High, would have called a "cacophony." That is, you couldn't hear yourself think.

Although I knew this marriage was gonna happen and it was gonna be good for everyone, the memory of Grandma's engagement to old man Rance smeared the moment like a big blob of dirty Vaseline.

Inside my head, I yelled, "Get a grip, April Grace!"

I had to do this about twelve times. And then I looked at good ol' Ernie. He was an awesome guy, patient and kind. He treated Grandma like she's his best friend. Although she'd had other boyfriends while the two of them dated, he'd waited, giving her time to find out if he really was the man for her.

I felt all warm and fuzzy in my heart.

Everyone in that kitchen was talking all at once, saying things like, "Oh, my goodness, will we have enough time?" and "Where do you plan to have the wedding?" and "What shall we serve at the reception?" and "What colors and flowers do you want?" And the thing is, because they were all saying it at the same time, no one was listening to anyone else. It was just a lot of racket.

After a couple of minutes, Isabel—who had been asking more questions than a two-edged sword, and not even giving Grandma or Ernie a chance to reply—cleared her throat and clapped her hands together twice.

Then, in that special way she has that scared the gizzard right out of all her students at school, said, "People, people!"

She clapped her hands together two more times, and I'm telling you it sounded like two gunshots. Everybody hushed.

I'm surprised nobody ducked.

"Listen to me, people!" she hollered, even though everyone was quiet and looking at her.

"Lamb-baby," Ian said with a slight smile, "we're all listening."

She gave him a narrow-eyed look. I thought for sure she was gonna holler at him, but she seemed to think the better of it. "Thank you, snuggles."

I think I'd almost rather hear them two squabble than use those goofy names.

"Grace, darling," Isabel said, looking at Grandma, "let me do it."

"Do what?" Grandma said.

"Why, the wedding, of course!" She pressed her long skinny hands to her chest "My dear, who is better qualified than I to take over the duties and details of your nuptials?"

Now, what in the world made that woman think she was better qualified than anyone else to take over Grandma's wedding? Maybe Grandma wanted someone else to do it. Maybe she wanted to do it herself. Maybe she and Ernie wanted something simple and plain.

"Why don't y'all just elope?" I asked. Nothing could be simpler and plainer than that, in my honest opinion.

Listen. The look they all gave me, you would've thought I'd suggested those two old people get married while riding mules down Howard's Hill.

Ol' Isabel picked up right where she left off, as if I hadn't said a blessed word. She went on and on about parties she'd planned—"Remember, Grace-dear, your birthday party a few months ago."—and places she'd shopped—as if that had anything to do with any of this business—and current styles, and the colors that were "in" this season, and did she want a church wedding, or an outdoor event, a formal, semi-formal, afternoon, morning, or breakfast ceremony. My ears like to have started bleeding just from listening.

I excused myself from the crowded kitchen—not that anyone noticed—and went out on the porch and plopped down on the porch swing. Daisy was lying in her favorite spot near the steps, but when she saw me, she knew I needed a friend right then. Good ol' Daisy does not ignore April Grace Reilly like everyone else seems prone to do.

Here's the situation—as much as I love my grandma and as much as I'm fairly happy she's getting married, I can't stand a lot of upset and chaos going on. We Reillys have a nice farm, and except for Myra Sue's occasional nonsense, we have a great life. We have lots of friends, our house is the best house in whole in entire world, we love each other.

And then, for some weird reason I have yet to figure out, last summer the world tilted on its axis and our peaceful life got scrambled like a skillet full of rotten eggs.

Number one, Ian and Isabel moved to our neck of the woods and acted all uppity until they finally saw the light.

Number two, my sister decided to starve herself nearly to death because she wanted to be as skinny as Isabel.

Number three, old man Rance tried to romance Grandma while all the above was going on.

Number four, one of my friends turned into a snob and a bully, which made life at school miserable.

Number five, Mama got pregnant and for a while I was afraid she was gonna up and die.

Number six, last winter, a couple of weeks after Christmas, Mama's mother, who had abandoned her not once, but twice, as a child showed up like she thought she was a member of the family—which she was but it took us all a long time to come to terms with that, let me tell you.

And then the worst, Number seven, Myra Sue ran away. She thought she was gonna become a famous TV star, but thank goodness we found out what was going on before Something Terrible happened.

Now, wouldn't you think with all this happening in one year, it was High Time the Reilly family had a break?

Grandma and Ernie getting married was fine, I reckon, but it was just one more rock thrown into the pond of life that was bound to stir up mud. And with ol' Isabel in charge, I figured mud was the least of what was gonna get stirred up.

Daisy rested her big white head on my lap and gave me the most soulful expression you can imagine from her brown eyes. She wagged her tail as I stroked her head and scratched her ears.

"Daise," I said, "I think you and me need to get a book and take off into the woods a lot this summer."

She smiled. I knew she agreed.

Fourteen

Imaginary Flower Girls
and
Grandma's Arms

Friday morning, I woke up to the fragrance of yummy, yeasty, spicy homemade cinnamon rolls. Mama doesn't make them very often, so they're always a big treat.

I jumped out of bed and ran downstairs. Mama was slathering thick cream cheese icing over the top of a pan full of fresh rolls.

Just as reached for the milk in the 'fridge, she said, "Wash your hands and face, April Grace. And brush your teeth and hair."

Y'know, I figured she'd say that. I should have done it when I first got up, but sometimes, you just can't help yourself when good smells wake you.

I washed and dressed in blue jeans shorts, yellow T-shirt, and my good ol' sneakers as fast as I could. When I raced into the kitchen, Grandma was sitting at the table with her big white #1 Grandma mug full of coffee. I liked the smell of coffee and cinnamon rolls mixed together. It made our kitchen the best place on earth to be right then.

"Mornin', Grandma," I said and started to pull out a chair, but she stopped me.

"Come here, child."

Uh oh.

Had she and Mama held off lecturing and punishing me about the Ernie-Grandma business until now?

Maybe they'd taken their time to devise the perfect punishment plan. And I'd bet they had added more because I'd been outside during all that wedding talk last night when I probably should have been sitting there, hollering out my own ideas and adding to the general ruckus.

The most awfullest thought occurred to me, so awful it like to have sapped my appetite for a cinnamon roll. What if they had decided I should be Grandma's flower girl?

Can you imagine anything more embarrassing than being a twelve-year-old flower girl?

Boy, oh boy, if that was their plan, those two women had come up with the perfect punishment. I'd get Grandma's darning needle and Daddy's Gorilla glue and Mr. Brett's duct tape, and I'd stitch and glue and tape my lips together so I could never utter another mumblin' word, forever.

"April Grace." Mama's voice hauled me out of that notion and back into reality. She and Grandma were eyeballing me like they thought I was sick.

"Yes'm?"

They sat there, waiting for me to say something more. I turned to Grandma with all the pleading and sorrowfulness I could muster on my face and in my eyes.

"Don't you think I'm too old to be your flower girl?" I even let my voice quiver a little bit. I doubted a voice on the edge of sobbing would help my cause, but I figured it wouldn't hurt to try.

Well, I tell you what. You should've seen her reaction. It was like I had said something completely dumb or totally unexpected, or both.

"Flower girl?" she echoed. "You want to be my flower girl?"

Before I could shriek out a protest, she turned to Mama. "What do you think, Lily?"

"No," I said, but apparently they didn't hear me.

"It's up to you, of course, Mama Grace, but I always thought of flower girls as young, under eight years old. But if April wants to do it—"

"No!" I hollered. "I do *not* want be a flower girl. I'll do *anything* else, I'll wash yours and Ernie's dirty dishes for twenty-five years, but please don't make me put on a foo-foo dress and scatter rose petals. I'd rather eat tar."

Grandma sat back, her expression completely baffled.

"Forevermore!" she said.

"April Grace, what are you going on about?" Mama sounded as perplexed as Grandma.

Here's the thing. When you have a vivid imagination like mine, you sometimes almost forget what you imagined and what's real. This can be a problem.

"I'm sorry," I muttered. "I just thought…" I didn't want to continue.

"Thought what?" Mama prompted.

"Well, I thought that… um… well, good gravy… I thought you were gonna punish me for talking to Ernie on the phone last week and for going outside yesterday evening when everyone was taking about the wedding. I thought you were gonna make me be a flower girl."

Mama and Grandma exchanged glances.

"Mercy on us," Grandma said, shaking her head like she could hardly believe what I said. Mama bit her lower lip like she might smile or cry. I wondered which one she wanted to do.

"Come here," Grandma said again, reaching out to me.

She pulled me down on her lap like I was a little kid, wrapped her arms around me and cuddled me close. After all that talk of me being too big to be a flower girl, you'd think I'd've been embarrassed, and would've squirmed and squiggled and struggled to get away.

Nope.

I put my head on her shoulder, snuggled against her like I used to. You know what? She still felt the same, warm and soft and comfortable.

"Now, listen to me, sis," she said. Her voice made her chest vibrate against me. "Are you okay with Ernie and me getting hitched?"

"Yes, ma'am." I lifted my head and looked right in her nice blue eyes. "Are you okay with it?"

"I absolutely am."

"You sure?"

"One thousand percent."

"What about Rob Estes and the Reverend Jordan?"

She smiled. "They are nice men. I like them both a lot. But I love Ernie."

"Love, like ooey-gooey love, like Mama and Daddy. Right?"

"April," Mama said, her voice gently admonishing.

"Yep," Grandma said, "just like that, ooey-gooey and sloppy-sweet. And I want you to know that I'm not mad at you. I was considerable put out that you took it upon yourself to try to order my life for me, but I realize you were doing what you thought was the right thing."

Well, I'm here to tell you that I was so relieved she wasn't angry at me that I wrapped my arms around her neck, burst into tears, and blubbered like a little kid. Grandma held me, and patted my back, and rocked back and forth like she was rocking Eli to sleep. I didn't care that I felt like a baby. Sometimes it feels good to be little and in your grandma's arms again.

After a bit, Grandma nudged me to sit up. She wiped my face with a paper napkin.

"Now, go sit over there and eat your oatmeal."

"Oatmeal!"

Sure enough there was a glass of milk and bowl of oatmeal on the table at my place.

"Mama!" I got up and sent her the saddest look in the world. "I want a cinnamon roll."

"These are for the Hoppers."

"Huh?" I was purely horrified. Not that they were for the Hoppers, but that there weren't any for us.

Mama laughed. "Oh, April Grace, you are so funny sometimes, honey. There is a whole other batch for us. And you may have one, after you eat your oatmeal."

You better believe I scarfed down that oatmeal like there was no tomorrow.

We three females were sitting at the table, enjoying a cinnamon roll each when the front screen door squeaked open.

"Lily? You home?"

"In here, Isabel," Mama called.

Boy howdy. I remember a time when Temple yoohooed at the front door, and Isabel thought it was the Rudest Thing Ever to walk into someone's house without knocking and announce your presence by hollering. As I've said before, Isabel has come a long way.

"My gracious," she said as she entered the kitchen with a briefcase, "there is a delightfully spicy smell is in this house."

"It's Mama's homemade cinnamon rolls," I said. "The best ever. Get you one, Isabel."

"Oh, my." She sat down at the table, put the briefcase on the floor beside her, and eyeballed my roll like she thought it might crawl off the plate and bite her.

"Try one, honey," Grandma said to her. "Lily, give her one."

"Oh, no!" Isabel said, rearing back. She eyeballed my roll again. "Well, just a small nibble, perhaps."

Mama cut a roll in half, put it on a small plate in front of Isabel, then handed her a fork. Grandma got up and poured her a cup of coffee.

"What d'ya got in that suitcase?" Grandma asked.

Isabel delicately cut off a tiny bit of the roll and put it in her mouth. She took a couple of chews, then closed her eyes.

"Oh, Lily," she said, "this is heavenly. The blend of cinnamon and butter… oh my." She opened her eyes and patted the briefcase. "This was my grandfather's attaché case, and it is full of wedding information. I brought it over so we can start planning your nuptials."

I still thought elopement was a good idea, but this time I kept my yap shut.

I want you to know Isabel ate every crumb of that cinnamon roll and she scraped her fork against the plate to get the every bit of the sticky filling and the cream cheese frosting.

"Told you it was good," I said, grinning.

She winked at me and laughed. "You were right. But do me a favor? Do not tell Ian of this transgression. I'd never live it down."

I hooted and giggled. It was good to see Isabel be so human. I promised her I'd keep her secret.

"Want the other half, Isabel?" Mama asked.

She held up both hands like trying to stop an oncoming bus. "No, no. I probably put on forty pounds from what I just ate."

Mama laughed and took away the plate. Isabel plunked that briefcase on the table in front of her and opened it. She started pulling out magazines and papers and pictures and I don't know what all.

"April," Mama said, "I'm going to go check on the baby. You wash up these few plates. When I get back, you and I will go to the Hoppers."

"Goody! I want to see Lacey again."

Mama smiled. "You liked her, didn't you?"

"She seems really nice. But kinda sad."

"If you had the life that child has had, you'd be sad too," Grandma put in. She'd made these mysterious little comments before, and my interest got keener every time.

"What do you mean?"

Grandma took a long drink. "Just that life hasn't been easy on her."

Well, that told me absolutely nothing. I could see by the expression on Grandma's face, she wasn't going say any more about it. Boy, oh boy, Grandma sure can be stubborn when she takes a notion.

Fifteen

Deep Roots,
Shallow Roots,
and
No Roots at All

When we got to the Hoppers' house, Lacey was sitting on the top step of the front porch, reading. She wore a pair of jeans and a sleeveless, red-checked blouse that hung loose on her.

"Look, April Grace. A fellow bookworm," Mama said, with a smile.

"I noticed that," I said.

Poor Lacey's arms and face were bruised and cut, but she looked better than she had the day before.

"Hi!" I hollered as I ran to join her on the porch.

"Hi," she answered in her soft voice.

"How are you feeling?"

"Sore. Especially where the stitches are." She looked past me, and smiled at Mama. Her lips weren't as swollen as they had been yesterday. "Hi, Mrs. Reilly."

"Hi, sweetheart." Mama gave Lacey her special smile. "Are you doing better today?"

"Yes, thank you." She glanced at the pan Mama carried.

"We brought y'all some homemade cinnamon rolls," I piped up. "The best in the whole entire world."

Lacey's eyes lit up. "I love cinnamon rolls!"

"Well, here's a whole batch for you and the Hoppers," Mama said. "Are they inside?"

"Yes, ma'am, they are. And thank you so much." She jumped up and opened the door, then we followed Mama into the house.

I've been to the Hopper house many times, and let me tell you, everything in it is old, including them. For instance, their names are Chester and Theodosia. Do you know anyone under the age of one million whose name is Chester or Theodosia? And their furniture is boxy and squishy-soft, covered with old quilts. Mrs. Hopper calls the sofa a daven-port, which I thought was a town in Iowa. The pictures on the walls are faded. In fact, that picture of Jesus praying in the Garden is supposed to be at night, but in their print it looks like broad daylight.Everything might be old in their house, but Mrs. Hopper keeps it so clean you can eat off the floors. It smells like lemon oil, Ivory soap, and Mr. Clean. I'm not sure the last time they had new clothes. For as long as I can remem-ber, she wears the same dark blue dress to church in cold weather and the same green dress in the warm months. Mr. Hopper wears overalls and a plaid shirt for everything from plowing his garden to attending services. But those old outfits are scrubbed, starched, and ironed smooth.

"Let's see what you've brought us, Lily." Mrs. Hopper lifted a corner of the aluminum foil wrap. "Oh, my! Those look good, and won't my Chester love himself one with a cup of hot coffee."

The old man was snoozing in an old recliner, a knitted brown and yel-low afghan across him from the knees down. He didn't budge a hair. That's because he's deafer than five fence posts all stacked on one another.

"You didn't bring that sweet baby boy?" Mrs. Hopper asked. She looked around the room as if she thought Mama had stashed Eli somewhere.

"Mama Grace, Isabel, and Myra are at the house. I have no shortage of babysitters."

"Ain't that a blessin'? Have a seat," Mrs. Hopper said, "and I'll serve us up these here rolls."

"No, no," Mama said, as she sat in a yellow and orange flowered rocking chair. It was the only chair that wasn't covered with a quilt. "Those are for you and your guest. We have plenty at home."

"Want some coffee?" The old woman smoothed the skirt of her apron. "I just put on fresh pot not ten minutes ago."

"Want to see my room?" Lacey asked me.

"Sure."

I followed her into a small room where sunlight poured through two big windows. White curtains hung in the window and were pulled back to let in the sunshine. Another faded but pretty patchwork quilt covered the narrow bed. A plump pillow in a snowy pillowcase lay at the head of the bed. There was nothing on the dresser except a hairbrush and a stuffed toy elephant.

"Not much to see in here," Lacey said. "I don't have many things, but Cousin Doshie said it was all mine for as long as I stayed here. I've never had a room all to myself before." She glanced around. "Do you like it?"

I don't think I'd ever known anyone who had almost nothing before.

"It's real pretty. I like the yellow and white wallpaper."

"I bet it's fifty years old," she said, giggling. She was probably right.

"An old quilt too, huh?" I touched the soft patches with my fingertips.

"Cousin Doshie said she made it the first year she and Cousin Chester were married."

I looked at those bits of material, marveling at how they were still around after all these years.

"Wow."

Lacey fingered the quilt too. "It smells a little funny, but I don't mind."

"Mothballs," I said. "My grandma has old stuff, too." I glanced at the book she held. "What are you reading?"

She held out the book. "*Bringing Home the Bacon*, by Alice G. Frost. Cousin Doshie found it on the side of the road. See?" She pointed to a place on the cover that had been scraped and torn. "I can hardly believe someone would throw it away."

"Me, either. Is it good?"

"It's okay. It has some funny parts, and some sad parts."

I scanned a page or two. "May I borrow it when you're finished?"

"Sure."

"I love books!" I said with a big grin.

She shrugged. "Reading is all right, but sometimes I'd rather do something else."

I'd hoped we could talk about all the super great stories we'd read and the authors we liked, but maybe she didn't read as much I did.

"What would you rather do?"

"Bike riding is fun, but I've never had my own bike before. Cousin Chester bought it for me the day I got here. He had it waiting for me on the front porch." She gave me a sad little smile. "That was so sweet of him, and then I went and wrecked it."

"I'm sorry that happened to you."

"It was okay until I wrecked. A little shaky and scary, but it was fun."

"Until you wrecked."

"Yeah." She smiled at me. "Until then."

"You like to take walks?"

Her eyes lit up. "Sure. I love to explore outside. Do you?"

I nodded so vigorously I like to have shook my freckles off.

"There are some good places around here."

She grinned real big, then pressed her fingertips against the cut on her lip.

"Maybe we can pack lunches and go exploring," I said.

"That will be super!"

"And Grandma can go with us sometimes, because she knows lots of stuff about what grows in the woods."

Lacey clapped her hands together. That's when I noticed she wore bright red fingernail polish.

"How'd you talk your Mama into letting you have that color of polish? I wanted Tahitian Sunset, but my mama said it had to be clear or light pink, like this."

I held out my hands. Lacey glanced at my fingernails, nodded, then turned her head so I couldn't see her face. She stared out the window and didn't say a word, so I continued.

"My sister, Myra Sue, likes to paint her fingernails all the time. Not me. This was just to make Isabel happy." I waited for her to say something, but she stayed quiet. Maybe her cuts were bothering her. "Boy howdy, wait until you meet Isabel St. James."

"Oh? Is she your best friend?"

"Isabel?" I hooted. "She's as old as Mama. Even older, maybe."

Lacey sat down on the edge of the bed and picked at her red fingernail polish. "Where'd you live before you lived here?" she asked me.

"I've always lived here."

She looked up. "Your whole life?"

"Yep. And my daddy and my grandma too. We have lived on the same farm since forever."

"Wow."

"Where do you live?"

She shrugged. "For now, right here."

"But before here?"

"Different places. Hey, let's go outside and look at the geese. You like geese?"

It was as plain as the nose on your face she didn't want to talk much about herself. I wondered what her secret was, and the desire to know gnawed on my brain like a rat on a hunk of moldy cheese. But I've learned a few things in my life. One of them is keep my big yap shut until the time is right. The time was not right to ask Lacey questions. Maybe, if we became good friends, she'd tell me what she kept hidden inside herself.

While Mama visited with Mrs. Hopper, and the old man snored away in his chair, Lacey and I went to the meadow where noisy white geese waddled about. A small pond provided them a place to swim and play. One goose spotted us, stretched its long neck out and flapped its wings. If Myra had been there, she would have run to the house, screaming like she thought she was gonna be murdered by goose.

Lacey and I watched the strutting and squawking and nonsense.

"Silly goose," Lacey said, then we both had a good laugh.

Sixteen

Ernie,
the
Bad News Bearer

Boy oh boy, you should be glad you weren't in our house that next week.

For one thing, Isabel and Grandma had taken over the dining room. They put all the leaves in that big old table and had spread so much wedding junk over it that I got dizzy just walking through the room. Bear in mind that our table has room for at least twelve people, and more than that if we scrunch so close we nearly eat off each other's forks.

One thing I thought but did not say aloud, not even to ask someone in private was, *Why don't you women do this at one of your own houses?* But I knew our house was bigger than either of theirs, and for sure no one on Rough Creek Road has a dining table as big as ours, but still.

You know what? I'll betcha Mama invited them to use our dining room.

That very next Tuesday, instead of Grandma going into town for her weekly trip to the grocery store, Ernie showed up at our front door.

Myra Sue, who was doing her best to be one of the wedding planners in the dining room, leaped to her feet and flung herself across the table.

"He can't see this!" she screeched. "It's bad luck!"

"Oh good grief, Myra, don't be a goose," I said. "It's supposed to be bad luck only if he sees *Grandma* before the ceremony on the day of the wedding."

She kinda froze right there, sprawled like a dry land octopus, across all those papers, and bits of material and books and cassette tapes.

"It's true," Grandma said. "Now get up from there before Ernie sees you spraddled out all over the table." She went to open the door for him.

"Dear, dear, dear," Isabel muttered, frowning as she straightened the mess Myra had just created.

"I'm sorry." The way Myra whimpered, you would've thought she'd burned down the house.

"It's fine, darling," Isabel said. "I can put this to rights. But, please, don't do that again. It lacks elegance and grace."

And good sense. I refrained from saying this aloud. I also refrained from pointing out that although Myra Sue is very pretty, she lacks elegance and grace anyway. All day, every day.

Grandma and Ernie came into the dining room after a minute or two, hand in hand, all mooney-eyed and smiling goofy at each other. Grandma's cheeks were pink, and I figured they'd been kissin' in the front room. I'm glad I did not see that. I prefer not to see old people kissin' and stuff.

"Howdy, ladies," Ernie said, grinning at us. "I seem to be a little outnumbered here."

Mama came into the room carrying Eli, fresh from his bath. He was wrapped in a soft blue towel and his dark red curls clung damply against his head. He seemed to be grinning all over himself. He smelled so sweet and cuddly that I wanted to smooch him a bunch of times. I tickled his soft cheeks and tiny nose.

"There is it least one more man in the room, Ernie," Mama said, laughing.

Ernie chuckled, and shook Eli's right hand like he was grown.

"What we lack in quantity, we make up for in quality, eh, little man?"

Eli squealed and squirmed, happy as could be. Everyone kept making a big deal over him until Mama said she had to get him dressed.

"I just brought him in to say 'hi'."

Ernie turned to Grandma.

"Gracie, I knew you were busy, so I took you some groceries over to the house and put them away for you."

You should have seen them twinkle at each other. I had to look away.

"Why thank you, Erns."

Okay, so now they had pet names for each other. At least "Gracie" and "Erns" wasn't obnoxious like "lambkins" and "snookums" and "bobo babykins." If they ever resorted to that kind of stuff, I was gonna go get my earholes sewn up.

"Look, honey," Grandma said, pulling Ernie nearer to the table. "Do you like this color, or this one better?"

She pointed to two pieces of material. Both were shades of pink, Grandma's favorite color. One was the color of my fingernail polish, and the other was the color of a rare hamburger.

"Well, um," Ernie said, looking like he'd been trapped.

"What's your favorite color, Ernie?" I asked. I had a feeling he was not going to say "pink."

He fingered the two swatches. "I've always been partial to brown."

"Brown?" Isabel and Grandma said at the same time.

He nodded. "Or dark blue." He looked up. "Why, Grace, don't look like that. I'd never insist you wear brown for a wedding dress."

"My dear sir," Isabel said, snooty as you can possibly imagine, "we are deciding the color for the matron-of-honor's dress, not the wedding dress."

"I see. Well, any color you decide will be just fine with me." His gaze traveled along that mess of plans and papers along the table. He dipped his head toward it. "All this for the wedding?"

"Yes!" Isabel said. "So much to do and so little time."

Ernie ran a hand over the top of his head and eyeballed that table full of stuff once more.

"I see," he said, slowly, looking confused. He let go Grandma's hand, took off his glasses and cleaned them with a white handkerchief. I doubted having clean glasses was gonna make things any less confusing for him.

"Want a glass of sweet tea, Ernie?" I asked.

He gave me a smile. "That would be right fine, April Grace. Thanks."

I went into the kitchen and filled a glass with ice. I poured it brim-ful, turned, and nearly jumped out of my skin to see him sitting at the kitchen table. He must walk as quiet as a cat.

I handed him the tea and he drained half that glass in one gulp.

"Want a cookie?" I asked.

He shook his head. I studied him, and it seemed like he had more on his mind than wedding plans. He'd been a bachelor all his life with no family around, so I knew he was used to being by himself. But maybe all that aloneness meant he needed someone to talk to.

I pulled out a chair across from him and sat down.

"You okay, Ernie?"

He drank more tea, taking slow, tiny sips as if he was stalling, or maybe searching for the right words.

"You look a little distressed," I added.

He nodded and sipped some more. I got up and filled his glass. Silence spread so heavy between us, I couldn't hardly stand it. I blurted out the very first thing that popped into my brain.

"Should I call you Grandpa?"

He choked a little. Tea dribbled down his chin. I handed him a paper napkin.

"I'm sorry. I just thought…"

He raised one hand and shook his head.

"No, no," he said, still coughing a bit and dabbing at his shirt. "You call me whatever you want to call me." His eyes crinkled with a big smile.

"I've never had a grandpa, you know. Voyne Reilly died a long time ago. And I think Mama's daddy is probably dead too."

"I've never had a granddaughter before."

"It might feel a little funny calling you 'Grandpa' when you've always been 'Ernie'. How about if I call you Grandpa Ernie?"

"Why, I think that sounds fine. And I do believe I'm going to like having such fine grandkids."

We grinned at each other, then bit by bit his happy look faded and worry settled across his expression. I had a feeling I knew what bothered him.

"Listen, Ernie—er, Grandpa Ernie, Isabel St. James likes to have a project. When she doesn't have one, she turns mopey and she makes life purely miserable for everyone around her. But when she *does* have project, she gets all carried away with herself, and she drives everyone else crazy."

"That's no fun," he said.

"I know! Either way it's unpleasant. But, at least if she's busy, she's happy, and everyone should be happy if they can be, don't you think?"

He nodded solemnly. "I agree with that, yes."

"Right now, she's over the moon about your wedding."

"Seems so."

"Well, I don't believe it was Grandma's idea for your wedding to be the big to-do Isabel is trying to create."

"No," he said, slowly. "I thought we were going to keep it simple."

"I suggested y'all elope, but everyone thought I was being a smarty-pants, so I didn't bring it up again."

He laughed. "We want our friends to celebrate with us. Why, it's taken me all this time to get Grace to the altar, so I want to make sure we have a party of it. If Grace chooses to have a fancy celebration, why, that's okay."

"I see. Well, just remember, if it starts getting out of hand, that'll be Isabel's doing, not Grandma's."

He tapped his index finger against his temple and winked. "I'll remember that."

So if Isabel's wedding plans didn't upset and worry him, I wondered what did, because that troubled look settled over his face again.

"Grandpa Ernie?" I whispered, leaning toward him. "Is something wrong?"

He hesitated a few seconds, then he said, "It's not that something is *wrong*. Just unexpected." He paused and made a face like someone just stepped on his foot. "I've got some relatives coming for the wedding."

"I didn't know you had any relatives."

"I do. Some elderly aunts and several cousins in Wisconsin. They're all the family I have left."

"I've never heard you talk about them."

"No, I don't suppose you have. It's been years since we've seen one another."

"And they're coming to the wedding?"

He nodded and stared down at what was left of his sweet tea. I jumped up and refilled his glass.

"That's nice. But you don't look so happy. Don't you want them to come?"

"Well, I do and I don't. That is, I'd like to see Clyde and Ruth. We were all youngsters together. But."

Somewhere in the back of my mind, a deep, mournful bell began to clang. Ernie had always been a strong, steady man, kind and gentle, and sweet. Something was wrong.

Since he was talking to me like I had some sense instead of like I was a bothersome kid, I decided it wouldn't hurt to ask a question or two.

"But what?" I said.

"I got a call at the store right before I left this morning." He blew out a deep breath. "They've decided to turn this into a family vacation. All of 'em, except Clyde and Ruth."

A little shiver shot down my spine.

"How many is 'all of 'em?'"

He rubbed his jaw and looked kinda sick.

"I'm not rightly sure, but it's a lot."

Uh-oh.

Seventeen

Lacey Paige Pickering's New Friend

For the next three weeks, Mama put Myra Sue and me to work like we'd never worked before. In fact, the only one who didn't work his fingers down to a nub was Eli.

Let me tell you, we scrubbed and scoured. We moved all the furniture around and cleaned behind, beneath, and down in the crevices of every chair, table, and doodad shelf. We washed, starched, and ironed curtains. We turned mattresses. We worked in the vegetable, flower, and herb gardens, even Myra Sue. Of course, she acted like she was Rapunzel who'd been dragged out of the tower by the hair of the head and forced to endure the unending agony of pulling weeds.

"We want Ernie's relatives to be comfortable and at home when they get here," Mama said. "They'll be our family, so let's make sure they feel that way."

Every single night I fell into bed so pooped I didn't even remember fluffing my pillow. All those walks in the woods with Daisy I'd hoped I could take with Lacey Paige Pickering and Grandma? Well, they didn't happen. Nosirree.

Most of the time, Grandma and Isabel were either off doing wedding things sixty miles away in Blue Reed, or huddled together over the dining room table, talking wedding. The only good thing I can say about all that business was that ol' Isabel had completely forgotten about not having a job. She laughed and whooped and hollered with Grandma as if they were two girls. But once the wedding was over, look out. I figured someone better come up with something for her to do.

I'd really been looking forward to spending time with Lacey Paige Pickering. Nearly every day, I asked Mama if I could go see her or she could come see me, but Mama said no, we were too busy right then. So, the only time I got to see Lacey was at church on Sundays, which were the only days we didn't work like cowhands.

The first Sunday after Lacey moved in with the Hoppers, I saw her sitting with them in their regular pew down in the front where no one but old people sit.

"I'm gonna see if Lacey wants to sit with me," I said.

Mama nodded and wiped some dribble off Eli's chin. He grinned at her and grabbed her nose.

"May I take Eli with me, just to introduce him, then I'll bring him back to you before Sunday school starts."

Mama doesn't leave Eli in the church nursery. She said she wants him to learn how to behave in church and other public places, so she keeps him with her and Daddy. She did the same with Myra Sue and me, and boy howdy, we know how to behave in church.

"All right," she said and handed him over, "but don't dally."

I hefted that chubby little kid in my arms and took off down the aisle with him. When Lacey saw us, her face lit up.

"Why lookee there!" Mr. Hopper said, grinning. "You get lost, youn-gun'?" he said to Eli.

Mrs. Hopper did a bunch of smiling and patting and cooing. I might as well have been a green and purple frog robot for all the attention I got—which was none. But that's okay. I was there to show off my baby brother.

"Hi, April Grace," Lacey said softly. "Who's that?"

"This is my brother, Michael Eli Reilly." I gave him a big smooch on his soft, round cheek.

"He's so cute!" She touched him with the tips of her fingers, al-most as if afraid she might hurt him.

"I'm heading to Sunday school class. You want to go with me?"

"Class?" She frowned and shook her head. "No, thanks."

"If you stay here, you'll be in the Mature Living class. They meet right here in these pews."

"Really? Well, okay then." She turned to Mrs. Hopper. "Cousin Doshie, is it all right if I go with April Grace?"

"Yes, yes. Of course. Go be with the kids your own age, honey."

After I gave Eli back to Mama, Lacey and I hurried downstairs to our classroom. You never want to be late to Miss Chestnut's Sunday school class. She makes a Big Deal of it, if you are.

"I wish Mama would let me wear jeans and sneakers to church," I said. "I hate hard, clunky shoes."

Lacey looked down at her clothes and grimaced. "I don't have any clothes other than jeans, and a few shirts. And this pair of sneakers."

My own personal self, I didn't care if someone wanted to wear a fancy dress or jeans to church. I reckon the ones who care are other people, not God. But I knew Lacey was going to stick out in her outfit. I just hoped no one would be rude.

We went into the classroom and there sat Lottie Furhman, Aimee Dillard, and Brittany Johnson in their own exclusive, whispering, snooty little group.

One thing you should know about me, if you haven't figured it out already, is I can't stand snobs, so I just try to ignore those three as much as possible.

I introduced Lacey to the class and nearly everyone, including those two bratty twins, Micky and Ricky Tinker, were nice and friendly to her. But then I caught ol' Lottie and her friends giving Lacey the once over. I pinned a look so hard on those girls, their faces got red and they stared down at their hands without saying a word.

In that instant, my resolved plan became if those girls, or anyone else, ever picked on Lacey Paige Pickering, they'd have to deal with April Grace Reilly.

Because we had worked so hard all that week, and Sunday is the only day we wouldn't be turning the house inside out, I wanted Lacey to come spend the afternoon. But I knew Mama planned to rest, so I didn't mention it that day, or even the following Sunday. By the third Sunday, though, our house had been turned inside out, upside down, and sideways so that it practically glowed in the dark. Even the knick-knacks gleamed and sparkled.

So that Sunday, the last one before Ernie and Grandma's Saturday afternoon wedding, I decided to ask at breakfast.

"May Lacey spend this afternoon with me?"

"Oh, honey, I don't know," Mama said. A slight frown creased her forehead.

"I promised her we'd do some stuff, but she's been by herself most of the time 'cause I've been working like a dog."

"You know we're expecting the Beasons on Wednesday," Daddy reminded me.

"I know. But Lacey is just one girl and besides, they aren't here yet."

"I don't want any messes made, not after we've worked so hard."

I sensed her weakening, so I pressed my advantage. "Mama. You know me. We won't make a mess, and even if we do, I'll clean it up. I promise. I just want to show her around the farm and stuff. We won't even be inside very much."

She looked right into my eyes as if pondering her decision. "All right, then."

"If April Grace gets to have company, then I should get to too," Myra Sue said. "Jennifer and Jessica haven't been—"

"No," Mama and Daddy said together. I don't blame them. Jennifer and Jessica had taken to giggling like hyenas about every little thing, plus they were as messy as my sister.

"But it's not fair!" Her lower lip pooched out.

"After the wedding, you may have the girls here for the weekend. But not today."

Ol' Myra seemed to have trouble digesting this information. She looked half-gleeful because she could have visitors for a whole entire weekend, but she looked half-sullen because that weekend was still a couple of weeks away. I knew one thing for sure, though. If she kept pouting and arguing, she'd not only be grounded, she'd be without any company for a while.

On the way home after church, the three of us—Myra Sue, Lacey, and me—sat in the backseat. While Lacey and I happily chatted, ol' Myra got grumpier and grumpier. Then she started muttering and mumbling how I was spoiled and always got my way.

Daddy told her, very politely, to please quit complaining.

She huffed, crossed her arms, and pushed out her lower lip.

"April Grace gets everything," she said, as if she couldn't help herself. Sometimes that girl just doesn't use her brain.

Mama told her she'd have to wash the Sunday dishes all by herself.

She sulled up like a possum in the corner, and left her lower lip hanging out about a mile. But a few minutes later, when Lacey said, "You have the prettiest hair and eyes I've ever seen," ol' Myra perked up like freshly inflated balloon.

She patted her big blonde curls and blinked twice, real big.

"Thank you so much."

"Are you a cheerleader?" Lacey asked.

Myra wriggled with joy. "Not yet. You can only be a cheerleader if you're a junior or senior."

Oh brother. I can just see my sister out there jumping around, shaking pompons, hollering "Go, team!" I am not trying to be mean, but while Myra Sue Reilly might be really pretty, she's about as coordinated and light on her feet as a mule. Likely as not, she'd get out there cheering where she shouldn't be, and she'd fall down, and the players would trip over her and lose the game.

"I'm going into tenth grade," Myra said. "What about you?"

"I'm not sure," Lacey mumbled, looking uncomfortable.

Confusion leaped into Myra's big baby blues. "But —"

I could see my sister had less sense than a goose about this and was going to pry into it, so I interrupted.

"Do you like dogs?"

Myra Sue glowered, but I didn't care.

"I think so," Lacey said. "I've never really been around them, but I like looking at them. Cats, too."

"Grandma has this awful ol' cat that hates everyone except Grandma and Isabel St. James."

"Cats are pretty."

"Do you have one?" I asked.

She shook her head. "No pets."

"Ever?" Myra Sue said.

"Never."

Wow. Think of that. I failed even to imagine a world where no animals were. Just the notion made me queasy. I changed the subject.

"Did you finish that book Cousin Doshie found in the road?" I asked.

She nodded. "I finished it a couple of weeks ago. There's not much to do at Cousin Doshie's except housework or feeding the chickens and geese. She doesn't want me to cook, and she won't let me get out of sight of the house. I can't even take a walk."

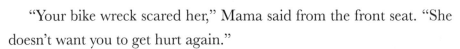

"Your bike wreck scared her," Mama said from the front seat. "She doesn't want you to get hurt again."

"I know. She kinda makes me nervous, the way she's always asking if I'm okay and hovering around."

"That's just because she's someone who likes to take care of people. She loves you," Daddy said. He met Lacey's eyes in the rearview mirror. "You'll find a lot of women on Rough Creek Road are like that."

He and Mama exchanged moony-eyed looks. I reckon they will do that until they are one hundred and ninety years old.

"I'll lend you some books, if you'd like. And when we go to the library, you can go with us. Right, Mama?"

"Of course!" Mama said.

Lacey smiled. "That would be nice, thank you."

"Do you watch the soaps?" Myra Sue asked. She leaned forward, all interested. Ever since she ran off last year thinking she was going to be cast in a big soap opera, Mama has forbid her to watch them anymore, forever. She said they were feeding unrealistic and dangerous expectations, and until Myra could get a grip on what was real and what wasn't, it was best not to feed her wild ideas.

"Cousin Doshie won't let me watch much television. She says it warps the mind."

"Your Cousin Doshie is right," Daddy said.

Myra Sue sat back and pouted some more. I figured she was reliving Mama's lecture.

"Cousin Doshie says there'll be plenty to do once the garden produce comes in," Lacey said. "I suppose I'll be helping in the kitchen then."

"Poor you," Myra said. "Gardening is wretched, backbreaking work."

She sounded like Isabel, who wouldn't know a garden seed from a green M&M's candy.

"Myra Sue," I said, "the only thing you've ever done in the garden is turn on the water hose."

I liked working in the dirt, but Myra hated it. In fact, Myra hated nearly everything that required physical exertion. She said sweating is bad for her health. How in the world she thought she'd be able to withstand all the activity it would take to be on the cheerleading squad escaped me. Mama let her get away with not working outside, as long as she did extra inside chores.

We turned off the highway and onto Rough Creek Road.

"Do we need to stop at the Hoppers to get you a change of clothes, Lacey?" Mama asked. "If you and April are going to explore the farm and woods, you'll want old clothes."

I cringed. I reckon Mama didn't know poor Lacey had almost nothing. I knew for sure she'd never hurt Lacey's feelings on purpose.

"That's okay," Lacey said softly. "These are all right."

Myra Sue ran her eyeballs over Lacey's outfit. She started to say something, but I pinned a look on her that was sharper and harder than the look I given Lottie and her pals. That look told her I would clean her clock and eat her lunch if she so much as peeped one rude syllable to Lacey. She said nothing.

Eighteen

Holey Cheese
on
Wheels

As soon as Sunday dinner was over, and ol' Myra was elbow deep in dirty dishes and hot, soapy water, Lacey and I took off on a tour of the farm with Daisy beside us.

You'd never know that Daisy was the first dog Lacey had met face to face. Boy howdy, with them two it was love at first sight.

"Daisy stood guard over you while you were lying in the road after your bike wreck," I said.

Lacey hugged that dog so hard, ol' Daisy's fur like to have turned blue. She wagged her tail and smiled during all that hugging. She even licked Lacey's face. Just one time, because she's not a dog that will slobber all over you.

"I love Daisy!" Lacey declared, hugging the big white furry neck again.

"She's the best dog, ever," I said, patting and rubbing Daisy's back. "Someday we'll go over to Mr. Brett's, and you can meet his dog, Taz. He's a really cool dog, too."

"Yay! I think I like dogs."

We walked all over the farm that afternoon, from the front yard to all the ponds, and even back to the big hayfield on the far side. We saw two huge, long snakes, and both of us screamed even though they were nothing but harmless black snakes that'd gotten big eating field mice. Then we watched a groundhog waddle around the edge of the woods, doing whatever it is groundhogs do when they're out doing groundhog business. Squirrels chased one another up and down trees. Bunnies skittered in and out of thickets. Birds were everywhere and all of them had a song or a twittering chirp to offer.

Lacey gawked and marveled at everything as if she'd never been out in the country. I don't know where she'd come from, but she was the kind of person who seemed curious and interested in lots of different things. Living with the Hoppers but not allowed to explore outside must have been tough on her. I wondered what Mrs. Hopper would say or do, if she knew Lacey and I had explored the farm most of the afternoon. Surely she trusted us not to let anything happen. After all, we'd saved Lacey's life and that should account for something.

"I want to live in the woods," Lacey said at one point.

She loved the cows, although most of them gave us the big eye and kept their distance. In the calf lot, the babies trotted up near the fence where we stood, bawling at us.

"They are so cute!"

"They think we're going to feed them."

"Can we?" she asked.

I shook my head. "Nah. We have to be careful what they eat and that they don't eat too much of it. Baby calves have delicate systems for a while."

We leaned against the wooden fence and watched them play and butt each other and run with their tails in the air. Lacey stretched one arm through the fence, trying to coax one of them closer to her. All of them stood back, looking at us, twitching their ears and tails, but since neither of us offered the feeding bucket, they stayed where they were.

By mid-afternoon, my lunch had worn off with all that walking. I figured Lacey was ready for a snack too, but if we went back to the house right then, Mama would probably take one look at our grubby selves and insist we take showers.

I'm not against showers, understand. But once you're clean and smelling good, you're supposed to stay that way, which means the outdoor fun kinda comes to an end.

"You want to see the cave?"

Her eyes got big. "You have a cave? Yes, I want to see it."

The cave wasn't a real cave, not like Blanchard Caverns or even Marvel Cave. Instead, ours was a sheltered place on the side of a steep hill with a humongous outcropping rock hanging over it like an extended roof. I didn't go there very often because I don't like places under the ground. They're dark and damp and creepy, but I figured Lacey would get a kick out of it.

While Daisy decided to stay with the calves and rest, Lacey and I tromped away, past the calf pen, past the hay barn, past the milk barn, and past the equipment shed where the John Deere tractor, the New Holland Haybine, the old baler, and all the other farm tools were kept. Beyond all that, the ground began to slope and once we reached the woods, the ground got so steep and rocky that this part of the farm was what Grandma called "hardscrabble useless." The woods were thick with undergrowth and briars. No one hardly ever went back there.

"This is like the witch's forest in the Wizard of Oz," Lacey said as we picked our way through.

"Yeah. Kinda spooky, huh?"

"But exciting," she said with a grin.

I got in front of her because I knew the best way to approach the cave.

"Be careful of the briars," I cautioned as I tried to clear a path. "And watch out for copperheads."

Instead of coming to a complete standstill and demanding to leave, Lacey cheerfully said, "Okey-dokey!"

Maybe she didn't know that copperheads were poisonous snakes that live in places just like those woods. I kept an extra sharp watch for 'em.

I pulled back a few branches and some brush that blocked the entrance, and we went inside. The cave was about the size of our living room, so there was no danger of getting lost in it.

Lacey looked around at the low ceiling and flat rocks in the walls. "This is so cool!"

"I hid in here one time."

"You did?"

"With Pilgrimette. She's a turkey. I thought we were going to eat her for Thanksgiving Dinner, so I brought her down here and stayed with her until Daddy and Mr. Brett found me. I like to have froze."

"Wow."

"We didn't eat her. I just misunderstood a conversation I overheard."

"Oh, good. Do you still have her?"

"She's in the chicken yard. I'll show you her later."

I wanted to get back into the sunlight and away from that place. I hated to spoil Lacey's fun, so for a little while longer we poked around some more, looking at moss and damp rocks and the tracks where animals had been.

"We better get back to the house before they come looking for us," I said. "We can come back another time. Maybe we'll bring a lunch or something."

"A cave-nic instead of a picnic?"

"Right."

We trudged out of the woods, back up the slope, and across the hay-field near the house.

I pointed at Grandma's place.

"See that little white house with the red roof? That's where Grandma lives." I paused, and stared at an unfamiliar blue van parked in front of her place. "I wonder who's there. Ernie drives a green car. "

Under normal circumstances, I would have lit off to her house and walked right through the front door to satisfy my curiosity. But I suspected that van might have something to do with Grandma's wedding plans. It was my desire not to get caught up in all that hoop-de-doo, so Lacey and I just kept walking toward our own house where I hoped we could get a good snack.

We were still a ways from the house when I heard loud voices and laughter.

"What's all that noise?" she asked. Then, "Golly, April Grace, there's a school bus in front of your house."

Sure enough, parked in our driveway, sat an old yellow school bus with the name of the school removed. A bunch of dots in various sizes had been painted all over that thing.

"Good grief!" I hollered. "What in the world is *that?* It looks like a hunk of holey cheese."

Nineteen

Hospitality Rains Down
Like a
Flood of Locusts
and
Prickly Pears

I was curious to the gills because that contraption was about the ugliest mess I'd ever seen on four wheels. I was about half afraid to find out what it was and why it was parked in our driveway.

"If that thing has anything to do with Grandma's wedding, I'm gonna hide in the cave until after the knot is tied."

Lacey laughed. "You say funny things."

"But I speak the truth."

"Mama and I stayed in a bus like that one time. It had beds and a little stove and places to sit."

"You did? For real?"

"Yep. It wasn't so bad."

How bad had her life been if she thought staying in an old school bus "wasn't so bad"?

"Let's go see what's going on," I said, and moved closer to that bus.

"Right-o!"

Now here is where Lacey Paige Pickering and my best friend, Melissa Kay Carlyle, differ. If Melissa had been there, she would've been hanging back, trying to talk me out of getting any closer. Lacey wasn't a bit timid about moving forward with me.

When I stepped around the corner of the house and got a gander at the front of the house, I nearly fell backward. In fact, poor Lacey yelped because I almost knocked her right over.

"What's wrong?" She stepped to the side as if she expected to me plow into her again.

"That."

I pointed to a mile-high pile of suitcases, boxes, plastic bags, paper sacks, and loose clothes on the ground, right smack in front of the steps.

On top of that whole mess was a big yellow triangle of fake cheese with holes in it and a big red foam hand with the index finger extended.

A burst of whooping and cheering erupted from the house and pretty near blew the front screen door off, and like to have startled me half to death.

We eyeballed that awful bus and we gawked at the horrible mound of junk. We grimaced as another bout of noise issued from inside the house.

"I kinda feel like Something is Going to Happen," I croaked because my actual voice box dried up like an old dead prune.

"Something like what?" Lacey whispered back.

"I don't know exactly. Sometimes I get these creepy-crawly feelings on the back of my neck."

I didn't need a special sense to know what was inside that house was Bad News. I shuddered. Usually, I'm pretty brave. Even when things are the most awfullest, I go right ahead and do what I need to do. But at that moment, I felt like I couldn't face alone whatever might be inside our house. I grabbed Lacey's hand.

"Don't be afraid. Maybe it won't be as bad as you think," she said in her normal voice, giving my fingers a nice, reassuring squeeze.

She looked so calm and peaceful that I felt better. She was right. After all, Ian and Isabel and Mimi had burst into our lives like the Day of Doom, but we all survived. Ian and Isabel had become friends, and Mimi turned out to be all right.

I gave another long hard look at that bus, then a double-barreled glare at that disgusting pile of junk. I sucked in a deep, noisy breath and straightened my shoulders.

"Let's go."

"I'm right here with you."

As solemnly and slowly as if we were attending our very own funeral,

Lacey and I mounted the porch steps. The noise swelled, and I could just imagine how loud it must be inside the house. Why did Mama and Daddy let this go on? Where were they?

Through the screen door, I could see my sister sitting on a stairstep halfway up. She put a finger to her lips in a shushing gesture and beckoned us to come inside. I opened the door like it was made of soap bubbles and we slipped inside and scurried silently across the entry and up the steps.

"What's going on?" I whispered-screamed, even though I figured I could yell those words out and no one could hear me over the racket in the other room. "Who is that, and why are they yelling so much? Why is there such a mess outside?"

"Come upstairs," Myra Sue said, and all three of us shot up the steps and into her room. She closed the door and leaned against it. Her big blue eyes were wide and startled. She held both fists against her chest and breathed like she'd been running for twenty hours.

"You look like you're gonna faint," I said. "Are you all right?"

Lacey took Myra Sue's hand and led her to the edge of the bed, then sat beside her and patted her hand.

I wondered if I should get Mama or Daddy. Then I wondered where they were. Had something happened to them? My heart stood still.

"Where's Mama?" I asked.

Myra jabbed her pointy finger down.

"With them," she croaked.

A horrible scene of Mama and Daddy tied up and helpless while noisy people shook the house off its foundation rose in my mind.

"Where's Eli? Where's Grandma?" I screamed.

"I don't know!" Her voice went up and up in pitch until it ended in a gasp.

It was like someone let out all my air and blood. I wanted to run downstairs and help my poor mama and daddy, but my legs let go of my body.

"Ufff," I said, sinking to the floor.

"April Grace!" Lacey said. She stretched out her free hand toward me.

Myra Sue flopped back on the bed, moaning. I tried to get up, but my knees failed and I slumped right back over.

Lacey let go of us as if we'd burned her fingers. The next thing, she's running out of the room like she's being chased. She'd probably run the entire two miles back to the Hoppers as fast as she could, and she'd never, ever, for the rest of her whole life, come to our house again because someone had opened a can of flat-out crazy and poured out a circus all over our lives.

The floor vibrated with the noise and activity from below.

Myra moaned, and I sighed. Lying on the floor, weak as a new kitten, solved nothing. I forced myself upright and gulped in air.

I told myself that surely those loud people weren't murderers and thugs. Surely Mama and Daddy were safe. Then Eli started to cry. I took in another deep breath and got to my feet, then stood there wobbling like I'd forgotten how to walk. Myra Sue lay on the bed like a princess who'd fainted and needed milk and cookies to revive her. Or those imaginary smelling salts she wanted to use on Isabel. She stared up at the ceiling.

"Sister?" I said.

She did not even blink, and that kinda scared me. Myra Sue has never been strong and determined like me. If she can't pout her way into getting what she wants, she tends to melt into a weak little puddle of helplessness.

Maybe she had died. Maybe all that ruckus had plain out killed my only sister. I stumbled to her.

"Myra!" I yelled, shaking her.

Right then Mama and Daddy rushed into the room with Lacey right behind them, toting Eli who fussed but didn't blubber.

"Girls, what's wrong?" Daddy said.

He went straight to Myra Sue who was rolling her eyes and moaning. Mama grabbed my upper arms and looked into my eyes. She felt my forehead. Daddy did the same thing with Myra Sue, then they switched places and looked into our eyes and felt our faces all over again.

Myra drooped in Mama's arms, and I sagged against Daddy.

"What's going on?" I said. "Who are those people? Why is our house so messy? Why is it so noisy? Are you and Mama okay?"

"Those are Ernie's relatives," he said.

"For real?" I shrieked. Those awful, messy, noisy people were going to be Grandma's new in-laws. I felt like I might throw up right there in front of everyone.

"Is that what's brought on this reaction?" Daddy asked.

With this news, I knew if I tried to speak, I'd bust out crying, or maybe screaming. I nodded.

"Myra?" he looked at my sister. "You too?"

She sniffled and tears poured down her cheeks. "They just walked in… and took over!"

"Did it seem that way to you, honey?" Daddy asked in his kindest voice. She nodded.

Daddy led me by the hand and sat me down on the edge of the bed next to Mama with my sister on the other side of her. Daddy hunkered down, close to all of us.

"They weren't supposed to be here until Wednesday," I said, as if that made a difference.

"They got here early," Daddy said.

"But why are they in our house?"

"We invited them in, honey," Mama replied. "They've been on that bus and the van for nearly four days, taking their time to do some sight-seeing on the way down. They're tired. They need a place to relax."

"Why can't they stretch their legs outside?" That was the most reasonable question my sister has ever asked in her entire life.

"Yeah," I said. "And why can't they do all that hollering outside too? What's wrong with 'em, anyway? Were they raised in a barn?"

Mama turned to Lacey, and said, "Honey, I think Eli has a little toy giraffe in April's room. Would you take him in there and let him play with it?"

"Sure, Mrs. Reilly."

I knew Mama was sending Lacey out because this was going to be a Private Talk, but she didn't want to say something like "Go away" or "This is none of your beeswax." Lacey probably knew it too. She quietly closed the door behind her as she and Eli went out.

"Here's the situation," Daddy said. "These are Ernie's people, his family. And because Ernie will be marrying your grandma, soon they'll be our family too."

"Oooh," Myra whimpered, and I nearly whimpered right along with her. "Do we have to be related to them?"

Trust her to ask something like that.

"Of course we do," Daddy said.

She sniffled and buried her face against his chest. One of us girls needed to say something smart, but Myra Sue wasn't the one to do it.

"But, Daddy, why are they in our house?"

"Why, honey, because we invited them in." He said this as if I was silly for even asking.

"But why are they making so much noise?"

"Because they're watching a ball game on television," Mama answered, stroking Myra Sue's head as it rested against her shoulder.

"A game?"

"Baseball," Daddy said. "The Milwaukee Brewers are playing against the Toronto Blue Jays."

"Oh." I guess that made as much sense as anything else. "But why is all that stuff piled up by the porch steps?"

My parents exchanged looks. Long Significant Looks, which were not mushy or moony-eyed at all. You know that sick feeling in my stomach? Well, boy howdy, it got worse.

"That's their luggage and other belongings," Daddy said. "They'll be staying with us for a few days."

Myra Sue sat straight up. *"ALL OF THEM?"*

"No, not everyone," Mama said. "Some are staying at Ernie's house in town, of course. And a few will be over at Grandma's."

"And the bus has come cots in it," Daddy added.

"How many will be in our house?" I asked in hushed tones. Not because I wanted to speak softly but because I couldn't catch my breath.

"Seven. More if the bus cots are too uncomfortable, I suppose." Mama chewed on her bottom lip a few seconds, then smiled reassuringly at me. But I did not feel better.

"Seven?" Myra and I screeched at the same time.

"How many of them are there?"

"Well, let's see," Daddy said, his forehead creased as he thought and counted. "I believe all together there are about twenty, give or take a few."

"Oooh," Myra and I groaned together.

Mama and Daddy looked at each other again, and as if they were reading each other's minds, they both pulled away from us and held us at arm's length.

"Now, girls, we've been through this sort of… situation before," Mama said.

"Yeah, a lot. But never with this many…" My voice trailed as her soft expression began to change.

"It doesn't matter if it's one, or if it's two dozen," Daddy said. "We will practice hospitality with them, and you girls will be respectful and courteous. Is that clear?"

Boy oh boy.

"Yes, sir." Said in unison.

"Now, go bathe your faces." Mama trailed a long gaze over me. "You better jump in the shower and put on some clean clothes before you go down to meet the Beasons."

"Um… what about Lacey? Poor Lacey might be overwhelmed by that whole mess, er, I mean, by all those people."

"Lacey handled herself very well when she came downstairs to get us. But she needs a shower and a change of clothes too."

"Mama, she doesn't have anything," I whispered.

"What do you mean?"

"She only has a couple of pairs of jeans and a few shirts and one pair of shoes."

"That's all?" My sister blinked about eighteen times.

"Well, she can't help it, Myra Sue," I told that uppity girl. I repeated what Grandma had said a couple of weeks ago. "Lacey has had a hard life."

Her mouth formed an "oh," and she said nothing else.

"I bet Lacey could wear some of my clothes, Mama. She's older than I am, but she's about my size."

"You find her something, honey, and take it to her. Then once you girls are clean and neat, you may come downstairs and be with everyone."

Trust Mama to make this depressing business sound like a party.

Twenty

Some In-Laws Should be Outlawed

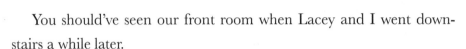

You should've seen our front room when Lacey and I went downstairs a while later.

Mama had instructed us to be "clean and neat," and we were. We both wore freshly laundered jeans, sleeveless button-down tops, and sandals. In my opinion we looked presentable when we walked into that room, but I still felt sick with dread. Those prickles on my neck kept wiggling like crazy back there so much that I wanted to scratch. But I didn't. Isabel St. James would've been proud. Besides, I figured someone had to show those loud-mouthed people some good manners.

A bunch of people with dark curly hair of various lengths sat clustered around the television like they'd never seen one before.

Potato chip bags, candy bar wrappers, cracker crumbs, and popped kernels of corn were scattered all over the room, as if someone had come in there and broadcast them like fertilizer. Coca-Cola and Pepsi-Cola cans cluttered the end tables and coffee table without any coasters beneath them to keep from making wet rings. Apparently all that leg-stretching those people wanted to do inside our house had extended to foot stretching too, because it looked like a sneaker and sock factory had exploded all over the floor. And it didn't smell none too sweet either. After all that scrubbing and cleaning we'd done, it seemed to me that Mama should've told those Beason people about that "clean and neat" rule.

To tell you the honest truth, I felt short of breath.

My sister might have felt right at home in that pigpen of a living room, but she was nowhere to be seen.

"Your mama is awfully sweet." Lacey's voice shook me out of my stupefaction. Her gaze fixed on my mother who was passing around a platter of sandwiches to that crowd.

Here's what I thought. I thought that bunch of Beasons should do more than grab a sandwich, mutter "thanks," and lean sideways to see the television as if Mama was a concrete pole that would forever block their view of that stupid ballgame. I felt like unplugging the TV and telling them to clean up their sorry mess.

"Mama?" I said. My voice kinda shook.

She turned and smiled as if she was standing in a field full of kittens and rose petals.

"Here's April Grace and her friend Lacey. Girls, come and meet our soon-to-be relatives." She said this with all the joy of welcoming Santa Claus to our family.

Believe it or not, all those people turned from TV and eyeballed us. And they were smiling and friendly. Every last one of them said hello to us. That might have been because a commercial was on instead of the ballgame.

Mama put her right hand on my shoulder and her left hand on Lacey's shoulder and steered us closer to our guests.

"Let me introduce everyone to you." She started with the man who had just taken a sandwich off the platter. "This is Roy Beason, and next to him is his son, Ranger. Then there is Pardner and Al, and Tillie, and Bixie, and Daphne. On the sofa is Dolly and Pat."

"And Benji is asleep on the bed in our room," the one named Roy announced, as if that explained all the secrets of the universe.

Don't think that "asleep on the bed in our room" got past me, 'cause it didn't. I'm sure he didn't mean a place in Wisconsin. He meant a room in our house, which he was claiming as his very own.

"Benji won't be a problem. When he isn't sleeping, he's sitting quietly with his toys," Bixie said.

"These are Ernie's cousins from Wisconsin," Mama said, her smile still as bright as ever.

Boy howdy. There was no way Jose I'd remember all those names. And let me remind you, this was not everyone. Mama had said earlier that more of these folks were at Grandma's house and at Ernie's.

As best I could, I smiled and said "Hello" to all those strangers. I pretended their presence, noise, and mess in our home didn't make me feel as if I floated in and out of my body like an uneasy ghost.

The back door on the service porch opened, and a second later, Grandma and Ernie came into the living room. Right behind them, a whole new cluster of people entered the house.

"Hey!" one of the younger men hollered. "Is the game on?"

"Brewers!" one of the women squealed.

"What's the score?" said another. They rushed past us without any introductions and joined the others.

"Where are the triplets?" asked the white-haired woman named Dolly.

Triplets?

"They said they weren't up to making the trip out here," Ernie said as he looked around the room in horror.

"Oh, well. Them." Bixie rolled her eyes and Dolly nodded. "Spoiled."

"To the core."

Oh brother. Just what we needed around here. Spoiled triplets.

Both women looked like they were about to say something to Lacey and me, but the commercial was over and every Beason eyeball, except Ernie's, focused on that television.

"Game's back on!" one of the boys hollered.

"Oh, no, it isn't," Ernie snapped as he stepped around us and stalked over to the TV. He switched it off and turned to glare at his relatives.

"*HEY!*" they yelled like they thought they were Gabriel's trumpet.

Ernie put a fist on each side of his hips and ran his gaze over the lot of them. Anyone with half an eyeball could see he was fit to be tied.

"What in the name of time is the matter with you people?" he said. "You come into the clean, comfortable home of a welcoming stranger and treat it like it's the city dump." He glanced at me. "April, run and get a garbage bag or two, sugar?"

"Yes, sir, Grandpa Ernie." I never thought fetching a thirty-three gallon sized Hefty bag could make me so happy.

He took the bag and handed it over to the Beason with black-framed glasses. "Roy, you pick up your mess and pass it to Pardner. Then, Pardner, you pick up your mess and hand the bag to Al, and on it goes like that until every last one of you have cleaned up this mess you made. Why, you ought to be ashamed. I'm ashamed for you."

"Sure thing, Ernie," Roy said. He scooped up two soda pop cans, a Snickers wrapper, and empty Lay's Potato Chips bag. He shot a sheepish glance at Mama. "I'm sorry, Lily."

"Me, too," said the fellow who took the bag next. "We just get so carried away…"

Boy, oh boy, was that the truth!

In about two minutes, the living room was back to normal. Well, normal except it was full of strange people.

"Thank you so much," Mama said to them graciously as the last person to add his garbage to the collection handed her that trash bag.

Grandma ran a critical gaze over the tops of the tables. I reckon she was checking for water rings.

"Girls, you're probably hungry after your busy afternoon," Mama said. "Supper will be very casual, with everyone helping themselves to whatever they want when they want it. There are plenty of sandwiches in the refrigerator, so help yourselves. April, honey, you make sure Lacey gets whatever she wants, okay?"

"Yes'm. And I'll take that." I took the trash bag from her, and Ernie took it from me. He said, "Here, Ranger, you carry this out to the trash can outside. It's through the service porch. Go on through."

That lanky boy stood up and slouched out of the room with that black bag in his hand. He never said a word.

I had completely lost my appetite, but not my desire to leave that room, especially when Roy turned the television back on and ballgame noises started again.

"C'mon, Lacey," I said, and led the way to the kitchen.

You probably won't believe me when I tell you that Myra Sue was sitting at the kitchen table, playing a card game with a curly, dark-haired boy and girl who were probably close to her age. I didn't realize we had more Beasons in the kitchen.

"What are you staring at?" Myra glared at me over the top of the cards she held.

"You. Playing cards."

You see, my sister was terrible at cards, even Uno. Even Old Maid. Regular cards messed with her brain.

The boy and girl eyed Lacey and me.

"Who are you?" the boy asked in a way that got my hackles up immediately. As you probably know by now, when my hackles go up, my mouth opens.

"Well, you're the one in our kitchen playing cards with my sister," I said, "so why don't you tell me who you are."

He just stared at me, like he was daring me to say another word. I started to speak, but Myra Sue beat me to it.

"This is Colby and Brie, spelled B-R-I-E," Myra Sue said. "They're Pardner and Daphne's kids. And this is my baby sister, April Grace, and her friend, Lacey."

Lacey smiled and said, "Hello."

"At least Lacey has manners," the boy said.

"Shut up, Colby." The girl smiled at us. "Don't mind him. He gets crabby when he isn't watching football."

"Why weren't you in there watching baseball, then?"

He sneered. "In case you haven't noticed, Red, they aren't the same game."

"Do you guys play Pitch?" Lacey asked.

"Yep," Colby said. "I can play any card game you throw at me."

I wanted to throw something at him, but it wasn't cards.

"May I play?" Lacey asked.

"Sure!" Brie said, smiling. Her brother shrugged, and Myra Sue blinked.

Well, now. I didn't want to play cards with my sister, who doesn't know a club from a spade, and that smart-alecky boy who'd probably run his mouth like a souped-up motorcycle, but in the effort to be a Better Person and get to know these almost-relatives, I shoved aside my own misgivings.

I sat down in the empty chair next to Lacey.

"What're you doing, Red? You can't play."

I gave that boy a look that should've shut him up. "Number one, yes, I can. Number two, stop calling me Red."

He leaned forward, his brown eyes sparkly and snappy. "Five people can't play Pitch, *Red.*"

Says who?

"For someone who's named after cheese, you don't have a lot of room to name-call anybody else."

He tightened his jaw.

"I'll call you anything I want to," he bit off the words, "and right now I want to call you Red. Tomorrow, I'll call you Freckles. And the day after that, I'll probably call you Skinny."

Boy howdy.

"You got a lot of nerve for someone born in a cheese factory who barged into our home, uninvited, *Cheesehead.*"

"April Grace Reilly!" Myra gasped.

I ignored her in favor of glaring at Colby, who glared right back.

"I consider 'Cheesehead' an honorable name," he said. "It tells the world I'm a proud Packers fan."

"It's a stupid name, and it's stupid to like it. And what's really stupid is that dumb hat out there on the pile of junk y'all dumped in our front yard."

You should've seen his face. It turned so dark red I thought his skull might burst into flames.

"I'd rather cheer the Packers than a bunch of hogs."

Now, you need to know something. I don't like sports very much. They're loud and chaotic, especially football. But I don't want some outlander, out-of-towner, Yankee tough-guy wannabe disrespecting the Arkansas Razorbacks.

I curled my fists and leaped to my feet.

"Take that back!" I yelled at him. Boy oh boy, I was ready to sock him into the middle of next Tuesday.

"I'll sit out the game, and you play, April Grace," Lacey said. She rested one hand on my arm.

Her soft voice seeped past the ringing in my ears and soaked into my brain. I turned my head slowly. She met my eyes, as calm as still water. Myra Sue twitched like a toad on a hot rock. I don't know what Brie was doing, but if I slugged her brother, he'd probably slug me back and so would she.

I knew I had to get out of there before I got in trouble. Ol' Myra would probably tattle on me, anyway, no matter what, but I needed to put some space between me and everyone else.

"No thank you," I said stiffly, and stalked away.

Lacey followed me outside. She sat on the porch swing and said nothing while I stomped around and breathed.

Boy howdy, why, why, why had those Wisconsin Beasons—who Ernie had never, not even once, mentioned before—felt it necessary to inflict their messy, noisy selves on us and invade our farm? That whole batch of 'em galled me like salt on a fresh cut.

It wasn't until a tan Buick that was older than George Washington's grandmother pulled into our driveway that I realized I had been acting out in front of Lacey whom I really wanted to be friends with. I wanted her to like me, too, and spend time with me this summer. After seeing me march around and mutter like a knothead, she'd probably never want to come to our house again.

Mrs. Hopper got out from behind the steering wheel of that tank of a car and tottered up to the front steps. She paused long enough to eyeball that pile of junk, then worked her way around it real carefully.

"Hi, Cousin Doshie," Lacey said, getting up.

"Hi, sweetie. I come to see if you're all right and to take you home."

"Why, Cousin Doshie! I'm fine. We had a lot of fun today. Didn't we, April Grace?"

I nodded, but said nothing about us walking all over the farm and out in the woods. If Mrs. Hopper knew that, she might never let Lacey visit again, even if Lacey wanted to.

"What's all that?" The old woman pointed to the bus and the junk.

"The Reillys' family has come to visit."

"They aren't our family!" I busted out. "They're Ernie's family."

"Well, that's almost the same thing," Mrs. Hopper said with a smile.

I wanted to scream out, NO IT IS NOT THE SAME THING AT ALL! But I didn't want to make Lacey dislike me any more than she might already, so I kept my big mouth shut, even though I felt like I might barf up everything I've eaten since I was in second grade.

"Well, honey, there's enough company around here, so you come on back home with me."

Lacey smiled sweetly at her and said, "Yes, Cousin Doshie. I'll go tell Mrs. Reilly."

I went with Lacey as she found my mom making coffee in the kitchen.

"Thank you for having me in your pretty home, Mrs. Reilly. And thank you for the food."

"You are so welcome, Lacey. Come back again one of these days."

"Thank you, ma'am." Lacey turned to me and said, "I had a lot of fun. Maybe I can visit again."

"I'd like that," I told her.

She smiled, and left with Mrs. Hopper. It wasn't until she was gone that I remembered I had planned to lend her some of my books.

I went out the back door to get away from everyone else. Daisy was lying on the edge of the backyard. From a distance, a stranger might think she was a polar bear. I flopped down on the ground beside her and sprawled across her big furry body. Beneath me, she was warm and breathing and I could feel her sweet doggy heart beating. She wagged her fluffy tail, lifted her head high enough to lap my face, then stretched out again and went back to sleep. I closed my eyes and wished the entire world was a dog.

Twenty-One

Aunt Pookie Cleans Up

I lay there for a while, thinking about the events of that day and wishing the upcoming week was over. I reckon you could say I was depressed.

After a while, I heard a woman talking nearby. Daisy squirmed beneath me, trying to get up. I sat up and squinted at the person who stood between me and the nearly setting sun. All I could see was a round outline against that bright light.

"That's a fine-looking dog," she said. "Will it bite?"

"No, ma'am. She's never bit anyone."

The only person in the whole entire world who thinks Daisy is vicious is Isabel St. James and that's because she doesn't realize when Daisy bumps Isabel's leg and tushy with her nose, it's because she wanted to be petted.

The woman moved to pat Daisy and the sun shot right into my face. I turned a little, and saw my companion was a short woman, as round as she was tall, in jeans and a green Packers t-shirt. She carried a great big old-lady style purse on her left arm and clutched a black cane in her right hand. She leaned on it as she admired Daisy.

"You're one of Ernie's relatives, aren't you?" I asked.

"I'm his Aunt Pookie."

"Pookie?" Those Beasons could sure come up with some weird names.

She chuckled and nodded. "My real name is Poughkeepsie, after my mother's hometown in New York, but my little brother had a hard time pronouncing it. He kept calling me 'Pookie.'"

In my own personal opinion, Pookie is a better name than Poughkeepsie for a human person, but what do I know? I'm not a Beason.

"You fixin' to go somewhere?" I asked her.

She glanced up from scratching Daisy's ears. "Am I fixing what?"

"You have your purse. Are you going somewhere?"

"Oh." She shook her head and went back to the ear-scratching. "No. I always carry my pocketbook."

"It's awful big."

"It has to be big because I take a lot of medicine, and I want my medicine nearby in case I have a spell."

"Are you sick?"

Golly, I hoped she didn't have a spell with me sitting right there. I wouldn't know what to do.

"Just old and fat," she said cheerfully. She stopped messing with Daisy and looked around. "I also carry my thread in my pocketbook."

"Thread? Why?"

"Why, to make little pretties for everyone." She popped the clasp, opened that suitcase of a purse, and pulled out a ball of crochet thread. She waved a thin, silver crochet hook around and jabbed it into the ball. "Crocheting doilies and tablecloths and suchlike is my hobby. I'll make you something."

I couldn't think of a single thing I'd use a doily for, and where would I put a tablecloth? But it was nice of her to offer.

"Thank you," I said.

"A lovely old farmhouse like this...surely you have a nice front porch, don't you?"

"Yes, ma'am. It's on the front of the house."

She laughed. "Of course it is, but I haven't seen the front of the house yet. I've been over at Grace's, resting. She left a note, telling me to call her when I felt up to it, and she'd drive over to get me." She looked across the hayfield at Grandma's house. "It's just a short walk, though. I'm not so old that I need to be hauled around. Actually, I've walked around a little here in the back, peeked at the barns and livestock." She heaved a deep breath in and out. "But I'm getting a little tired now."

"I'll take you to the front porch and you can sit there, if you want to," I said.

"Aren't you a sweet, pretty thing?" She smiled real nice and took my arm. Her purse hung between us. "Let's go find that porch."

She walked awful fast for a round old lady with a cane and carrying a big purse. When we came around the corner, and she saw that pile of stuff in front of the steps, she halted so fast I stumbled right smack into her.

"I recognize that mess," she said. She let go of my arm and stomped the rest of the way to the porch, up the steps, and to the front door. Without even pretending to knock, she opened the screen and went inside. I was right on her heels.

The television was on, but this time the noise level was down. Although they all leaned forward, eyes glued to the screen, the living room was tidy.

"Ernest Charles Beason," Aunt Pookie said in a dreadful voice. Everyone turned to stare at her, even Grandma, who was sitting all snuggled up to Ernie on the sofa and holding his hand like they were in junior high.

He jumped up, looking alarmed.

"Something wrong, Aunt Pookie?"

"I should say so. Come with me."

She grabbed his hand and ushered him out to the porch.

"Old Ern's in trouble," Roy said. Everyone laughed like they thought it was the joke of the year, then they turned back to the ballgame.

I had a feeling the rest of them were in for it too. And I was right. About thirty seconds later, Ernie and his aunt stormed into the house and glared at their relatives. I moved over to a corner and tried to shrink out of the line of fire but I couldn't wait to hear what was about to be said.

"Turn off that television." Ernie's voice was as cold and hard as a piece of granite.

"But it's the bottom of the ninth, Brewer's leading six to five."

"I don't care if the bases are loaded and they've shipped in Roger Clemens to bring 'em all across home plate. Turn it off and ever' last one of you come outside."

"Do what he says or you'll have to answer to me," Aunt Pookie said.

They switched off the game and trooped outside like a bunch of sad, downtrodden kids. The Brewers had to win or lose without them.

You know me. I had to know what was going on so I slunk outside right behind them and watched.

Aunt Pookie pointed her cane at that pile of suitcases and clothes and cheesehead hats.

"What possessed you to unload your belongings out here in front of the house and leave them? Do you think the Reillys should carry your things inside and put them away for all of you? What is the matter with you?"

"Well, Auntie, the game was on, and we—" said the Beason named Pardner.

"I don't want to hear another word about another game the rest of the time we're on this trip! All the way down here we listened to games of one sort or another on the radio until I prayed the Lord would make me deaf."

"But we have a whole stack of tapes with the last two years Packers' games!" This outraged cry came from Colby. "We even brought the player in case they don't have VCRs in Arkansas."

Well, that was a stupid thing to say, but I realized I could expect nothing smart to come from his big yap.

Aunt Pookie drew a bead on him with her cane and she didn't move it, not even a fraction of an inch.

"If you so much as bring one of those tapes into this house, Colby Beason, I'll crush it to pieces with this walking stick, I promise you I will."

"You tell 'im, Aunt Pookie!" I shouted inside my head.

It was dark by the time they'd sorted out their belongings and split up to go to their various sleeping places. Some of them slept on cots in the bus. Colby and Ranger shared my room, Brie bunked with Myra Sue. Roy and Bixie took Mama and Daddy's room, while Mama and Daddy slept on the service porch on a small rolling bed that folded up during the day. Eli's crib had been moved into the living room where the sofa had become my bed. Aunt Pookie and Dolly stayed at Grandma's house, and I'm not sure where everyone else stayed. And I did not care. I just hoped they'd all get a good night's sleep and go home first thing in the morning.

That night, when the house was quiet, I could hear Mama and Daddy murmuring quietly from their bed on the service porch. Eli was sound asleep in his crib, God bless him. I wondered how he was able to be such a good baby with all that racket and carrying on, but he grinned and cooed most of the time.

I slipped off the sofa and padded to the kitchen door that led out onto the service porch.

"Mama? Daddy?" I called out real soft.

"What is it, April?" Mama answered.

"May I come in?"

"Sure, honey."

I slipped into the room, and Mama sat up. She scooched over and patted the little bit of space that was available on the side of the bed.

"What's up, punkin?" Daddy asked, yawning.

"You're upset about everyone being here, aren't you?" Mama said as she pulled me into her arms. She was soft and warm and smelled like Camay soap. My mama's arms were my favorite place to be.

"Why are there so many of them?" I asked.

"Because they want to see Ernie get married, honey."

"But why… I just don't understand why people always have to barge in on us, like we're the hotel for the world, or something. I mean, first it was the St. Jameses, then it was Mimi, and now it's all these Beasons."

Daddy sat up on his elbows. "Punkin, we understand how you feel. Truly we do. And I know you understand how we feel. We've been blessed with a wonderful home and lots of love and when people come to our door, we share with them."

"I know. But aren't there any rules? Can just anyone show up and say, 'Hey Mike, I want to move in with you, and I want Lily to cook for me and April Grace to clean up my messes.' Can't you just say, 'You look like an ax murderer to me. Go away.'"

"Oh, April," Mama said, but she and Daddy laughed.

"We won't let anyone who looks like an ax murderer into the house, I promise," Daddy said. I reckon he did not get a good look at Pardner Beason, who had squinty eyes and a scar on his face. "And we won't let anyone overstay their welcome. There are limits to hospitality, and your mother and I promise not to let anyone abuse our home and good nature."

You don't know how relieved I was to hear that.

"But what about that awful mess they made? Mama, after all that hard work—"

"Honey, they were road weary, hungry, and in need of some time to relax," Mama said. "I knew that. I gave them some time to shake off that trip, but I wasn't going to let them trash the entire house. If Ernie hadn't intervened, I would have asked them to clean up after themselves when their ballgame was over."

Mama always told the truth so I knew she wasn't saying these things just to make me feel better.

"All right," I said slowly. "I'll put up with them as best I can."

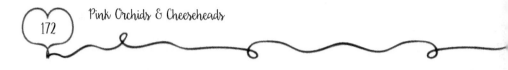
"That's good," she and Daddy said together.

"But I hope they go away the very second Grandma and Ernie say 'I do.'"

Twenty-Two

The Many Sides
of
Aunt Pookie

I reckon it was hard for those people to sleep in our house because one or the other of them was up all night, getting drinks, getting a snack, using the bathroom, looking out windows, going outside and coming back in. I would've slept better if I'd bunked down on action alley at Wal-Mart in Blue Reed.

I got up early to help Mama make breakfast. She was cooking a big one, with bacon and eggs and hashbrowns and grits and biscuits and gravy. I thought giving 'em Corn Flakes would be quicker and easier to clean up, but she said it was only right to serve guests a nice big breakfast after all that time they'd spent on the road to get there.

Mama has some strange reasons for doing things sometimes.

The bacon sizzled in two cast iron skillets, grits cooked on a back burner, hashbrowns were frying up nice and brown in another skillet, and a big pan of biscuits baked in the oven.

I was turning strips of bacon when Grandma came in through the back door toting a basket of eggs. Aunt Pookie toddled in right behind her and Dolly trailed along.

"Law, Lily, why didn't you wait?" Grandma said. "I got the eggs."

"Lily, you just sit down and let Grace, Dolly, and me finish this," Aunt Pookie said. She didn't give Mama a chance to reply. Instead, she steered her toward a chair and more or less shoved her down on it.

"But—" Mama said, starting to get up. Aunt Pookie rested both chubby hands on Mama's shoulders and held her down.

"We'll get it done." She looked at me. "Pour your Mama a cup of coffee, sweetheart."

"Yes'm."

I poured the coffee and set it down in front of Mama. I met her eyes and grinned like a monkey. It was about time someone besides just me helped her.

Pretty soon that big ol' breakfast was cooked and on the table. You should have seen Al, Colby, Ranger, and Pardner shovel down the biscuits and gravy. Those four needed some manners. I was taught not to cram food down you gullet so fast you could choke on it.

"Haven't y'all ever had biscuits and gravy before?" I asked.

"At McDonald's," Colby said. He didn't even look up.

I'll tell you something. Benji was seven years old, and he acted more mature than those boys. He sat on the Sears catalog in a chair and quietly ate his food. I don't think he could talk, because the whole entire time they were in our house, he never uttered a word. As Bixie had said earlier, all he did was sleep or sit quietly. His "toys" were an empty peanut butter jar and a white teddy bear.

"Wonderful meal!" Bixie said, sitting back. She wiped her mouth with her napkin. "Thank you so much, Lily."

"Your hospitality has been amazing, Lily," Roy added.

Al nodded, took a toothpick *out of his shirt pocket* and jabbed it between his teeth as if he'd been eating logs instead of biscuits and gravy and grits. I shuddered to think how long he'd been carrying around a toothpick. G-R-O-S-S.

"Thank you, but Mama Grace, Dolly, and Pookie did most of the work on breakfast this morning," Mama said.

Actually, Mama did most of the cooking, but she seemed disinclined to mention it.

Colby and Ranger scuffled at the table for the last of the biscuits and gravy.

Roy gave them a dirty look. I think Pardner was Colby's father, but I got so mixed up at the introductions, I wasn't sure.

"Boys!" Aunt Pookie said. She thumped the tip of her cane on the floor one time and they froze. "You will clean off the table and wash the dishes."

Boy howdy. I liked Aunt Pookie better all the time.

Colby caught me grinning, and his face turned redder than a boiled tomato. He shot me a glare that might have scalped my head if we'd been living in the Old West and his eyeballs had been hatchets. I grinned even bigger.

While the adults moved away from the table, Brie went upstairs to take a shower, and the boys started to clear away the dirty dishes. Myra Sue grabbed my arm and pulled me out of the dining room.

"Don't you think Colby and Ranger are the cutest things ever?" she asked in an excited whisper.

I shook off her hand. "Colby Beason! Are you kiddin'?"

"Shh!" She looked like I'd just stepped on her big toe. "He's a doll."

"Yeah. One of those sock monkey dolls."

Myra Sue folded her arms as if I'd insulted her personally. "You're just rotten."

I grabbed up my book from the end table by the sofa where I'd put it down yesterday. I hoped there'd be a chance to read it today. If nothing else, I'd sneak off to the hay barn or even to the cave. No matter what Mama and Daddy said about hospitality, I needed to get away from so much company. All those people in the house had made me dizzy the day before, and that feeling remained unchanged.

But I wasn't rotten, no matter what my sister declared. She's not the queen. Or even the princess.

Myra Sue glared at me and stomped off toward the staircase. I was right behind her, only I planned to head outside, not go sulk in my bedroom. In fact, I'm not sure I wanted to sleep in my room ever again, after three boys had been using it, especially Colby. One thing was for sure, I planned to disinfect every inch of that room with Ajax, Comet, Clorox bleach, Lysol, rubbing alcohol, and Raid the very minute they left.

An odor reached us about two seconds before that door opened. Temple Freebird walked in, a big tattered basket in her arms.

"Hello, hello!" she sang out. "Aren't you two the prettiest things on Rough Creek Road! And Tootsie-Roll, we're going to have to put a brick on your head to keep you from growing so fast."

Myra Sue stepped back like she thought she could get away from the smell. Let me tell you. There is no getting away from the Freebird Odor. Especially inside the house.

"Is your mama here?" Temple asked, looking around. "I heard you had a big bunch of company show up, and wanted to help out a little." She held up that old basket.

Boy oh boy, I hoped it wasn't filled with nature cookies. For some reason, Temple thinks I love those awful things and she brings them to me from time to time. They look like big chocolate drop cookies, but they have no chocolate, flour, sugar, eggs, or butter. I think the brown color comes from smashed up prunes or maybe pinto beans.

I guess I should stop saying "Thank you" and choking one down every time she brought them. She probably thinks she's doing me a favor when she brings a batch. Listen, don't tell her, but I offered one to Daisy once, and she took it off and buried it near the barn lot.

"Mama's on the service porch, I think," I said.

She breezed past us, smiling and humming a little tune. Myra Sue gagged and shot off upstairs. I hurried outside into the fresh air.

That big yellow bus sat right smack in the front yard. It truly was a blight on the landscape of our farm. Not only did it remind me of school —which I wanted to forget for the entire summer—it was pure-dee ugly. Plus, a bunch of Beasons were in there, milling around like ants.

The screen door squeaked open behind me. I'd never known that door to squeak like that. I reckon with everyone coming in and out, those poor hinges were tired.

"I'm going over to your grandma's house, April Grace," Aunt Pookie said. "You want to come along?"

Oh boy, did I!

"Yes'm," I said happily and went down those porch steps with her and her cane and her big purse.

"Want me to carry your purse for you?" I asked.

She shook her head. "No one carries my pocketbook but me."

"Grandma loses her purse a lot."

Aunt Pookie frowned. "That surprises me. Why would someone as smart as Grace lose her pocketbook a lot?"

"Well, she doesn't actually *lose* it. She lays it down and forgets where she put it. I guess you could say she misplaces it."

"Really? I fail to understand that."

She tsk-tsked between her teeth. I never should have mentioned it at all. I made Grandma sound like a real dummy when I was only trying to have a conversation. I decided not to tell Aunt Pookie that I have found Grandma's purse in places like the refrigerator, under her pillow, and in the clothes hamper. If I could've kicked my own behind, I would've.

"Well, she doesn't do it all the time. Just when she's really busy and stuff."

"If you keep your pocketbook on your arm at all times, you always know where it is."

"How do you wash dishes or take a bath with your purse on your arm?"

"Others do my dishes for me, of course," she said just as matter-of-fact as you please, "and I lock the door when I take a bath, so my pocketbook is perfectly safe."

This conversation unsettled me a little, and I didn't know why. Maybe it was the careless way she talked about other people doing the dishes, as if she never had to do anything. Or maybe it was just knowing that Aunt Pookie had such little trust in others she locked herself and her purse in the bathroom.

As you know by now, I like Ernie Beason a lot. He's kind and smart and quiet and generous. He treats Grandma really well, and he fits right in with us Reillys. I don't mind him being my Grandpa. But I betcha his weird relatives is why he moved to Arkansas all those years ago instead of staying in Wisconsin.

Aunt Pookie then asked me something about school, and we talked about that disgusting old school building and Mrs. Patsy Farber until we got to Grandma's front door.

Isabel St. James's pickup was parked in her driveway. I heard her and Grandma chattering away about flowers.

"But orchids are so expensive, honey," Grandma was saying as Aunt Pookie and I went inside.

"But if they're what you want, price isn't an issue," Isabel said in that snooty-snoot uptown voice of hers. Had she forgotten that she and Ian were no longer rich city folks?

"Really, carnations and roses would be just fine."

Aunt Pookie butted right into the conversation even though we hadn't been through the door but about ten seconds.

"They're so common, roses and carnations," she said. She shooed Queenie out of Grandma's favorite chair and lowered her pudgy self into it. She filled it right up too, and even hung over the edges some. "Pretty, but common. You should have something with some zing in it, Grace."

"Exactly!" Isabel said. "You keep saying you want simple yet elegant. Well, my dear, it doesn't get more elegant than orchids."

"I keep saying I want simple. *You* keep saying elegant, Isabel."

Isabel blinked about twenty times.

"The groom's family pays for the flowers," Aunt Pookie said, brushing cat hair from her slacks. Queenie glared at her from the middle of the room. "You get the orchids. We'll pick up the tab."

Grandma's mouth fell open, and Isabel beamed.

"There! A perfect solution!" Isabel said.

"Oh but —"

"No buts about it. The decision has been made." Aunt Pookie set her mouth in a straight line. I figured if anyone ever argued with her when she looked like that, that person might end up with a knot on the head from her cane.

Grandma sputtered before she found her voice. "Well, Pookie, that's mighty generous of you. Thank you."

Aunt Pookie nodded and took a crochet hook and the ball of off-white thread from her purse. She started whipping that thread into shape with the hook so fast it made my eyes blur.

"This'll be for Ernie and you," she said, holding up a long thin lacey looking strip. "A tablecloth. You do want an ivory colored one, don't you?"

"Why, yes," Grandma said, still flustered it seemed. "That would be right pretty. Thank you."

"I've made one for everyone in the family, and you'll soon be part of the family."

The thought of Grandma being in any family but our own made me want to holler "No way!" But I swallowed my words then shot off to the kitchen to wash them down with a glass of water.

When I came back, I noticed Grandma was wearing one of her best pantsuits. The shoes she had on always hurt her feet and made her legs ache and she only wears them when she's gussied up for church or a date.

"You going someplace, Grandma?" I asked.

"Isabel and I are going into Blue Reed to pick up my wedding dress."

Now, as a rule, a booster shot would sound more appealing than a trip to Blue Reed with Isabel St. James. But I'd do anything to stay away from that Beason clan as long as I possibly could.

"May I go along?"

"Sorry, honey. We've got to pick up a lot things for the wedding while we're in town, so we won't have room."

"You stay with me, sweetheart," Aunt Pookie said warmly, smiling. "Dolly will likely stay over at your house with the others. Say! I'll teach you how to crochet."

She beamed like the sun, but I wasn't sure I wanted to learn. Even though Aunt Pookie was bossy as all get-out, she seemed like she had a good heart and was pretty nice. She spoke her mind, but she took a real interest in people. And everything she'd said about our family and our farm had been nice. Well, except that bit about Grandma and her purse. I reckon that was just an observation, not an insult.

"Maybe you should go help your mama," Grandma said to me as she peered around the room. "Has anyone seen my purse?"

"It's right there," I said, pointing at it on top of the kitchen stove. "Good thing you didn't have a burner on."

Grandma rushed to pluck it off the stovetop.

"My goodness, Grace, get yourself a real pocketbook while you're in town and keep it with you," Aunt Pookie said. "That dinky little thing is hardly bigger than an envelope. And you shouldn't let that cat get up on the countertop. It's unsanitary."

Whoa. No one ever said anything about Queenie to Grandma without getting told off. When Grandma didn't reply, I figured ol' Aunt Pookie could get away with anything.

"Don't fret about Lily," she continued. "Our girls are over there to help her. April and I are going to have a crochet lesson."

"Crochet?" Isabel sniffed. "I thought that went out with bustles and mutton-sleeves. Does anyone even do that these days?"

"Yes, they certainly do." Aunt Pookie ran her gaze up and down Isabel's long bony frame. "You could use a hobby, I think."

Isabel blinked and shmooshed up her mouth.

"I beg your pardon," she said, so uppity it would curl your nose hairs.

"I agree with Aunt Pookie," I said. "If you had a hobby, Isabel, you wouldn't feel so all-fired depressed when you run out of projects. You oughta learn to crochet or knit or quilt or something, 'cause you're gonna need something to do after this wedding is over."

Believe me, if she failed to find herself something to do, I might pack a bag and go stay with Mimi out west for a few years.

"Why, I believe Grace told me you live on a farm," Aunt Pookie said. "A farm wife's life is a busy one, so you should have plenty to do."

You should've seen the look of horror that came across Isabel's face.

"Our Isabel is not a farm girl." Grandma gave Isabel a fond smile. The two of them have become best friends, in spite of their ages and differences. "She's brought some new life into our country ways."

Boy, that was the truth, but I kept my mouth shut. Aunt Pookie stopped crocheting to pin a hard stare on Isabel.

"But surely there are enough activities around here to keep you busy, lady," she said.

Ol' Isabel pulled herself stiff until she was as straight and wide as a crowbar.

"I daresay you're right, but I choose to pursue a more cultural path."

Aunt Pookie and Isabel eyeballed each other for a while. Then Aunt Pookie focused her attention on the lacy bit in her hand.

"High and mighty," she muttered. That crochet hook flashed like a silver streak as lace formed.

Isabel sniffed, lifted her nose in the air and stalked out. Grandma watched her go, then gave Aunt Pookie a grim look.

"Isabel is a good friend and neighbor," she said. It was plain as day she wanted to say more, but restrained herself. She smiled at me instead, and said, "Have fun, sugarbabe. See you later."

Aunt Pookie just kept crocheting and never looked up.

Twenty-Three

Aunt Pookie
and
Elmer's Glue
Have a Lot in Common

"I suppose I offended your grandmother." Aunt Pookie whipped up a few more stitches. "But I believe in speaking the truth. Don't you?"

You know me. I like to tell it like it is. So I did.

"I surely do. Sometimes, I blurt out things when I shouldn't. I don't like to hurt people's feelings, so I'm trying hard to be more careful about what I say and who I say it to."

"I don't set out to hurt anyone. That is never my intention." Boy, those stitches flew off that hook.

"You can apologize when they get back," I said. "Grandma is pretty good about forgiving people."

Of course, it did take her a while to get over being upset at me about my phone call to Ernie.

Aunt Pookie stopped crocheting and looked me right smack dab straight in the eye.

"Poughkeepsie Alameda Beason does not apologize."

"Ever?"

"Never."

Good gravy Marie.

"But what about when you've done or said something wrong?"

She went back to her crocheting. "I take care not to do that."

"But you just offended my grandma. You said so yourself."

"But it wasn't intentional." Poke, poke, poke, that hook into thread.

"So when she comes back, you won't say 'I'm sorry' or anything?"

Instead of answering, she said, "Sweetheart, would you mind to get me a nice cool glass of water? I need to take my medicine."

The way she was crocheting, like someone set her backside on fire, told me she was upset. Upset old people can get sick.

"You aren't fixin' to have a spell, are you?" I asked.

"Am I fixing what?"

"I mean, are you going to have a spell?"

"No, no, honey. Don't worry. But I have to take these pills right at ten o'clock every morning, on the dot."

"Okay, I'll get it for you right away."

I looked for Grandma's favorite glass, the one with roses on it. It was from a set that had belonged to her mother. All of them but one had been broken long ago. If Grandma was here, she would probably serve water to Aunt Pookie in that glass. It wasn't in the cabinet, nor in the sink or on the countertop. In fact, I saw it no place in that whole entire kitchen.

"Honey? What's taking you so long?" Aunt Pookie called. "I need to take my pill right on time."

I didn't want her to have a spell because I'd spent too much time looking for the company glass, so I got a regular glass that had nothing special about it. I filled it with cold water from the pitcher in the refrigerator.

Aunt Pookie had moved from the chair to the sofa. Her crochet work lay in her lap on top of her purse, and she was looking at the old photograph album Grandma keeps on the coffee table.

She took the glass from my hand, popped a tiny pill in her mouth and slugged down that entire glass of water.

"Thank you, honey. Now here, take this glass back into the kitchen and put it in the sink. Then come back in here and tell about all these people in your family album. With all her wedding plans, Grace hasn't had the time to tell me who's who."

"Okay!" I loved that album. I loved looking through every page at every face of all those relatives who have gone on before me. Not that there were very many of them.

Aunt Pookie's personality was hard to figure out. She was friendly and generous, but also bossy and hard. I wasn't sure if I liked her or not, but I figured things would go smoother if I tried to like her.

She patted the sofa cushion next to her and said, "Now, sit here and tell me about your people."

"There's not much to tell," I said as I settled close beside her. "All those frowny-looking people were grandma's grandparents and her mother, aunt, and uncle. Most of them died in the flu epidemic in 1917."

She had leaned close to look at the stiff-looking, unsmiling quintet in that photo, but when I mentioned the flu epidemic she sat back like she thought the picture had germs on it.

"All of them?"

I nodded. "Except her." I tapped my finger on the youngest person. "She was a flapper in the 1920s. See?"

I turned the heavy page and showed her the photograph of a laughing young woman with a cloche hat and a dropped waist dress with lots of fringe on it. The beads she wore hung clear down to her waist.

"That's my great-grandmother."

"Grace's mother, eh?"

"Yes, ma'am. Isn't she beautiful?"

Aunt Pookie studied the photo for a bit. "Well, it's hard to tell with that hat pulled down to her eyes, but she has a pretty smile. Like yours."

I grinned. I always thought it would be fun to be a flapper and do the Charleston and stuff, but Grandma said flappers were nothing for a girl to aspire to be. She always seemed a little embarrassed by her own mother, and she had told me very little about her. Which only made me curiouser of course, but she didn't care.

We went through the pages of that album, and I told her what I knew about the people who had lived and died long before I was born.

"I have to say," she said as she closed the album and laid it on the coffee table, "I don't understand a family as small as yours. Why, I don't know what I'd do without my clan of relatives."

I wanted to tell her I thought her clan of relatives was far too big and noisy and messy, and she'd be better off with a small family like ours. But I didn't. I'm trying to be a Better Person.

Female voices, chattering and giggling, grew close.

"Who's that?" she said, leaning forward, cupping her ear.

Myra Sue and Brie came into view, and a moment later, they entered the house. Brie gave us a big smile, but ol' Myra gawked around like she was in an unfamiliar place.

"Where's Isabel?" she asked, without so much as a howdy-do.

"She and Grandma went to Blue Reed."

Her expression crumpled like a snotty Kleenex. "But I wanted Brie to meet her!"

"Why?" said Aunt Pookie. "She's a most unpleasant person."

Boy howdy, you should've seen Myra Sue. Her mouth wagged open and shut, she blinked hard and fast about thirty times, and I think she even staggered a little. I don't know why Aunt Pookie's words surprised her. Hardly anyone up and down Rough Creek Road or in Cedar Ridge likes Isabel St. James. She was probably none too popular back in California, either.

"She's beautiful and cultured, and she's brought grace and elegance to this backwoods armpit!" Myra shrieked.

"Oh, good grief," I said.

"For heaven's sake, child." Aunt Pookie sat back as if Myra's voice had shoved her against the sofa. "It's not healthy to get so distraught. April Grace, go make your sister a cup of tea."

"Oh, but she—" I began.

"I don't want any tea!" Myra said.

"Do it." Aunt Pookie fluttered her fingers at me like she was shooing me into the kitchen. By then, I knew better than to argue.

She pointed to my sister. "You. Sit. There." She pointed at the wing chair by the window. "Brie, you go get her some tissues. I don't see any in here."

"There's a box of Kleenex in Grandma's bedroom," I told her.

Myra plopped down on the chair, slouching like an undercooked hotdog. She pooched out her lower lip about three feet and fixed those baby blue eyes on Aunt Pookie like she was about to bust into a squalling hissy fit. Brie brought the Kleenex from Grandma's bed table and handed them over.

"Don't look at me like that, girl. And stop your pouting. Sit up like a lady, and act like you're older than five."

Right then I loved Aunt Pookie. I went to fix the tea.

"Make some for everyone," she called to me. So I did.

Once Myra had gagged down her tea—she does that when she doesn't want to eat or drink—Aunt Pookie excused her and Brie to go back to the house. In fact, she ordered them to go.

"And, Brie, don't you be picking up any bad habits from that girl," she said, pinning her gaze on Myra. "Throwing fits and sulking is not a practice I want any of us Beasons to develop. If necessary, I'll send you to Ernie's house in town, and you can stay with the triplets."

I'd found out that the spoiled triplets Bixie and Dolly had complained about yesterday were not three rotten little kids. Della, Stella, and Ella were three old maid great-aunts who were older than dirt.

"Don't worry, Aunt Pookie." She smiled and gave a little wave, then she and Myra left. Myra Sue didn't bother to say "goodbye," "thanks for the tea," "see ya later," or nothing. Aunt Pookie was right. Myra Sue wasn't a person anyone else needed as a role model.

"Well, now," Aunt Pookie said, "let's start to crochet, shall we?"

She pulled out a skein of bright pink yarn from her purse and thrust it into my hands. She continued to dig around in that purse like she was looking for a lost peppermint Lifesaver.

"Well, my goodness," she muttered, scrounging like crazy. "I thought I had another crochet hook in my pocketbook."

"Do you have bad eyesight? You want me to look for you?"

"No, ma'am, you may not! There is nothing wrong with my eyesight, or my hearing. I am sound of body and mind. Obviously my other crochet hook is at Mike and Lily's house."

"How come you need a cane?" I bet you could have taped my mouth shut and shoved me in the cellar while John Philips Susa played the Washington Post March out in the yard, and I would have still blurted out those words for the whole entire world to hear.

Aunt Pookie clutched her purse with both hands like she had twelve live chickens in there clucking to get out.

"I use my cane when it suits me," she said in a voice that sounded like rocks. Hard rocks. Rocks with pointy places and sharp edges.

I gulped, but I met her eyes. "You mean you don't really need it?"

"Sometimes I need it."

"Like when you want to make a point?"

I remembered how ably she went up the porch steps the day before and how quickly and easily she walked across the hayfield.

Then guess what? You won't believe it, but I saw a twinkle in her eye. Sure enough.

"Exactly," she said. "There are times the Beasons need to have a point made. If I'm not around to make it with my trusty cane, why, those silly people would be living like tramps."

Boy howdy.

I decided I liked Aunt Pookie, no matter how bossy she got. She only did it to hold her family together.

Twenty-Four

Cellar Secrets

The phone at Grandma's rang while Aunt Pookie was crocheting and telling me about Ernie when he was a boy.

"You need to come home," Myra Sue's snippy voice said the moment I picked up the receiver.

"And you need telephone manners," I reminded her.

"Oh, boo hoo. Mama said."

"Mama said 'boo hoo'?"

"No!" she screamed at me. "Mama said come home. Lacey's here."

"Okay. I'll be there in a minute," I said, even though Myra had already hung up.

"I need to go back to the house, Aunt Pookie. My friend is waiting for me. Do you want to come along?"

"Not right now, sweetheart. I want to finish this row and maybe work another couple. It's nice and peaceful to crochet here in Grace's little house."

I knew what she meant about the peace in Grandma's house. If you listened, you could hear meadowlarks and redwing blackbirds out in the pasture, along with the mooing of the cows. Grasshopper wings made crackly noises as they flew from one grassy stalk to another. The cicadas hadn't started twirping yet, but they would once the weather got hot. The only other sound was the breeze in the trees outside as it came through the open windows, brushing the curtains across the sills. I loved Grandma's house almost as much as I loved ours, and I was happier than you can believe that she lived so close.

"Okay, then. Have fun crocheting, Aunt Pookie."

"Wait, wait!" she said just as I opened the door. "Would you like to fix me another glass of cold water before you go? My goodness, this country water is good."

"Yes'm."

I saw no reason she couldn't get up on her own two chubby feet, walk the few feet into the kitchen and pour herself a glass of water, but I think Aunt Pookie was used to being waited on. She'd probably not take too kindly to me suggesting she fetch her own water—not that I'd ever say it anyway.

I'm trying to be a Better Person.

When I got to the house, Lacey was sitting on one of the front porch steps. She grinned when she saw me.

"Hi!" I flopped down on the step beside her.

"Hey!" she said.

"What's going on?"

Her grin got bigger. "Cousin Doshie and I have been talking about how crowded it is here and everything, and I asked her if you could come and stay with us while all these people are filling your own house."

Her smile kinda wavered, like she thought I'd say no.

"Are you kiddin'?" I hollered. "Oh, boy, I would love that!"

"Your mom said it was okay, and that she'd drive us to Cousin Doshie's and Chester's when she has a free minute. That'll probably be a while, because she's really busy. I asked if I could help her, but she told me to stay out here and watch for you."

We grinned at each other. Right about then, Colby and Ranger came outside, the screen door banging shut behind them.

"Hey, there, Freckles," Colby said.

"Hey, Cheesy," I replied.

Ranger snickered, and Colby snarled his upper lip at me, and turned to Lacey.

"You gonna teach me that card trick you were talking about a minute ago?" he asked her.

"Sure," she said, smiling like she was happy to talk to that drip.

He pulled out a pack of cards from his shirt pocket and handed them to her. He sat down right next to her on the other side. If he'd sat that close to me, I would've chunked my lunch right on his sneakers. Apparently Lacey did not mind. She turned toward him and shuffled the cards.

A minute later Myra Sue and Brie joined us. Myra carried a battered old shoe box. She and Brie sat four steps above us. When I turned to see what they were up to, she stuck her tongue out at me for no good reason. Those two girls put their heads together and looked at the contents of that shoe box, which happened to be Myra Sue's collection of fingernail polish.

Everyone was laughing and talking and having a good time. Except me.

An odd feeling shuddered through my insides, something I didn't like. It made me feel oddly alone. It was such a strong and ugly sensation that it kinda took me by surprise. I just sat there, feeling bad, until I realized I might blurt out something dumb. I jumped to my feet.

"I'm going in the house for a minute," I said.

Inside, the women were in the kitchen. Temple had gone home, but her basket was there, on the floor near the door to the service porch. I lifted the top of the basket with the toe of my sneaker and saw a pile of nature cookies and a lump of bark bread. I hoped Mama had put that basket there to go in the trash.

On the other hand, if she served Temple's concoctions to our company instead of that good stuff she cooks, they'd probably all go stay in town at the Starshine Motel and eat at the Rootin' Tootin', which is a falling down old icky tavern, but most of those Beasons would probably fit right in.

Mama, as usual, scurried about, fixing food. Bixie, who is married to Roy, leisurely peeled potatoes, and Daphne, who was married to Al, was frowning at a loaf of bread like she'd never seen such a thing before.

"Mama, you want to serve these nature cookies and bark bread for lunch?" I asked.

Mama looked up and said, "April Grace, honey, take a basket from the service porch, run down to the cellar and bring up three jars of green beans and a jar of pickled beets. And two jars of the apples."

The cellar? Me? And she did not answer my question.

"Oh, Mama. Not the cellar." I hate the cellar. H-A-T-E it. It's a root cellar in the backyard, a few yards from the house. It was built even before our house, probably built before Grandma was born. It's damp and dark and creepy, and things like mice, lizards, frogs, and snakes tend to find their way into it.

"Do it, April," she said. Her face was damp with sweat and her eyes looked tired.

I glanced at the two women who were half-heartedly helping prepare lunch and the others who were playing cards at the table and drinking sweet tea like they were at the country club. It seemed to me one of them could volunteer to fetch that stuff, but no one did.

One thing about it, I wasn't going to make extra work for my mama, even if a snake as big as my daddy was curled up inside that awful old cellar.

I swallowed hard, went outside. There was a dim path in the grass from the door of the service porch to the crumbling concrete steps that lead down to the cellar door. I paused before I took a step down.

"You can do this, April Grace," I said aloud. "You'll be a teenager next year, almost a grown-up, so stop being a baby."

I gulped in a deep breath, squared my shoulders, straightened my spine, lifted my chin. Then I lowered my chin because I had to see where I was going. Those steps are steep.

About halfway down, I encountered a little brown lizard on the half-wall along the steps.

I'm not afraid of lizards and skinks, so I did not scream or faint. I think they're cool with the way their tiny faces look intelligent, and they tip their heads as if they're thinking about something interesting. That lizard and I both stood perfectly still and eyeballed each other. I admired his tiny little feet that looked like hands. He tipped his head sideways as if he was studying my freckles.

When I realized we were wasting time, I turned my attention to that door. It stood open about two inches, which is unusual because we always keep it fastened.

I wondered if there was a snake on our farm big and strong enough to push open that door and slither inside.

I shuddered. With all the guts I could gather, I shoved that old wooden door wide open. And what do you think I saw in the dim light of a single bulb that dangled from the ceiling? And what do you suspect I heard?

There sat Al and Roy and Pardner on concrete blocks they'd dragged down into the cellar from somewhere, hunched around a battery-powered radio, listening to a ballgame. Those men jumped liked I'd pulled a shotgun on them.

"Well, it's… uh… it's, uh… what's your name again, Red?" Pardner said.

As polite as anything, given the situation, location, and my state of mind, I said, "My name is not Red. It's April Grace, and I'm here to get some jars of food for Mama."

I pointed to the shelves behind them. Those shelves were nearly empty, but soon the garden would be producing plenty of fresh vegetables and Mama would be canning them, replenishing what we'd already eaten. Of course, with all these Beasons and the way they scarfed down the grub, the whole entire cellar might be empty before the end of the week.

Al stood and said, "I'll make a deal with you. I'll grab you what you need off the shelf, if you'll not tell Aunt Pookie we're listening to the game. She'll be in a foul mood all the way home if she finds out."

Since he, or one of the other men, would have to reach the beans and beets for me anyway, I didn't see why he thought this was a good deal. I had no intention of tattling on those grown men. What purpose would it serve? But I'll tell you this, I thought that since they promised Aunt Pookie no more ballgames while they were here, they should honor their promises.

"I'm no snitch," I said.

"Good. Now, what do you need? Carrots? Corn? Pickles?" He was plucking ever' last one of those off the shelf as he named them.

"No, sir. Three jars of beans, two apples, and one beets."

"Yes, sir, little lady, at your service!"

It sounded to me like he was trying to butter me up, or something, but he didn't need to. In fact, I was pretty glad to find those men in that old cellar. If there'd been any snakes down there, they would've already seen 'em and chased 'em out.

He handed me the beans and beets, then ran his gaze along the rest of the shelves.

"Did you say apples?"

"Yes, sir. They're usually over there." I pointed to the corner where Mama and Grandma always placed the canned peaches, pears, and apples.

He walked to the corner and eyeballed every jar there, shaking his head.

"Sorry, little girl. Not an apple in sight. You want these peaches instead?"

"No thanks, but if Mama wants peaches, I'll probably be back."

I turned to leave, but Pardner spoke up.

"Now, you remember our little deal? You don't tell Aunt Pookie anything."

I looked over my shoulder. The light from the door made the scar on his face stand out sharp and white. I met his eyes straight on.

"My older sister is a tattletale, not me. If she catches you, you'll probably have to promise to buy her a gallon of perfume and two hundred bottles of nail polish."

To which those men laughed like that was the funniest joke of the year.

I hurried out. Even with three big strong men in that nasty ol' cellar, it was still the creepiest place on earth.

I plunked the jars of beans and beets on the countertop in the kitchen and said, "Here you go, Mama."

She was chopping onions and the kitchen smelled like it.

"Thanks, honey." She glanced at my plunder. "Oh, April Grace, I wanted apples, too. Get two jars. In fact, bring up three."

"There aren't any apples."

She paused chopping. "What do you mean, there aren't any apples? I put up twenty quarts of apples last fall and I know we have not eaten them all."

"They aren't there."

She rinsed off her hands and dried them on a blue and white dish towel. "You must have looked in the wrong place."

Her voice was tense, and I knew she must be plumb wore out. Mama always speaks sweet and calm unless she's tired or put out with someone.

"In the far corner on the left, with the peaches and pears? They weren't there."

"You didn't look in the right place," she said again and headed outside with me on her heels.

"Mama, wait!"

"April Grace, I have a lot to do today, so don't bother me, please."

"But, Mama!" I followed her all the way to the cellar, hoping to head her off. "I promise, I looked and they weren't there. You don't have to check."

"You left the door open, April Grace. How many times have I told you to keep the cellar door closed?"

Mama trotted down those steep steps and opened the door all the way.

Twenty-Five

Breaking Promises While Sitting on the Premises

Daylight from the open door shone once more into that dank old room and illuminated those three men. They all jumped up like guilty boys on the playground.

Mama jumped too, except she wasn't guilty. They had startled the liver out of her.

"What in the world?" She pressed her hand to her chest. "Why are you men in the cellar?"

Right behind me, a voice shouted, "Roy Alexander Beason! What do you think you're doing?" Bixie stepped into the cellar.

Dolly pushed past me and screeched, "Are you boys drinking *moonshine?*"

The sunlight coming in dimmed as more and more Beasons piled up on the steps to the cellar to see what was going on.

Pardner got to his feet and took a step toward me. He was so big and ugly and the thundercloud look on his face was so awful, I felt cold all the way to the middle of my bones.

"Why, you lying little redheaded brat! What did you tell them?"

I shivered and stepped close to Mama. She put an arm around my shoulders and drew me nearer.

"Never speak to my daughter like that! Don't look at her so menacingly."

Pardner waved his arm toward me. "But we had a deal –"

"I don't care! No one, not you or anyone else on the face of this earth makes threatening gestures toward my child."

He stood there like a big ol' dummy.

"All I said was there weren't any apples," I choked out. "I didn't say anything else."

"What is the matter with you, Pardner?" Bixie leaned forward and glowered at him.

"Where's that moonshine?" Dolly hollered. "I'll pour every drop of it down the drain! You just watch and see if I don't." She looked around that cellar like she expected to find a still hidden in the shadows.

Roy stood between Mama and me and Pardner. He even elbowed that man back a couple of steps.

"Everyone just calm down," he said, as if we were all about to riot. "Dolly, there is no moonshine, so take it easy."

"If I find a drop of it, I'll pour it out, I swear I will."

"We know, Dolly, we know. Believe me when I say there is no moonshine here." Roy turned to Mama. "The thing is, Lily, we sneaked down here to listen to the game on Pard's portable radio. And your girl walked in on us."

"A ballgame?"

He looked uncomfortable and nodded.

"And this is a reason to call her names, to frighten her?" Mama's hand tightened on my shoulder.

"That wasn't intended —"

"Oh, I think it was. It surely seemed that way just now. I don't know what might have happened if I hadn't been here to stop you." She fastened her angry gaze on Pardner's face. "I don't want to be inhospitable to Ernie's family. However, I refuse to put my children in harm's way. Pardner, you gather your things and go stay in town with Ernie, or at the Starshine Motel. You are no longer welcome in our home."

Wow.

Boy howdy. I have seen my mama riled only a few times. Mostly, she's quiet and kind and sweet. But I've seen her pushed to the edge, and this was one of those times.

You'd've thought ol' Pardner would get all mad and nasty, but instead, he kinda shrank in on himself. He looked down and shuffled from one foot to the other.

"I'm sorry, Lily. I… well … it's just that the Brewers are doing so well this year."

He lifted his head and his expression was all enraptured, like Myra Sue's when she's talking about Isabel. "Aunt Pookie forbade us to listen to or watch any more games while we were here. If she knew we were, why, she'd take this radio and likely smash it to bits."

His words fell on deaf ears. Mama stood her ground.

"That is a poor excuse for scaring a young girl. Take your radio into town and listen to all the ballgames you want. Immediately."

She turned me around and guided me through that mob of Beasons crowding the cellar. It looked like most of the clan was there, except for Aunt Pookie and those kids who'd been on the front porch. When I glanced over my shoulder, I saw them all shuffling along, silent and stoop-shouldered. Maybe I should've felt sorry for them, but I didn't. At least not right then. They'd barged into our home like it was a playground, and only when Aunt Pookie was around did they act like decent people.

"Lily?" Bixie approached, looking white-faced and uncertain. "Do you want the rest of us to go?"

"No, of course not," Mama said. "But surely you understand my reasoning?"

"I do, yes. If you feel uncomfortable with Pardner around, I don't blame you for sending him away. He is a hot head, but not a bad person. It's just that …" She took a step closer to Mama and lowered her voice. I strained to hear. "It's just that none of us want to upset Aunt Pookie. She's the rock and foundation of this family, and we love her. Her health has diminished a lot in the last year or two. She's had two heart attacks, so we try not to upset her."

Hmm. That sounded nicer and friendlier than Pardner's concern about that stupid radio and ballgames. Didn't he care about poor ol' Aunt Pookie's health at all?

"I'm so sorry to hear she's that ill," Mama said. "I can see that you're devoted to her."

"Yes. She raised all the boys on her own. The triplets were of no help. In fact, she has played nursemaid to them most of her life. If you want to meet three spoiled old women who believe the world revolves around them, you should meet Ella, Della, and Stella."

I'll tell you something. That Beason family had as many layers as a rotten old onion, and I had a strong suspicion the onion-peeling wasn't over.

Twenty-Six

When Things
Go Missing

While the Beasons went back into the house, Mama returned to the cellar. I waited for her at the top of the steps.

She came out carrying three jars of pickled peaches. A frown pinched her eyebrows downward.

"April, honey, why are you standing here?" she said as she reached the top step.

"Just waitin' for you. Thank you, Mama, for sending him away."

She looked into my eyes.

"I'm sorry he scared you, but that's not going to happen again. I will never let anything happen to my children. Never."

Just hearing those words made me feel all warm around my heart.

"And I'm sorry I didn't believe you about the apples," she continued. "There's not a single jar of them down there, so we'll have pickled peaches for dessert instead of apple cobbler. I just can't understand it. Surely, we didn't eat all those apples."

"Maybe Grandma got some of them."

"I'm sure she did, but she didn't take them all."

"Mr. Brett?"

"Well, honey, Mr. Brett knows he's welcome to anything in the cellar he wants, but he always asks before he takes even a pint jar of bread-'n-butter pickles."

We walked toward the back door. I opened it for her.

"It's a mystery to me," she said, shaking her head as she entered the service porch.

Mystery, huh?

The kitchen was warm and fragrant, and mostly empty. Bixie was checking on a humongous ham baking in the oven, and Lacey was rubbing a hunk of cabbage across a vegetable grater for coleslaw. Voices and sounds of activity came from other parts of the house.

Myra Sue and the other kids were nowhere to be seen. Which failed to surprise me even a tiny little bit. I figured all of them were as lazy as pigs in the sun. Even Brie, who seemed nice enough, had shown no signs of ambition beyond eating, playing cards, and primping.

Mama handed me the peaches.

"Find a bowl for these, honey, but don't open the jars yet," she said as she walked out of the room.

"Yes'm."

"April Grace, is everything okay?" Lacey asked.

I glanced at Bixie, who was watching me. Her ears practically grew antennae. I didn't want to say anything that would cause a problem.

"Things are all right." I said.

"Some of the family is leaving here to go stay at Ernie's in town," Bixie said. She gave me a nervous little smile.

"Does that mean you won't be coming to stay with me?" Lacey's voice brimmed with disappointment.

I really, really wanted to go to the Hoppers and stay until the Beasons left. But I hated leaving Mama with all those Beasons hanging around in every nook and cranny. If she needed me to help clean and cook and pick up after those people, I'd stay home. At least Isabel had taken over all the wedding details and Mama didn't have that mess to deal with.

A moment later, Myra Sue came galumphing into the kitchen, her lower lip "all a-tremble," as Jane Austen might have written in one of her stories.

"Where is Mama?" she said, glaring at me.

"She's around somewhere, probably nursing Eli in private. Why?"

"Because Colby and Brie are leaving! She threw them all out."

"She did not!" I hollered.

"She did too. Pardner said so."

"No, she didn't," Bixie said. "She told Pardner he had to leave, but she did not say Daphne and the kids had to go with him."

Myra Sue's baby blues swam with tears.

"Just when Brie and I were having so much fun!" she squealed and stomped her foot. She turned and clomped from the room.

"Should you go to her?" Bixie asked me.

"Nah. She's just having a hissy fit. She has them about three times a day, like a meal. If you mollycoddle her, she gets even worse."

"Oh."

Lacey went back to grating the cabbage, taking long even strokes. Every stroke sounded like she was ripping a seam. I wondered what was on her mind, but she said nothing, just grated that cabbage like it was the most important thing in her life.

I opened up a cabinet where we keep the serving bowls. The peaches had been preserved, whole, so they needed a large bowl. I took out a yellow and white checked one. "This is my favorite."

"That's pretty." Lacey gazed at the bowl like she'd never seen one before.

"Mama has had it since she and Daddy got married. It was a present from Grandma."

Lacey glanced up at the open cabinet and pointed to a bright red bowl.

"I like that one too."

I got it down and when she saw it had a pattern of red poppies on a white background inside, she touched it with her fingertip, leaving a tiny bit of cabbage on the rim.

"Ooh, I love it."

"Shall I use it instead of the yellow one?" I asked her.

"Oh, yes! It's beautiful."

I thought it was strange she would react with such emotion to a serving dish, but I still didn't know Lacey very well. Unlike the Beasons, whose layers peeled like smelly onions, Lacey unfolded bit by bit, like a rose.

Mama came into the kitchen looking more like herself than I'd seen her that day.

"We have it under control in here, I think, Lily," Bixie said. She took the lid off a steaming pot as if she'd been slaving over it all day. I don't even think anything was in it but the hot water Mama had used for cooking potatoes.

Mama glanced around. "Good." Her gaze landed on me. "Honey, you want to run across the hayfield and tell Aunt Pookie lunch is nearly ready?"

"Can't I just call her?"

"I tried. She's not answering the phone."

"That's Pookie for you," Bixie announced. "She doesn't like the telephone and refuses to talk on it."

It seemed to me that refusing to answer the telephone was about as inconsiderate a habit a person could develop in this modern age. What if someone needed her, really, really badly?

"I'll go with you," Lacey said, "if this is enough for coleslaw. Mrs. Reilly?"

Mama patted her on the head. "I'll finish it up, honey. You go with April Grace, if you want to."

"I think it's so cool your grandmother lives so close," Lacey said as we walked toward Grandma's house. She sighed. "You're so lucky."

"I think so too. Well, except for the all those Beasons hanging around right now."

"I think they're interesting."

"I reckon that's true, but they don't have much couth. I mean Bixie and Roy are okay. And at least Bixie is helping Mama around the house some while everyone is watching TV or just lousing around."

"That's not fair."

"I know, but Mama is patient with people like you would not believe."

"Why are Pardner and those guys leaving?"

"Because Mama went into the cellar and they were in there listening to a ballgame and Pardner thought I'd ratted them out when I promised I wouldn't. I didn't. I tried to stop her from going down in there, but she went anyway. And then he got kinda mean, and Mama told him to hit the road."

"Wow. So her patience has limits, huh?"

I remembered when Mama had enough of Isabel St. James last year and pretty much told her to shape up or ship out. And there was the time when Mimi came and Mama seemed to have no tolerance for that old woman. Not that I blamed her. Mimi was a pill until she let her guard down and we finally understood what was going on. One thing I was beginning to realize, Mama's patience wasn't selfish or focused on what was best for her. Instead, the limits seemed to be linked with us kids and our welfare.

"For sure. I reckon that man wouldn't have hurt me, but he like to have scared me out of ten years growth. His eyes were all…" I shuddered.

"Yeah." Without Lacey saying another word, I knew she knew exactly what I meant.

I stopped on the far edge of the hayfield.

"One more thing, please. Don't mention this to Aunt Pookie."

"Okay, but why not?"

"Ol' Pardner said not to say anything because he didn't want to get in trouble for listening to ballgames when he promised he wouldn't. Imagine a grown man like him afraid of getting in trouble! But Bixie said Aunt Pookie has a bad heart, and they don't want her to get upset."

"I'll be sure not to upset her. But won't she find out, sooner or later?"

"I reckon. But not from us."

"Gotcha."

We hurried across the yard and into the house.

Aunt Pookie had moved back to the comfy chair. The crocheted piece in her hand was several times larger than it had been when I left her earlier.

"You do that fast!" I said, touching the lace.

She held it up proudly, and the three of us admired it.

"I doubt I'll get it done in time for the wedding, though." She sighed, then smiled at Lacey. "Who might you be, pretty girl?"

"This is Lacey," I said. "She's a new neighbor and a new friend."

Lacey and Aunt Pookie shook hands and smiled at each other.

"Mama sent us over here to tell you lunch is ready."

"Oh? Your mama is a nice lady, my dear. I hope you appreciate her."

"Yes, ma'am, I do."

She jabbed the hook into the ball of thread, wound the worked piece around everything and stuffed it all into her purse. I finally realized what a benefit that big purse was for her. By the time she was finished, she'd be toting around a full-sized tablecloth. Pretty soon, her big ol' purse would be full of lace.

She grabbed up her cane and we all set off to the house.

Of course, Aunt Pookie noticed right away Pardner, Daphne, Colby and Brie were gone—although how anyone could tell someone was missing from that noisy bunch is a puzzle.

"They decided to stay in town so the kids could use the city swimming pool," Roy lied when she asked. He didn't even look guilty when he did it, either. Which made me wonder if people could lie and look normal, how can you trust them to be telling the truth when they're being honest?

"I don't recall those kids being so crazy about swimming." Aunt Pookie pursed her lips as if she was pondering this situation.

"I wished they'd at least stayed for lunch," Mama said. She looked kinda upset. Daddy, who'd come in for lunch, reached out and touched her hand gently. They smiled at each other. It was a nice comforting feeling to know Daddy noticed Mama's upset. He'd talk to her about it later, if they hadn't already had a discussion.

Aunt Pookie waved one hand like chasing away a fly.

"Pardner gets crazy notions sometimes." She settled down at the dining table and tapped the side of her head with her index finger. "I think all the sports he watches and listens to have addled his mind. I hope he properly thanked you for your hospitality, Lily."

"Everything is fine, Aunt Pookie," Mama said. "I believe the triplets will be coming out here to stay with us. I'm looking forward to meeting Ella, Della, and Stella. Now, let's say grace. I'm sure you're all hungry."

Since Pardner had taken his crew away in the converted school bus, I wondered where some of the clan was going to sleep. It would be just like Mama and Daddy to give up their place on the service porch and sleep on a blanket in the hay barn.

It seemed to me, right then, the less spoken in front of Aunt Pookie about this situation, the better. I didn't know if she'd have a spell or not, but for sure, the more we discussed Pardner and them being gone, the more agitated folks were likely to get. And the more agitated people got, the more stress it would cause Mama, and it might mess with Grandma's wedding. So I kept my mouth shut.

The absence of those four Beasons had no effect on the appetites of the rest of that family. They chowed down on the smoked ham, the potato salad and coleslaw, and slurped up the pickled peaches until there were no leftovers for even a small snack. If this kept up, there'd be no food for us Reillys to eat once they all finally went back to Wisconsin.

And thinking of that, my thoughts went back to the missing apples.

Let me tell you something. Several jars of canned apples don't just get up and walk out of the cellar all by themselves.

"April Grace, you clear the table," Mama said. "Myra Sue, you help Bixie with the dishes."

"But—" Ol' Myra slapped her trap shut right quick, when Daddy leveled The Look on her.

"I'll help April Grace," Lacey said. Everyone else got up and skedaddled before they had chores assigned to them.

As Lacey and I stacked plates, she asked me, "Are you going to stay with me at Cousin Doshie's?"

"I'll talk to Mama," I said.

"Talk to me about what?" Mama said. I didn't know she was right behind us, sweeping up the crumbs. The broom made little swish-swish noises across the dining room floor.

"About staying with Lacey at the Hoppers'."

She looked up from sweeping and smiled at us.

"Oh, yes. Of course, honey. I think that's a good idea."

"For real?"

She laughed softly. "For real."

"But don't you need me —"

"I have Myra Sue to help. And Bixie. And I'm sure the other ladies will give an assist. Plus, without the bus, we're going to need more sleeping space, so you're actually doing me a big favor by staying with the Hoppers."

"You and Daddy and Eli won't have to sleep in the barn, will you?"

"Of course not! Now, as soon as you get the table cleared and put a fresh cloth on it, you may run upstairs and get your stuff together. You'll need to come back for the rehearsal party on Friday."

Lacey and I looked at each other and grinned so big our faces nearly fell off.

"Okay."

Lacey and I carried the last of the dishes into the kitchen, and I toted the soiled tablecloth out to the washing machine on the service porch.

I reckon it was the orneriness that persuaded me to sidle up to Myra Sue who was drying dishes with all the enthusiasm of scrubbing fly-specks off the walls of the barn.

Out of the corner of my mouth like a gangster from an old movie, I said, "I'm going to go stay with Lacey for a few days. Nannynannybooboo."

She flopped her mouth open and shut about eighty times.

"No fair!" she hollered. She slammed the plate down on the counter and glared at me. Lucky for her it didn't break.

It occurred to me that I probably shouldn't have said anything. Now, not only would she throw a hissy, she'd give Mama grief. So much for engaging brain before putting mouth in gear.

"Maybe I can talk Daphne into letting Brie come back." Bixie smiled at Myra Sue, even though I had told her earlier mollycoddling—which means giving in—was not the way to handle that girl. But, I'd be at Lacey's, so I didn't care what Myra Sue did or didn't do.

I got a fresh tablecloth from the hutch in the dining room. That's when I noticed the little ceramic elves were gone. Ever since I can remember, those two little elves have sat side-by-side in a mossy little glade. I looked to see where Mama had put them, but they were nowhere in sight.

"Mama?" I called.

She came into the dining room, her arms full of naked baby Eli and his bath toys.

"What is it, honey? I'm about to give the baby his bath."

"Where are the elves?"

"The elves?"

"Yes'm. They aren't in here." I pointed at the empty space.

She frowned.

"Why, I don't know! Did you move them?"

"No, ma'am."

Lacey stood at the far end of the table and smoothed the tablecloth, but she was watching us closely.

"Honey, have you seen them?" Mama asked her. "They're mostly green, about four inches high. They belonged to Mama Grace's best friend when they was young."

Now, why didn't I know that? I thought I knew everything about this family.

"No, ma'am," Lacey said, "but I can help you look."

Mama's smile included us both. "No, that's all right. April, have you packed your things to take to Lacey's?"

Twenty-Seven

This Whole Situation Needs a Thorough Think-Through

You should've seen my room. After only one night with Colby, Ranger and Benji staying in it, it looked like the end of the world had come and gone. I knew Benji had made none of that mess. Poor kid had to sleep in it, though.

"Oh, those disgusting boys," I growled. "Why didn't they at least make the bed?"

"Or pick up their dirty clothes?" Lacey started to pick up a pair of jeans, t-shirt, socks and underwear. I stopped her.

"Don't touch those. I'll take care of it. Be right back."

I found Benji sitting on the sofa with his empty peanut butter jar and teddy bear. He hardly moved at all. Ranger was outside, sitting on the ground in the front yard with Daisy's head in his lap.

"She's a nice dog," he said, surprising me. Ranger had said very little since he'd been here, so I didn't dislike him the way I did Colby. "She's old, huh?"

"Yeah. Older than me."

He kept petting Daisy and murmuring to her. I decided if she liked him, I'd at least tolerate him. I'd never seen her around Colby, but she's a smart dog. I bet she would have eaten his foot, and had his gizzard for dessert.

"Um, you left your dirty clothes on the floor my bedroom," I said.

He didn't look up. "No, I didn't."

"Excuse me, but you did. I saw them just now."

"Any dirty clothes on the floor belong to Colby. My mom makes me keep my stuff picked up."

"Oh. Well, does she ever tell you to make the bed?"

"Sometimes."

"When you're finished with Daisy, would you do that? Please?"

"No problem."

"Thank you, Ranger."

He never looked up, and he said nothing else, so I went back to the house. I got a trash bag from the service porch and took it upstairs.

"Hold this open on the floor, please," I said to Lacey as I handed it to her. Without touching that boy's clothes with my own personal fingers and taking care that none of them landed on Lacey's hands, I kicked them into that bag, tied it closed and set it in the hallway for whatever Beason wanted to tend to it. Lacey laughed at me as I dusted my hands together then shook them to make sure Colby's cooties weren't on my fingers.

I packed my necessaries in a little flowered suitcase.

"Hey, Lacey, you want to pick out some of those books to borrow?" I pointed at my bookshelf.

"Sure! How many?"

I shrugged. "Whatever you want."

We sat side by side, cross-legged on the floor, in front of the bookshelf. I'd read most of them and showed her my favorites. If I'd've been her, I'd've taken a big ol' bunch of them, but she is more ladylike than I am. She chose only four.

"We should pack some cookies to take with us," I said as we got up off the floor.

"Cousin Doshie has baked a whole batch for us."

"Super. She makes good molasses cookies."

"Yes, she does. She's a good cook." Lacey went to the window and leaned on the sill. "I love this. From up here, it's like you can see the world."

I stood beside her. "If I'd been up here when you had your bike wreck, I would've been able to see you lying there." I pointed to the place. "Right there."

"Golly."

While she gazed out the window, I put the books she chose in the suitcase and started to close it. I glanced at Lacey, giving her a sharp once over. She was a year older than me, but just about my height. She had more of a figure than I did, that's for sure, but we were still about the same size.

I pulled out a pair of jeans, a couple of dresses, some shirts, and a pair of church shoes from my closet and stuffed them in the suitcase. The cloth sides of that suitcase bulged, but I was able to zip it closed.

"Guess what?" she said, still gazing outside.

"What?"

"This is the first time I've had a sleep-over."

"For real?"

"For real."

"We'll have fun."

"I know. Because you're fun, April Grace. Fun, and funny. It's nice to have a friend."

My heart got all warm and fuzzy.

"I think so too."

It seemed reasonable that Lacey might turn into a best friend, just like Melissa Kaye Carlyle. I wondered for a few seconds if it was okay to have two best friends. It didn't matter. I was going to have two of them, and that was that.

As we started to leave the room, Lacey spied a doll on my shelf. It was a baby doll I'd gotten for Christmas a few years ago. She was dressed in a soft pink and green sleeper I didn't play with her very much. Not that I had anything against baby dolls, but I preferred to hike in the woods or to read.

"Ooh. May I look at her?"

"Sure." I handed the doll over.

Lacey ran her hands delicately across the round face and rosy cheeks as if the doll was a real baby. She smoothed the sleeper, then cradled the tiny feet.

"What's her name?"

"Kylie."

"She's soooo sweet."

Without even thinking about it, I said, "Would you like to have her?" Her eyes bugged at me.

"Oh, I couldn't."

"Why not? She just sits on my shelf, collecting dust."

"But…"

"I have a lot of dolls. Honest. I don't need that one. Please take her."

Actually I had three more, but they'd been stored in the attic. Two were baby dolls, and one was a Barbie doll. I don't know why Grandma gave me that thing, but I guess she thought since all the other girls my age loved to play Barbies, so would I. Let me assure you, I'd rather play with set of rocks.

Lacey's eyes filled with tears. When I saw that, my own filled. I had no idea why we both cried, but we did. She hugged that doll to her. Tight.

"Thank you." Her voice was hardly above a whisper.

Downstairs, I set my suitcase out of the way and we went into the living room. Mama sat in Grandma's favorite rocking chair. With slow, deliberate rhythm, she rocked Eli, who was all snuggly and sweet-smelling from his bath. His head rested on her shoulder, his dark red hair in damp, soft ringlets, and his eyes nearly closed. He spotted us, smiled sleepily, then his eyelids drifted shut.

Aunt Pookie stretched out on the sofa, one hefty leg stretched out on the cushions, the other with a foot on the coffee table. Apparently Mama was going to let her get away with that. She was crocheting the tablecloth as fast as killing snakes.

Benji had moved to the far corner on the floor with his peanut butter jar and teddy bear. Not for the first time, I wondered what it was like in his head. Was he happy? Did he experience anger, or fear? His expression never varied, no matter where he was, or with whom.

The rest of the Beasons roamed on the porch, or hogged the bathroom, or clomped around upstairs, or took naps on various beds. Except for Al. He was at the dining table, eating a bowl of Cheerios like he hadn't been fed in a year.

"He's the cutest thing ever!" Lacey tipped sideways as she looked at Eli. "I wish I had a baby brother." She patted Kylie's vinyl body and moved slightly, mimicking Mama's rocking motions.

"You girls ready?" Mama asked softly.

I nodded.

"As soon as Eli is sound asleep, I'll drive you up to the Hoppers. She continued to rock him, slow and even, lulling my baby brother deep into dreamland. I know she'd done the same to me when I was his size. I just wish I could remember it, because it seemed like that would be a fine memory to have.

I'll tell you one thing, though. It was hard to imagine Myra Sue as a cute little baby being rocked to sleep.

"Where you two ladies off to?" Aunt Pookie asked as she eyeballed the corner of her handiwork. She frowned and yanked the thread, unraveling several inches.

"We're going to Lacey's house," I said.

Lacey turned her face to me, her eyes wide and shining. "My house. But it's not really. It belongs to Cousins Doshie and Chester."

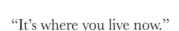
"It's where you live now."

Mama got up slowly and quietly. She'd moved Eli's crib onto the service porch. Those Beasons always used the front door for their coming and going, so it was way too noisy in there for Eli during the day.

Aunt Pookie's crochet hook glinted in the light as she stitched. Lacey seemed transfixed by it.

"What're you doing?" she asked.

"I'm crocheting Ernie and Grace's wedding present."

"Wow."

Lacey sank down on the sofa next to Aunt Pookie's stretched out leg and watched every little movement.

Aunt Pookie paused. "You want to learn to crochet, Lacey?"

"Yes, ma'am."

"Well, if I hadn't lost the other crochet hook I thought I'd packed, I'd teach you. But, it seems to have gone missing." Mama walked into the room. "Lily, do you have a crochet hook?"

"I never learned, believe it or not, but I bet Mama Grace has one in her workbasket."

"I wish I'd known that earlier." She grinned at Lacey. "Why don't you run over there and get it, honey?"

"But we're fixin' to leave," I said.

"You're fixing what?"

"We're getting ready to go to Lacey's house."

Aunt Pookie went back to making those fast stitches.

"But if you'll go get me a hook, I'll teach you both a couple of beginning stitches. Smart cookies like you two will learn how to make a slip knot and chain stitch in no time at all. You can practice at Lacey's house. Keep you from getting bored. "

I started to protest because I wanted leave before the Beasons invaded our space or the spoiled triplets showed up. Lacey's excitement stopped me. It was plain as day that poor girl needed some good things in her life. If learning to crochet made her happy, I'd go along with it.

"Check Grandma's wicker workbasket in her bedroom," Mama said. "She keeps all kinds of goodies in that." She glanced at Aunt Pookie. "You know, I think Mama Grace even has a tatting shuttle in that basket, though I've never seen her tat a thing."

"Tatting! Now there's a dying art."

While those two women talked about tatting—I had no earthly idea what that was, but it sounded painful—Lacey and I left.

"If your grandma has two hooks," Lacey said, as we walked, "we should borrow them both, then we won't have to take turns."

"Good idea."

Learning to crochet was about number 712 on the list of things I wanted to do. But having a good friend was always in the top five, so I was willing to do this with Lacey. If it turned out to be fun, we could teach Melissa what we learned, and we could be a trio of crocheting friends.

Grandma's house was quiet and empty, clean as a whistle. Lacey followed me into the bedroom, which is cluttered because Grandma has a lot of keepsakes from when she was a girl and when she and my grandpa were first married.

All the interesting little knickknacks and pictures distracted Lacey for a while. I ended up explaining the history behind each object and told her who was in the pictures.

"My favorite is the photo of her and my grandpa, though I reckon she won't have that sitting on her bedside table once she and Ernie get hitched."

I turned to get photo from the table but it wasn't there. I looked

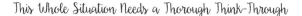

around, but couldn't find it. Gone. Just like the special company glass. Just like the canned apples. Just like the ceramic elves.

"Lacey," I said, scouring that room with my eyes, "there is something weird going on, and I think the Beasons are behind it."

She had opened the wicker workbasket and found several steel crochet hooks in different colors and sizes. She held out the assortment like a fan.

"Which one do you want? And what do you mean?"

"The blue one is fine. I mean things are missing around here. And none of 'em disappeared until the Beasons barged in."

"Really?"

"Yep."

"What about money and jewelry?" she asked.

My glance went straight to Grandma's polished mahogany jewelry box on the dresser. She didn't have much jewelry, and none of it was worth much money, but still…

I opened it and there lay a couple of brooches, a round one with blue stones and the other a plain gold bar. Her class ring, from 1942, was in there, and Grandpa's pocketwatch that he'd got when he was boy. There were a few broken chains, all snarled in a big tarnished knot. Two old wedding rings, both of them thin, plain gold bands were tied together with a blue ribbon. Grandma had quit wearing her wedding ring last year. It used to bother me some, seeing her naked hand. I reckoned she'd be wearing a new wedding ring soon enough.

"Nothing missing out of this," I said. "I'll look and see if anything is gone from anywhere else."

All the kitchen stuff was in place, and the same in the bathroom. I thought for a minute nothing had been taken from the living room, but then I noticed the little glass horse she kept on the end table next to her Bible was gone. Not that it was such a big loss. Old man Rance bought it for her last summer. I don't know why she kept it, other than she thought it was pretty.

I sat down on the sofa to ponder. Lacey, who had yet to complain or demand anything in my hearing, sat down with Kylie in her arms. She stroked and patted the doll, waiting as I gave this whole situation a thorough think-through.

Twenty-Eight

We Have Ourselves a Problem and It's Not Just Myra Sue's High Heels

"What are you going to do?" Lacey asked me after a while.

"I reckon I need to talk to Mama or Daddy. If Grandma was here, I'd tell her, but she's off gallivanting with Isabel for the wedding. And I reckon even if she was here, she wouldn't want to know about this right now. It would upset and distract her."

"Have you noticed anything other than those elves and the canned apples missing from your place?"

"I haven't looked." Our eyes met the second those words were out of my mouth.

"Maybe you better check before we go to Cousin Doshie's."

"Yep. You want to help?"

"Of course! But I don't know what to look for."

I crimped my mouth, then I thought of something. "You can take notes."

She beamed. "I'm a good note taker. But what about Aunt Pookie and our crochet lesson?"

"We can do that after we investigate."

I hoped Aunt Pookie wouldn't demand we plop down and learn how to do that business the minute we stepped inside the house. We had important work to do first.

"Let's go."

"Let's do it!"

She still had the crochet hooks in one hand and the doll in the other as we tore off across the field. Quiet as two country mice at a funeral, we crept inside the house and eased upstairs. My bed was made, all nice and neat. I hoped Ranger or one of his family had done that. Anyone but my mama who had enough to do feeding those starving Beasons.

I got Lacey a pen and notebook from my school backpack in the closet. She put the doll and the hooks on the bed and immediately wrote something.

"What's that?" I asked as she wrote.

"Just notes of what was taken, from where, and when you noticed. In case you forget, or get mixed up, or something."

"I won't forget, but it's a good idea, anyway."

When she finished, she put the blue cap on the Bic ballpoint and said, "What's next?"

I knew this was going to take some time and thought, but we didn't have a lot of time. I mean, even while we were discussing this, that guilty Beason—or Beasons, as the case may be—might be swiping more stuff. And if they went back to Wisconsin before we figured out who was taking what, they'd be taking our stuff.

"We should go through every room in the house. Do a 'sweep.' That's what they call it on those TV cop shows. Since my strongest suspect is that rotten ol' Colby, and since he stayed in this room, let's start here."

"Very good idea, Sherlock." She grinned, and tapped the pen against the side of her head.

I looked over my room like you wouldn't believe, eyeballing every inch. The only things I didn't use were a magnifying glass, a microscope, and a trained-to-find-stolen-stuff dog.

"Everything is here," I said, finally, and with considerable relief. "Let's check my sister's room."

We walked in, and there was ol' Myra, whirling around in a party dress like she was dancing. She had on bright red lipstick, a pair of ultra-high heels that looked like something Isabel had donated to her. She wore a glittery headband like she thought it was Crown Jewels.

When she saw us, she stumbled to a stop and wobbled around like a Weeble. That's when I saw she had padded her bra until her chest looked like it ought to be on Dolly Parton.

I started laughing, and like to have passed out when I couldn't catch my breath.

"April Grace Reilly, you little sneaking, snooping sneak of a snoop!" she screamed. "What are you doing in my room? Ever hear of knocking?"

By that time, I was on the floor, snorting so hard with laughter I nearly ripped out the back of my headbone.

"I'm gonna tell Mama!" she yelled like a five-year-old. She tried to stomp out of the room, but ended up tripping over her own feet and crashing to the floor.

"Oh, my!" Lacey said, rushing to her. "Are you all right?"

Myra was in a tangle of skirts. She stayed there, kicking like a bug on its back, trying to get up.

My sides ached so hard, I had to cross my arms and hold 'em.

"April Grace, stop laughing or you'll be sorry!"

"Here," Lacey said, tossing aside the notebook, "I'll help."

Myra Sue paused all the flailing and kicking and screeching and whimpering and moaning and groaning and sighing. Something must've clicked in her little pea brain and told her Lacey was someone who would pamper and pet her and call her pretty.

"Thank you," she said pitiably, and grasped Lacey's hand as she struggled to her feet. Then she limped/staggered/swayed/stumbled to her bed where she sank like the Titanic.

"Shall I get you a cool cloth?" Lacey said worriedly.

"Yes," Myra whimpered.

"No!" I said. "Myra Sue, sit up. Lying down like that will make you feel worse."

Lacey tried to pull her into sitting position, but my sister was a dead weight, floppy as a ragdoll.

"Myra Sue," I said, "if you lay like that in high heels, it will make you light-headed and you might throw up. And your feet will swell like an old lady's."

Boy howdy, she shot up like a wild onion in the springtime. I had no more idea than the man in the moon if lying on the bed that way in high heels would make you throw up or your feet swell, but I figured it could, and what my silly sister didn't know wouldn't hurt her. At least when it came to this.

"What are you doing in my room?" She sounded well on her way to full recovery.

"We're solving a mystery," Lacey said, "but you have to keep it secret."

Well, that probably wasn't the smartest thing my new friend could say, but Myra Sue nodded as if it made perfect sense.

"What's the mystery?" she asked in a whisper.

"Girls, what's going on?" Mama stood in Myra Sue's open door and narrowed her eyes at us like she was the police and we were the crooks.

Myra Sue looked at Lacey. Lacey looked at me. I looked at Mama. Mama folded her arms and frowned.

"Why in the world are you wearing that dress, Myra?" she asked. "That's for the wedding." She looked more closely. "And wipe that lipstick off your mouth, for goodness sake."

When Myra reached into the bodice of her dress and pulled out a tissue, I thought Mama's eyes would pop out of their sockets. I had a hard time trying not to laugh. I turned it into a cough. A long, hard cough.

Mama wasn't through yet.

"Whose shoes are those? Take them off this instant before you fall and break your neck."

"That's what I did, Mama," she said, her eyes filling. "I fell. Right there. I might have already broken my neck."

She pointed to the middle of the floor with one hand and clutched her throat with the other, as if she thought breaking her neck was something like tonsillitis. I thought even Myra Sue was smarter than that. She conveniently forgot to tell Mama she had attempted to charge across the room like a bull elephant and fell off her shoes.

"And you two," Mama said, looking at Lacey and me, "I thought you in such a hurry to get to Lacey's house. Why are you up here in Myra's room?"

"Mama, we kinda have a problem."

"Oh? What is it?"

I slipped over to the door, closed it, and took Mama's hand. I led her to the bed where she sat down, looking at me with considerable concern.

"April Grace, what is it?"

I met her eyes and tried to look as serious and grown-up as possible.

"Mama, some of them Beasons are thieves."

Twenty-Nine

Escape From
the
Beason Herd

"Why do you say that?" Mama didn't seem a bit surprised by my announcement.

"Number one, Grandma's company glass with the roses on it is missing. Number two, our ceramic elves are missing. Number three, all the canned apples are gone. Number four, Grandma's little glass horse is missing, and worst of all, number five, so is the photo of Grandma and Grandpa on their wedding day."

"And Aunt Pookie's other crochet hook," Lacey added.

"Yeah. That."

"And Eli's little blue hat," Myra Sue put in. "I was going to put in on him before taking him outside yesterday, but I couldn't find it."

Mama frowned. She sat there for a minute, quieter than a tomb, staring down at her clasped hands. I reckon she was thinking about thieves and Beasons and missing items. Finally she heaved a deep sigh and looked up.

"Have you girls seen someone take any of these things?"

"No, ma'am."

"Me, either," Lacey said, and Myra Sue shook her head.

Mama met our eyes, in turn.

"I understand your concern, but it's wrong to accuse people of something as serious as stealing when you have no proof."

Lacey jumped up and walked over to the window. She said nothing as she stared outside. Mama eyed her but didn't call her back.

"You should ask 'em, Mama," I said. "Interrogate each Beason until the guilty dog barks. Or call the sheriff and let him do it."

"No, honey." She ran her hand along my hair, smoothing back lose strands. "These missing items have very little value beyond sentimental."

I frowned so hard my face hurt.

"But the photo on Grandma's table! It's not like Grandpa Voyne is around and we can take a picture of him."

"There's another just like it in the picture box in the attic, so don't worry about that."

"But the ceramic little elves. And Grandma's—"

Mama put her fingers over my lips. Her expression was kind, but stern.

"We are not going to ruin Grandma's big day, April Grace. If someone took these items, let that person keep them, because they aren't worth creating a rift between our family and Ernie's."

Lacey and Myra Sue kept quiet, but yours very truly refused to be silent.

"But if you'd just ask…"

"No." The word dropped from her mouth like a rock. "And you aren't to ask, either. I don't want you talking about this to anyone else. Not to the Hoppers, not to Temple and Forrest. Not even Isabel and Ian." Mama pinned a look on Myra Sue, who rolled her eyes.

"Mother, you know I'm no blabber mouth," she said, all snooty.

I was pretty sure if I said one more word, logical as it would be, I'd be sleeping in the attic with the cobwebs instead of going home with Lacey. I clamped my lips together.

"Agreed?" Mama asked us all.

"Yes, ma'am," we said, sweet as baby lambs.

We sat in complete silence, not daring to move, while Mama met our gazes once more.

"Lacey?"

She looked over her shoulder at Mama.

"You all right, honey?"

"Yes, Mrs. Reilly. And I won't say anything."

Mama finally seemed satisfied that she had made her point. She stood.

"If you two are ready to go to the Hoppers, I'll run you up there."

"Mama?" Myra Sue said, oh-so-pitifully because she was staying behind. I don't know why she acts like she's a thousand years younger than I am.

"You change out of that dress and those ridiculous shoes," Mama said. "After we drop off April Grace and Lacey, you and I will go to Ruby's Place for a Pepsi Slush. Want to?" She tilted her head slightly, smiling as if the two of them were in on a secret mission all their own.

Myra grinned so big the braces on her lower teeth shone like treasure.

I just about hollered out "No fair!" because I dearly love Pepsi Slushes, but I didn't. For one thing I didn't want to sound like a baby, or like Myra Sue. And another thing, I was too excited to stay with Lacey to care about an ol' Pepsi Slush, anyway.

"My suitcase is packed and ready to go."

Lacey dashed into my bedroom and got Kylie the doll, the notebook, and the pen she'd used for notes.

"You're taking your doll, April?" Mama said. "You haven't played dolls in a long time."

"Kylie belongs to Lacey now," I said.

Lacey stopped stone still and gave us both a look full of uncertainty. I bet she thought Mama was gonna make her give it back to me.

Mama looked surprised for about three seconds, then she bathed Lacey with her warm smile.

"Good! Kylie has been by herself too much lately. She can use some cuddling and lots of love."

Me and Lacey grinned at each other and took off down the stairs.

"Get in the car, girls, and I'll be there as soon as I check on Eli."

"Whoa, whoa, whoa!" Aunt Pookie hollered as we dashed toward the front door. "You girls haven't had your crochet lesson yet."

Well, shucks. I was beginning to think we'd never get out of the house.

Mama popped her head into the living room and said, "I'm sorry, Aunt Pookie, I need to get the girls to the Hoppers before Doshie begins to fret."

"She's a real worrier," Lacey added. "Maybe you can show us in a day or two?"

Aunt Pookie frowned, bunched her lips, and wrinkled her nose. It was clear as glass she disliked not being the boss of everything.

"All right, but don't forget! Girls these days need to learn some kind of handcraft. Girls with nothing to do tend to get into mischief." She eyeballed us both, a clear warning.

"Yes'm," I said.

"Yes, ma'am," Lacey said. "We won't forget."

"My sister will be here, though. You can teach her."

"Ah!" Aunt Pookie said gleefully. "Wonderful!"

I figured she wouldn't say "Wonderful!" once ol' Myra threw a hissy fit, but I figured if anyone could handle a hissy fit and come out on the winning end, it would be Aunt Pookie.

"Grandma's crochet hooks are on the bed in my room."

"Run up and get them," she told me. "I don't want to drag my crippled hips and knees up and down stairs."

I reckon she forgot I knew she could get around as good as anyone else but before I could say a word, Lacey piped up. "I'll get them for you, Aunt Pookie."

The old woman watched her hurry away. "Now that young lady will get far in life, if she keeps her sweet spirit and doesn't let anyone take advantage of her."

I sorta kinda thought she directed that remark at me, but I'd never take advantage of Lacey Paige Pickering, and I'd probably slug anyone who tried.

Thirty

Confessions
at a
Freshwater Spring

You would've thought the King and Queen were coming to have supper with us at the Hoppers that night.

Mrs. Hopper might be older than dirt, but boy howdy, she sure can cook and she cooks a lot. We had fried catfish, hushpuppies, broccoli salad, macaroni and cheese, fried potatoes, baked apples, biscuits, brown beans with ham, and molasses cookies for dessert. Mrs. Hopper kept asking if I wanted more of this or that, and I ate so much I like to have busted my own bellybutton.

Mr. Hopper said almost nothing, except the blessing and "Pass the biscuits."

To tell you the honest truth, I don't think he's as cranky as folks say. I think he's just quiet and most of his talking is inside his head. He looks grumpy and frowny because he has worked outside his whole entire life and the sun has baked his squints until they turned to wrinkles.

Lacey loved the clothes I gave her. She had to try on everything right then, and squealed every time she looked in the mirror. I was happy I had given her a couple of my favorite shirts.

That night we went to bed and talked so much our throats got tired. When we fell asleep, Kylie was squished between us on that narrow bed. The next morning, Mrs. Hopper made us a giant breakfast of sausage, grits, gravy, and biscuits.

"I hope you girls slept good," she said as she put the food down in front us.

"I did," I said.

"Me too," Lacey added. "We talked for a long time. April sure is funny, Cousin Doshie. She told me all about when the St. Jameses first moved here. And her Mimi. And all Grandma Grace's boyfriends."

Mrs. Hopper gave me what you'd call a tender smile and stroked my head with her warm, wrinkled old hand.

"It's nice to have you here, April Grace. Our little Lacey needs a friend like you."

I glanced at Lacey, and she smiled.

"I want you girls to have fun while April is staying, but we can't neglect our chores," Mrs. Hopper went on. "So after you finish breakfast, y'uns go out to the garden patch and pull up any weeds that might have popped up since yesterday. Dead head the flowers in the flower beds. Water all the plants in the window boxes and hanging on the porch, then the rest of the day you can do whatever you want."

Doing chores is pretty fun when you have someone to talk to and laugh with while you're working. It's almost not work. Except you do get sweaty pulling up weeds while the sun beats down on you.

After the chores, we hung around with the geese for a while. Four goslings followed their mother around, and boy howdy, did she get ticked off when we tried to get closer.

All morning we stayed within eyesight and earshot of the house. Mrs. Hopper called us in for lunch of cornbread and beans.

"Mrs. Hopper," I yelled because she couldn't hear well and didn't wear a hearing aid, "you cook almost as good as my mama."

She laughed. "That's a right fine compliment. Thank you, April Grace."

"Cousin Doshie!" Lacey hollered. "May April Grace and I walk over the hill?" She pointed toward the back of the property where the land rose steeply.

Mrs. Hopper pondered a minute, then she nodded.

"I reckon it'll be all right. April was raised in these hills, and knows her way around the woods and hollers. But don't be out past dark. And be careful."

We scrambled up the hill, plowing through old fallen leaves and undergrowth. We finally got to the top, huffing and puffing a little. And then we stared.

The hill sloped into a small valley. A beautiful meadow lay within it, filled with wild flowers. We walked down to that field and stood in the middle while the red Indian paint brush, purple coneflower, brown-eyed Susans and Queen Ann's lace nodded and waved in the wind.

"I've never been in such an awesome place in my life!" Lacey laughed then whirled around like Julie Andrews in *The Sound of Music*. "I love the Ozarks!"

For a long time we ran around in that meadow, looking at the different wild flowers, watching the redwing blackbirds balance on stalks of tall, thick grass. We caught grasshoppers and looked at them closely and let them go. One time we found a brown and yellow box turtle. He immediately folded in on himself. I picked him up, and we stroked his sun-warmed shell. He peeped at us, but never poked his head out.

"He's so cute!" Lacey said.

"I'll put him back down so he can go on his way. We don't want to scare him."

I gently placed him where we'd found him. Although we stood there for a while, watching and waiting, he remained all wrapped up in his shell. We moved on.

On the far side of that meadow, just a few feet into the woods and tucked in among an outcropping of mossy rocks, fresh water bubbled up from the ground and formed a clear little pool.

"A spring!" I said. "With watercress."

"Feel that cool air." Lacey lifted her face and closed her eyes.

"And smell the woods."

We both drew in deep breaths through our noses. We got on our knees, cupped our hands in the spring and drank the fresh clear water. It was so cold it made my teeth ache. I broke off two sprigs of watercress and gave one to Lacey.

"It's good to eat. I read a book where people ate watercress sandwiches, but I like it like this." I bit about half the sprig. The spicy, peppery taste was yummy.

Lacey tasted hers. "Mm. I love that."

For a while, we munched watercress and washed it down with cold spring water. I dried my fingers on the front of my T-shirt.

"Do you like living with the Hoppers?"

Lacey nodded. "It's nice there. They're really good to me. When I grow up, I want to build a house right back there." She pointed toward the meadow. "My children will have a lot of space to play and they can come back here to this spring and cool off and get a drink."

"You want get married and have kids when you grow up?"

She nodded. "Lots of kids. I want to have one house where we live always, not moving around."

"That means we'll always be neighbors, because I will never move away from our farm."

"Good!"

We grinned at each other. Settling side by side on a large mossy rock, we locked our arms around our bent knees.

"I want to be a detective when I grow up," I said, "so I know I'll have to be away from home, going places, looking for clues, talking to people and chasing down leads, but I'll live on Rough Creek Road so I can see my family every day."

"Why do you want to be a detective?"

"Number one, I am always full of curiosity and if I'm a detective I can ask questions and snoop around."

Lacey giggled.

"Number two, I watch people. I notice things about them that no one else does. People ignore my observations because I'm just a girl, when I have my very own April Grace Reilly Detective Agency, folks will listen. And number three, the world needs more detectives like me."

"Do you want to have a husband and kids?"

I shrugged. "Maybe. Maybe not. It depends on if I find a boy who's smart and nice. I'm not going to marry a knothead. But no matter what I do, when I think of being grown-up, I think of being grown-up at home." I paused. "You know what's a pain? That you can't be a kid and a grown-up at the same time, that's what."

"Some grown people act worse than little kids, though."

"True. But they are knotheads."

Lacey nodded, and we lapsed into silence. We sat without speaking for a long time, staring at the sparkling water, listening to birds and insects while the spring splashed gently into the pool.

Lacey took in a deep breath and spoke without looking at me.

"My mom is in prison for killing my dad," she said.

It was like the whole entire world stopped spinning. Even the birds stopped singing. Although the sun still shone and there wasn't a cloud in the sky, the day seemed to turn dark.

"Wha…?" I gawked at her so hard my eyes nearly fell out of my head. She just sat there, not meeting my eyes, calm as a summer day.

"It happened when I was really little, about three years old." She plucked at the moss. "I don't even remember him. But Mom told me later that he was mean, and she was afraid he was going to hurt me like he hurt her. So one night, she shot him in his sleep."

Good gravy Marie.

I'd never known anyone who committed a crime, or even someone related to anyone who committed a crime. Well, except those Beasons who stole memorabilia from us, but right then that didn't count.

I swallowed hard and stared at her, but she never looked up from that mossy rock beneath us, not even once.

"After Mom shot him that night, she grabbed me and our clothes and we took off. We never stayed in one place longer than a few weeks. I never even went to school, or anything."

"But you can read."

"Mom taught me. We lived in cars and shelters most of the time. A few times we stayed at a public park and lived in the culvert that ran under the road."

Boy howdy.

"A few weeks ago, the police found us."

She still had not looked at me. There were so many questions rising in my mind that my brain nearly boiled. Something told me to keep my mouth shut and let her talk.

"We were staying in a house in some little town in Tennessee. The lady who ran the place told us it was a shelter. The third night we were there, she and Mom talked long after I went to bed. The next morning, a couple of deputies showed up with a warrant for her arrest. She told them over and over that she'd killed my dad in self-defense, that he had beat her and she was afraid for my safety, but they told her if that had been the actual truth, she wouldn't have shot him while he was asleep and she would have gone to the police instead of running from them. She tried to explain that she had wanted me to be safe, didn't want me to go into state care. She won't ever get out of prison."

Lacey stopped talking and crimped her mouth so tight I knew her heart hurt. I reckon she was trying hard not to cry.

I stared at her, at this girl who was so sweet and pretty and gentle. I played over in my mind how it must have felt to have no home, no daddy, no one to trust. I'm sure she and her mother made no friends. How could they when they wouldn't be in one place long enough? Even though I hated going to school, at least I had the opportunity to go and to learn.

Now, Lacey didn't even have a mama to turn to, and she never would. I couldn't imagine life without my mama. Or any of the rest of my family, for that matter. I swallowed hard. While Lacey had been living, unsettled, without friends, family or home, I'd been right here on Rough Creek Road, safe and warm and loved.

I didn't understand how something like that could happen. Lacey was good and kind, a lot nicer than me. And she seemed to like everyone. I think most people in her shoes would be angry and bitter, hating the whole world.

"So you probably don't like me anymore," she said, still looking at the water.

I jerked like I'd been poked. "Huh? Why do you say *that?*"

"Because my mom is a murderer and my dad was an abuser." She sent a sideways glance at me.

"You can't help what your parents did."

"You might think I have bad blood or something."

"I don't think any such thing."

"But you hardly know me."

"So what? We've spent time together and I've watched how you act with my family, and Daisy, and even those Beason cheeseheads. I like you, Lacey, and so does Grandma and everyone else. Nothing you can do other than being mean to my folks or Daisy will change my mind."

"I'd never do that."

"I know. That's what I mean."

In the whole entire time since I'd met her, Lacey had never once shed a tear. But right then tears sprang into her green eyes, clung to her lashes for a second or two, and dropped to her cheeks.

"You'll be my friend forever?"

I figured it was time to make sure she understood what I meant.

"Here's the thing, Lacey. I'm kinda hardheaded sometimes. I'm not patient, at all. Plus, I get super irritated by people who act like they don't have a lick of sense. Even though I'm trying to be a Better Person, I call my sister names and think bad things about her. And Isabel, too. Not only that, I blurt out stuff when I should keep my big mouth shut. A lot. So, knowing this, the question should be, do *you* still want *me* to be your friend?"

Her lower lip trembled just a skosh, but she steadied it and nodded with enthusiasm.

"Yes! I don't care if you are green and covered in purple dots! You're smart and funny, and if you do say things when you shouldn't, you're still kind."

I held up one hand, pinkie extended. "Then let's pinkie swear we'll be friends forever."

"Best friends?"

I had already decided there was no rule stating a person could have only one best friend.

"Yup!"

We linked pinkies and promised, "Forever'n ever!"

"Gosh, April Grace, I wish you had always been my friend."

Thirty-One

Here Comes the Bride.
And Groom.
And Everyone Else

"Happy is the bride the sun shines on, Grace!" Isabel sang out Saturday afternoon.

We were in the Sunday school classroom where she was fiddling with the flowers that went in Grandma's hair.

"I think you're right, honey," Grandma said. "But goodness me. What a to-do this has been."

I stood to one side, out of the way, during all this getting fancied up. I wished Lacey had been with me, but Mama picked me up at the Hoppers that morning so I could get all gussied up for that wedding. We had left way early to get to the church, and there was nothing for me to do but watch.

Ol' Myra hovered near Isabel, watching every move that woman made. You would've thought getting underfoot the way she did would've got on Isabel's last nerve, but it didn't. Instead, she showed Myra how to do things with hair and makeup for a wedding.

I was glad she hadn't spotted me, or she might've thought I needed a few lessons my own self.

Once again I pondered how it would have been a far better idea if those two old people had eloped. Grandma had been so nervous this past week, she could hardly eat and ended up losing weight. Right then, she kept twitching her dress front.

"My bosoms have plumb shrunk and now this dress hangs funny."

"It does not," Mama said. "You're hunching your shoulders. Stand up straight and your bosoms will come forth again."

Grandma did, and they did.

Her dress was the ivory color of antique lace and it had lots of small, embroidered pink flowers and teeny sparkly beads had been stitched to the bodice. The gathered skirt flowed soft and silky to just below her knees. Her ivory colored shoes would probably make her feet hurt before she got down the aisle, but I reckon if you wear sensible SAS shoes, or sneakers, with your wedding dress, you're setting yourself up for a lot of snickering from onlookers.

Instead of a veil and all that mess, Grandma wore pink orchids in her hair, sorta like a wreath. As silly as it sounds, it looked really pretty. And thank goodness Isabel had not overdone Grandma's makeup.

"Grandma," I said when everyone hushed for a minute or two, "you look beautiful."

And she did. She sparkled and shone and looked happy as an angel.

The door to the Sunday school room opened, and Miss Chestnut popped her tiny little head inside. She had appointed herself the director of keeping everyone in their place and on time. That had flustered Isabel a bit, at first, but I guess when she realized that no one argues with Miss Chestnut and wins, she gave in. She even expressed her appreciation on more than one occasion.

"Everyone who isn't part of the wedding should go sit down," Miss Chestnut said. "We're about to commence."

All those Beason women who'd cluttered up that room for no good reason filed out. Mama ushered Myra Sue and me toward the door, but I turned and rushed back to Grandma. I didn't want to crush her dress or smear her makeup or make her late, so all I did was take one good long last look at her before she changed her name. She smiled, reached out and touched my hair and cheek. With all the dignity you can possibly imagine, I walked out of that room with my mother and my sister.

Let me tell you something. The Cedar Ridge Community Church was packed with folks dressed up to beat the band. Big pink and white bows festooned the end of every pew. Although it was the middle of the afternoon, pink and white candles burned in every window. Soft, romantic music came through the sound system.

I sat next to Mama and Myra Sue. Ian and Mr. Brett sat on our pew too because they are like family. Eli was in the church nursery with Christy Sanchez, a nice girl in the youth group, to watch him. Daddy was going to give the bride away, which I thought was sad and weird. No one should give away Grandma.

All the Beasons sat where they should have, on the groom's side of the church.

The music stopped, and so did all the soft murmurs. No one moved. Nothing made a sound. Then the door on the right side of the platform opened and Pastor Ross, Ernie, and Paul Esdon, the manager of the Grocerteria and Ernie's best man, came out of the little room.

Pastor Ross was in a nice dark blue suit and pale green shirt with a dark blue and green striped tie. All over the church, women blew out soft sighs. Not only is Pastor Ross young and handsome, he is also single.

Ernie and his best man stood on the preacher's left side. Both wore dark gray suits, white shirts, and silvery-gray ties. A little swell of pride tickled my chest. Ernie was going to be my grandpa, for real. I betcha he'd be the best grandpa in the whole entire world.

The music started again, a nice quiet tune, instead of the "Here Comes the Bride" song I'd expected.

Isabel, wearing a petal pink dress of something silky that flowed and draped over her skinny body, glided down the aisle as graceful and pretty as you could hope for. She carried a bouquet of pink and white rose buds. Her hair was fluffier than her usual slick-backed style, and her makeup was soft. She smiled, and her eyes shone.

Twittering and soft chuckling started in the back of the church and moved forward like an ocean wave. I craned my neck to see what amused

Here Comes the Bride. And The Groom. And Everyone Else

251

everyone. Four-year-old Lauren Ayres, dressed in pink lacy ruffles, carried a white basket full of rose petals. Her face was in a pout that perfectly mimicked Myra Sue's, and she took her own sweet time coming down the aisle. In fact, it looked like she might turn around and leave.

"Toss the petals," someone called softly to her.

She stopped, looked around, frowned at the white basked full of pink rose petals. She dumped them in a pile, kicked them a couple of times, and stomped to the front of the church. Isabel beckoned Lauren to stand beside her, but the girl went to stand behind Ernie instead. Everyone laughed at that, and she buried her face against his leg.

Without a speck of warning the music went from gentle flutes and violins to loud trumpets. Ever' last one of us jumped like we'd been shot.

The volume went down to a reasonable level right quick, as if someone had turned a knob that should've been turned earlier. The wedding march played and everyone stood.

Well, I tell you what. When you are a kid, you are shorter that the grown-ups surrounding you. It's hard to see a bloomin' thing with adult bodies blocking it all. Finally, though, I saw Grandma, her hand on Daddy's arm. There she was in the pretty dress and her bouquet of pink orchids, her whole face smiling. I don't believe she took her eyes off Ernie the whole entire trip down the aisle.

When she got to the front of the church, Ernie stepped out to meet them. Daddy placed her hand in Ernie's, then stepped away and came to stand beside us. He was grinning from ear to ear. Grandma and Ernie faced the preacher. The rest of us sat down.

After Pastor Ross started his little "We are gathered here" talk, Lauren must've got tired. She squatted down right there on the platform, like she thought she was fixing to play in the dirt. She put the flower basket on her head, and that's how she stayed during the rest of the wedding.

I reckon it might have been better if I had been asked to be the flower girl, after all. I wished Melissa had been there to see everything. She would've gotten a kick out of it.

Almost before you knew it, Pastor Ross announced them married, Ernie kissed Grandma, and they trotted up the aisle toward the back of the church.

"Is that *it?*" I asked Mama. "After all these weeks of crazy wedding busyness, it's over, just like that?"

Mama laughed. "It takes a lot of work, even for a nice simple wedding. Just think what it would have been like if Isabel had persuaded your grandmother to have that fancy wedding. Besides, it's not quite over. Remember, there's the reception in the Fellowship Hall."

Oh, yeah. Cake!

Once the guests started to move, I went hunting for Lacey. I found her a few pews away, surrounded by a bunch of old ladies who were smiling and telling her how pretty she looked. I agreed with them. She wore the green and white floral dress and shiny black shoes I had given her. Her green eyes sparkled and her long brunette hair shone like a polished stone.

When I reached them, the ladies stood back to open their circle and let me in. They smiled at me and told me how nice I looked, and how tall I was getting, and how red my hair was. I thanked them for their nice words, even the remark "hair red as fire," which I wasn't so sure was a compliment.

"Oh, April Grace," Lacey said, all excited, "this was fun! Miss Grace was so beautiful with those flowers in her hair and that pretty dress. Oh, and that little girl cracked me up. Did you see her flop down on the stage?"

"I did. She nearly—"

"Honey," Mrs. Hopper interrupted, toddling up to us. She looked at me. "Chester wants to go home now, but I think Lacey'd enjoy the reception. Reckon your folks could drop her off on your way home?"

"Sure, Mrs. Hopper," I said so loudly some people turned to look at us. Boy, it can be embarrassing when you talk to old people who won't wear hearing aids. "We'll bring her home."

"Thanks, April Grace." She turned and hollered, "Come on, Chester. The Reilly's will bring Lacey later."

Lacey and I moved along with the herd, heading slowly to the back of the church where Grandma, Ernie, Isabel, and the best man stood in a line, shaking everyone's hand.

When it was my turn, I stuck my hand out to Ernie and you know what? He did not shake hands with me, that's what.

Instead he bent down a little, pulled me into his arms, hugged me super tight and kissed my check.

"You call me Grandpa Ernie from now on, kiddo. Okay?"

I felt warm and fuzzy around my heart.

"You betcha!" I said, grinning like a monkey.

I hugged Grandma, and kissed her cheeks ten million times. I hugged Isabel and hoped I didn't break her skinny bones, and I shook hands with Paul Esdon because there is no way Jose I am going to hug someone I don't know, even if he's Grandpa Ernie's best man. Lauren Ayres was nowhere to be seen. In my own personal opinion, shaking hands with a little bitty kid would be weird.

Lacey and I went to the Fellowship Hall where the wedding guests were congregating. It was decorated real pretty in there, with pink and white balloons and flowers. A big bowl of pink cloud punch sat on the table near the four-tiered wedding cake.

The Beason men and boys were clustered around the table, looking at the refreshments, and eyeballing that wedding cake like they were fixing to grab fistfuls of it before Grandma and Ernie even got a chance to cut it. The women and Benji clumped in a wad along the wall. They whispered among themselves, except for Benji who held his peanut butter jar and his bear and never moved.

Three silent old women sat in folding chairs. Dressed alike, with identical curly white hair and silver-framed glasses, those had to be the triplets. Their relatives griped a lot about them, but I'll tell you something. They were the only Beasons I trusted because things had gone missing from our farm before those old ladies ever set foot on it.

I noticed an uncomfortableness in the room, kinda the way the air feels before a storm.

A shiver went down my back.

Thirty-Two

Cheeseheads
Go Missing

I grabbed Lacey's hand and said, "Let's walk around and look at everything."

"Sure!"

"Listen," I whispered in her ear, "if you see anything that seems peculiar, let me know."

"What do you mean?"

"I'm not sure exactly. But help me keep an eye on that bunch of cheeseheads. I think they're up to something."

"Really?" She glanced at them. "Are you sure you aren't feeling this way just because you don't like them?"

I reckon she had a point, but it bothered me, the way they stood there, eyeballing things and whispering. Besides, I had a good reason not to like them. I don't like thieves.

"Remember what I told you the other day by the spring? I notice things that a lot of people don't. Let's walk around, but keep our eyes open."

She nodded.

We meandered and mingled with the guests, often getting stopped by folks who said things like, "You've not lost a grandma, you've gained a grandpa" and "My, what a pretty bride your grandmother is!" A couple of times someone asked, "Why weren't you the flower girl?"

Each and every time I made polite answers, and the whole entire time I acted as grown up as possible. I made sure to introduce Lacey to everyone. But I also kept an eye on the Beasons.

We walked to the refreshment table where everything was laid out with white plates, shining silverware, and burning pink taper candles. The wedding cake stood four tiers high with two white lovebirds on the top instead of a tiny bride and groom.

"Look, April Grace. The frosting is as white and glittering as snow, and those tiny pink orchids look just like the ones in your grandma's bouquet."

"Ernie's favorite color is brown and Grandma said that because they didn't use a bit of brown in the wedding, the entire cake is chocolate."

"Yum!"

"Yeah, yum!"

We grinned at each other.

The Beason men still lingered in the vicinity of the refreshments, but at least they were hanging back, being polite. I glanced at the women and realized for the first time that Aunt Pookie was not with them, and neither were Pardner, Daphne, Colby, and Brie. That was really peculiar.

I started to ask Bixie where they were, but Lacey clutched my arm and said, "Presents!" She tugged me across the room to a table piled with gifts.

There sat Aunt Pookie in the comfy big chair someone had hauled out of the pastor's office for her. She sat close to the gift table as if she were keeping watch over it. Her arms were wrapped around that big old suitcase of a purse, and she smiled like she was listening to angels sing. She was also fanning her face with an old Sunday school bulletin. I wondered where in the world she'd dredged that thing from since I knew the Fellowship Hall had been cleaned and completely decluttered for this occasion.

"Hi, Aunt Pookie," Lacey and I said, nearly at the same time.

"Look at all those presents," Lacey said, her eyes big and shining. I bet that girl had never had a wrapped present in her whole entire life.

"Have you been having a good time, Aunt Pookie?" I asked.

"I have been, but I'm a little tired right now." She ran her gaze over Lacey and me. "My goodness, don't you two girls look a picture. Pretty as a pair of peaches you are."

"Thank you," I said.

"You look nice too," Lacey said. "I like that pretty pin you're wearing."

Aunt Pookie looked down like she'd forgotten she had it on. "Just a little trinket."

I had to ask. "Where is Pardner and them?"

"Who?" She frowned as if she'd never heard of her very own relatives.

"Pardner and Daphne and their kids."

She stopped smiling and fanning. "Aren't they here?"

"Well, they aren't standing near the cake with the rest of your family."

She reared up, stretching her chubby neck to look across the room.

"Run over there, April Grace, and tell Bixie I want to talk to her."

Bixie looked upset when I delivered the message. She followed me across the room to Aunt Pookie.

"Where are Pardner and Daphne?" Aunt Pookie fixed a hard look on her.

Bixie swallowed hard. She cleared her throat. She said "Um" and "Uh" about twelve thousand times.

Aunt Pookie's face turned into a thundercloud.

"Where are they?"

"Well, um, actually… um, they're gone."

"Gone? Gone where?"

"Home. They left right after the wedding."

"Home? You mean back to the Reillys, or home in Pitney, Wisconsin?"

Golly, you should've seen Aunt Pookie's expression. It was scary enough to make a rattlesnake swallow his own fangs.

Poor ol' Bixie looked terrified.

"Home. Wisconsin," she squeaked.

"How they getting there? Airplane?"

Bixie moistened her lips with the tip of her tongue.

"They took the bus," she choked out.

"A Greyhound, I hope."

It was like poor ol' Bixie had to dig for words. "No. Our bus."

"Our bus? The bus that we need to take us home?"

"Yes, Aunt Pookie."

Uh oh.

Aunt Pookie's face got red. Really, *really* red. Her eyes bulged. She made a strangled sound and reached out one hand. She toppled right out of that chair and onto the floor.

"She's having a spell!" I yelled.

I grabbed her purse strap and tugged it out from under her while Bixie stood there and hollered, "What do we do, what do we do?" like a silly goof.

"I'm getting her pills."

The reception came to an abrupt and silent halt. The wedding guests rushed to us, crowding around, sucking the air that Aunt Pookie needed.

I opened her purse. And froze. Inside was Grandma's favorite glass, Eli's little blue hat, the photograph of Grandma and Grandpa. For a minute, I didn't understand. Had Aunt Pookie found the missing items? Or, had she…?

Roy grabbed that purse out of my hands, dumped everything out on the floor and snatched up a medicine bottle. He fumbled, getting a pill out of it. He shoved it in her mouth, beneath her tongue.

I stared down at Aunt Pookie and wondered if she was dead.

Thirty-Three

Spilled Secrets
and the
Need for Understanding

Aunt Pookie did not have a heart attack, or a stroke, or anything like that. She had got so upset by that crazy Pardner driving off in the biggest part of their transportation that she passed out.

People crowded around, gawking at her until she finally came around. She sat there on the floor until a pair of emergency workers showed up with a blood pressure cuff and an oxygen mask and I don't know what else. I reckon seeing those medical men revived her better than anything, because she shooed them and their equipment away, got to her feet, and settled herself in the comfy chair again.

"Enjoy the party," she ordered everyone, flapping one hand toward the room. "I'm fine. Go, go. Have fun."

She fanned her face with that bulletin and clung tightly to her purse. I saw no purpose in doing that. Her secret had spilled out onto the floor for all the world to see.

The wedding guests hadn't understood what the rest of us did— that Aunt Pookie Beason was a thief who stole mementoes from people who fed her and gave her a place to say. If they had, they might not have returned to their merriment so quickly. They might have wanted to call the cops instead.

We all had cake and punch, though I could barely swallow anything with Aunt Pookie the Thief sitting right there. She appeared to be having a regular high ol' time.

Lacey enjoyed her cake and punch, but she wasn't as excited about it as she had been. I guess she wasn't too happy with Aunt Pookie, either.

The newlyweds opened their gifts, had a dance, then they left for their honeymoon.

When the wedding guests had all gone home, it was us two families, facing off. Poor Lacey had to witness the whole mess. To tell the truth, Mama and Daddy didn't seem as upset as much as they seemed hurt. And the Beasons appeared to be more embarrassed than defensive.

"Mike, Lily," Roy said. "I can't begin to tell you how sorry—"

"You don't have anything to be sorry about, Roy," Aunt Pookie interrupted. "It wasn't you or any of the rest of our family. It was me."

Roy held up one hand.

"But Aunt Pookie, I share the blame. I knew you'd do it. I hoped you wouldn't, not here, not with our new family around, but, well, we know you can't help yourself. We know that, and we should have kept a closer eye on you."

That was the craziest bunch of words I'd ever heard.

"It was only a few things," she said, "just to remind myself of my visit here." She opened up that purse and frowned. She dug around in it like a squirrel hunting for a nut. "Who's been in my pocketbook? Where are all my souvenirs, my keepsakes?"

Well, you should know by now that there are times when I have to speak up, and this was one of those times. Even if my tongue had been super-glued to the roof of my mouth, I had to say what was on my mind.

"I have them," I said. I ticked off the items on my fingers. "The ceramic elves, the glass horse, the picture of Grandma and Grandpa, Daisy's brand new dog collar, Eli's little hat, Mama's favorite wooden spoon, Grandma's favorite drinking glass, Myra Sue's bright blue hair ribbon and one of my favorite books. I reckon you took it after I went to stay with Lacey. Did you think I'd put them back in your purse for you to haul back to Wisconsin?"

For once, no one gave me a look to silence me. Which was a good thing, because I was wound up and couldn't stop, no matter what.

"You have a mighty big purse, Aunt Pookie, and it holds a lot of stuff. I can see why you kept tight grip on it all the time. But what I can't figure out is where are the jars of canned apples? Did you stuff them down your bosoms?"

Aunt Pookie, head down, plucked at the clasp on her purse.

"You're right, April Grace. My pocketbook would never hold canned apples. I put them on the bus." She sighed long and slow. "That bus which is now on its way home without me."

Well, I tell you what.

"You know what, Aunt Pookie? I liked you. You and me, we had fun. I was even gonna let you teach me how to crochet. But I gotta say it. Stealing things that mean a lot to other people makes you the biggest cheesehead of them all—and believe me when I call someone a cheesehead, it's not a compliment."

"April Grace," Mama said. She didn't sound mad, but she did sound disapproving. I knew I'd overstepped the lines, but I didn't care.

Aunt Pookie looked up. Her brown eyes filled with tears. She slumped down in her chair and lowered her head.

Roy hunkered down in front of me. He took both my hands in both of his and met my gaze. I'd never seen so many brown eyes in all my life as I'd seen since the Beasons had been around. But you know something else? All that week, I don't think I'd ever looked into any of those eyes, except with anger or mistrust. It surprised me that Roy's eyes were kind and gentle, and their expression seemed to beg me to listen to him.

"April Grace, there is a disorder called kleptomania. Have you ever heard of it?"

I nodded. "It means people steal things."

"Actually, it means people steal things because they can't help it. What happens—"

"Stealing is stealing. It's not like sneezing or sleeping or anything like that. You don't have to swipe stuff that belongs to other people."

"People with kleptomania can't help themselves, April Grace. There is something that's wired in their brains and it sometimes causes them to take what doesn't belong to them. It's an illness, of sorts." He looked around at the rest of us. "Aunt Pookie doesn't take things out of deceit or to deprive you. She… just takes them because she's compelled to."

"I've heard of this," Daddy said.

Mama nodded. "So have I. It's a sad thing—"

"Well, I've heard of it, and I think it's disgraceful!" Isabel butted in, all high and mighty. "If it's an illness, then take her to the doctor and get her medication."

"I've been to the doctor," Aunt Pookie said, softly. "I've been to a lot of doctors. I take medicine, but medicine doesn't stop it. It just helps me to control it a little more."

"So did you leave your medicine in Wisconsin?" I asked.

"When Aunt Pookie is overly tired," Bixie said, "or there is too much stress and excitement around her, she lapses into taking things."

"I suppose that's why she sat near the gift table," Isabel sniffed. Boy, she wasn't going to give the woman any slack.

But then again, neither was I. To me, stealing was stealing. The way not to steal is to refrain from taking something that doesn't belong to you. Period. I was suspicious of this whole klepto-mess, and furthermore I thought it was probably nothing but a bunch of excuses.

"So if you can't help taking things, are you willing to give them back?" Daddy asked

"Of course."

"Then how come you were looking for your 'souvenirs'?" I piped up. "And why did you call them yours when they belong to us?"

Mama put her hand on my shoulder. It wasn't exactly a gentle touch, either. I knew I needed to hush right then, but I just couldn't. The need to talk just dragged me right along with it.

"It seems to me, if you don't mean to swipe things, you wouldn't plan to hang on to them and call them souvenirs and take them back home with you once you've been caught."

Mama's hand got heavier on my shoulder, and Daddy pinned me with The Look. Roy let go of my hands and got to his feet.

"I don't know how to make you understand, honey," he said. "I wish I did."

"I think I know how." That was Lacey speaking. Everyone looked at her with considerable surprise. Especially me.

"You think you can make April Grace understand Aunt Pookie?" Bixie asked.

Lacey nodded. Boy howdy, what was that all about? Aunt Pookie was stealing us blind, but everyone, including my new best friend, was ganging up on me when all I did was say the truth. Lacey sat real straight with her hands clasped in her lap. She met my eyes. I didn't see any meanness there.

"Remember what you told me at the spring?" she asked. "You said you spoke up when you shouldn't, and you knew you shouldn't, but you just couldn't help it. Remember when you said that?"

"Yes, and I do. Because sometimes if I don't speak up, I feel like my brain might explode and—"

Hoo, doggies!

I heard those words come out of my very own personal mouth. They hung in the air like a bad smell.

"But talking isn't against the law." That was a lame defense, but I had to say something.

I realized what I'd just told myself. I pondered, for about the billionth time, as you know, how words and observations come pouring out of me even though I want ever so bad to hold them off. I thought of how often I'd gotten in trouble, at home and at school, for mouthing off. I thought of how I'd said hurtful things to other people, especially people who annoyed me. Like Myra Sue. Or people who got my last nerve, like Colby Beason. Or people I sorta kinda liked, such as Aunt Pookie.

"Maybe I have a disorder," I said, in a very small voice as I shrunk back against the chair. I wished everyone would quit looking at me.

"I sincerely doubt having a big mouth is a disorder," said Myra Sue, "but if it is, you've got a big order of it."

No one said a blessed word to her about being sassy. I bit my lips to keep from mentioning it my own self.

I kept my head down, but at one point I did glance up and catch a glimpse of Aunt Pookie. She and I were sitting in the exact same way, both of us embarrassed to the gills. It was like looking into a mirror, if I had been a chunky, white-haired old lady.

She gave me an uncertain little smile.

"Uh oh, Aunt Pookie," I said.

"Yes, April Grace. Uh oh, and I'm so sorry."

I swallowed hard. "Me too."

She held out one hand and I went over to take it. Her skin was cold and her fingers trembled.

"I'm trying to become a Better Person," I said.

"I know you are, dear. I think you are a wonderful person already." She took in a deep breath and pushed it out. "I'm going to work extra hard to control my own faults. I have plenty of them, you know. Let's encourage each other, shall we? I'll even call you up from time to time, if that's all right with you."

"Yes, ma'am, Aunt Pookie. That's fine."

Tears swam in her eyes as she met my gaze. Before I knew what happened, Aunt Pookie and me were hugging each other tight enough to cut off our air. Lacey was nearby, patting the tops of both our heads, smiling as big as the moon.

Boy howdy, I reckon everybody has secrets and flaws they'd rather not have, and I guess we could all use a little understanding and forgiveness. And I was gonna keep trying to become a Better Person, even if it took me the rest of my life.

The End

Acknowledgements

While the act of writing is solitary, no author writes her book alone. Others accompany every step of the creation.

My appreciation goes first and foremost to my long-suffering husband, who not only has a nine-to-five job, but takes over the shopping, dishwashing, dog sitting, errand running, and phone answering. He never complains.

I'm grateful to my daughters, Holly Hawkins and Joy Ross, who patiently help me remember what growing up in the 1980s was like for them.

No greater thrill exists for an author than the loyalty and support of readers. My thanks to Miss Kylie Cook, whose enthusiastic support of all things April Grace helps keep me writing these stories. The character of Lacey Paige Pickering was named and inspired by Kylie.

Of course, no acknowledgment page is complete without remembering with gratitude those professionals who help birth a book. Casey Cowan, president of Oghma Creative Media, who works so hard for so many, but lets me cry on his shoulder if I need to. Clay Mitchell patiently answers my questions of the editorial nature. My wonderful editor, Jessica Nelson, is a fantastic cheerleader and spirit-lifter. For all the rest of the Oghma team, I give thanks. They are amazing.

CPSIA information can be obtained
at www.ICGtesting.com
Printed in the USA
FSHW012017040919
61730FS

9 781633 7307